PAWSITIVELY

PAWESOME

THE ULTIMATE DOG LOVER'S TEXTBOOK

Cartrell Cooper

Dedication

To my dear father, Cartrell Cooper, whose unwavering dedication to the art of coon hunting story telling and passion for the music has inspired and shaped my own journey in the world of dogs. Thank you for imparting your knowledge, skills

, and wisdom to me and instilling in me a deep respect and love for these

magnificent creatures. Also, to my sister, Phyllis Cooper, whose unwavering love and devotion for dogs began when she gifted me my first dog, a spirited fox terrier. Thank you for introducing me to the joys of dog ownership and showing me the unconditional love and loyalty that only a dog can give. And not least my mother, Lucille Cooper, whose unwavering support and dedication to my education have allowed me to pursue my passion for dogs and to share my knowledge with others. Thank you for instilling in me the importance of education and encouraging me to follow my dreams. With love and gratitude, this book is dedicated to you for all you have done for the dogs that have touched our lives and me.

Acknowledgment

Writing a book on dog training is a significant undertaking, and it would not have been possible without the help and support of many people. I want to take this opportunity to express my gratitude to the following individuals:

First and foremost, I want to thank my family members, who have always been my biggest supporters throughout my journey in the dog training world. I am grateful for their love, encouragement, and unwavering belief in me.

I also want to thank my mentor, Cartrell Cooper, for sharing his wealth of knowledge and expertise with me and for being a constant source of inspiration and guidance.

Dr. William Dudley	*Duck Trammel*
John Quimby	*PT Jay Cox*
Officer Banum	*Lora I Delany*
Don Hudson	*Ron Shara*
Jay Johnson	*Jim Couch*
Kirk Anderson	*PO Pervis*
Mr. Maze	*Mrs. Perro*
Mrs. Bunton	*Mrs. Wilson*

All my Military Comrades

I am grateful to my clients who have entrusted me with the care and training of their beloved dogs. My children (Maria, Loretta, Ivana, and Levi), who I love and will never be forgotten. All the dog pros who have trust and confidence in me have been instrumental in shaping my approach to dog training.

I want to express my appreciation to the veterinary professionals who have provided me with valuable insights and advice on dog health and wellness. Their expertise has been invaluable in helping me create a comprehensive approach to dog training.

Finally, I want to thank my publisher and editors for their support and guidance throughout the writing and publishing process. Their expertise and attention to detail have helped to shape this book into its final form.

To everyone who has played a role in the creation of this book, thank you from the bottom of my heart.

Contents

About the Author

"Cartrell "Daryl" Cooper" is the owner of Big D's Dog Training, which is a dog training company based in Minnesota, USA. Cooper has over 52 years of experience training dogs and has trained dogs for law enforcement, military, and private individuals. He specializes in obedience training, field training, service dogs, and behavior modification, a professor of canine consulting and personal protection training for dogs. Many would say is that all? No-op! Big D's Dog Training offers a variety of training programs, including private training sessions, group classes, and board and train programs. Cooper is known for his effective and compassionate training methods and commitment to helping dogs and their owners achieve their goals.

Page Left Blank Intentionally

Unit 1: Can I Get a Dog?

"The only creatures that are evolved enough to convey pure love are dogs and infants."

- Johnny Depp

Cooper had always been fascinated by the outdoors, and he loved nothing more than spending time in nature with his father. From a young age, he had been tagging along with his dad on hunting trips, eagerly listening as his father shared his knowledge of the woods and their inhabitants. "Son, no, you can't have a dog."

As they walked through the forest, Cooper's father would point out different plants and animals, explaining their characteristics and behaviors. He would teach Cooper how to identify animal tracks and scents, how to follow a trail, and how to stay hidden from the game.

Over time, Cooper learned a lot from his father about the outdoors. His father taught him how to identify different types of plants and trees, how to recognize different animal tracks, and how to stay safe in the woods. Cooper loved the feeling of being surrounded by nature, and he soaked up every bit of knowledge his father had to offer.

But it wasn't just about the hunting. Cooper loved spending time with his father and shared a passion for the outdoors. They would talk about everything from school to sports to their favorite TV shows, and Cooper felt like he could tell his dad anything. He treasured these moments, knowing they were building a special kind of relationship that lasted a lifetime.

As Cooper advanced in years, he started to experience a sense of incompleteness. "I was in the second grade." He yearned for a companion who would accompany him on his expeditions and share in his joys and sorrows. Someone who would be a constant presence in his life, providing him with the support and companionship that he desired. It was clear to him what that would be, and he was determined to find that special being to fill the void in his life. A dog!

"Dad, can we get a dog?" Cooper asked as they walked through the woods, their shotguns slung over their shoulders.

His father smiled, knowing this question was coming. "A dog, huh? Well, let me tell you a bit about dogs first."

As Cooper and his father strolled through the fields,

his father took the opportunity to impart some of his knowledge about the history of dogs. He began by discussing the domestication of dogs and how they have been bred for different purposes for thousands of years. He explained that dogs were first domesticated over 15,000 years ago and have since become one of the most diverse species on the planet, with over 400 breeds recognized worldwide.

Cooper's father went on to describe how dogs have been bred for specific tasks such as hunting, herding, guarding, and even as companions. How his family growing up had a coon dog. He explained that certain breeds were developed for their strong sense of smell, while others were bred for their speed and agility. Cooper jr was fascinated by this information and listened intently as his father shared stories about the various breeds of dogs and their specific characteristics.

As they continued their walk, Cooper's father began to talk about their own dogs on the farm. He spoke with pride about how their dogs were essential for keeping the farm running smoothly and putting food on the table. He shared stories about how the dogs would help round up the cattle and keep the predators away. He described how their loyal companions would accompany them on long walks through the countryside and always be there to greet them when they returned home.

Cooper's father also explained how their dogs were trained from a young age to be obedient and well-behaved. He emphasized the importance of establishing a strong bond between a dog and its owner through consistent training, direction, and reinforcement. He shared tips on how to train a dog to follow commands and behave appropriately in different situations.

As they reached the end of their walk, Cooper felt a newfound appreciation for dogs and their importance in human history. He realized that he wanted a dog not just as a companion but as a partner in adventure, a loyal friend who would always be by his side. His father's words sparked a desire in him to find the perfect dog to join him on his future expeditions and share in his joys and triumphs.

Cooper's father paused for a moment as if reflecting on his words before continuing. "The relationship between dogs and humans is truly unique. It's a bond that goes beyond words or actions. Dogs have a way of sensing our emotions and responding to them in their own way. They can comfort us when we're sad or anxious, and they can bring us joy and laughter when we're feeling down. They offer us a kind of companionship that is hard to find elsewhere."

He went on to explain how dogs have been used in therapy for people with mental health issues and disabilities, providing a source of comfort and support. He recounted stories of how dogs have been trained to detect certain medical conditions, such as seizures or low blood sugar, and alert their owners to potential dangers. He also mentioned the many ways in which dogs have served in law enforcement and search and rescue operations, demonstrating their incredible intelligence and bravery.

"Dogs truly are man's best friend," Cooper's father concluded. "They have been by our side for thousands of years, and I believe they will continue to be for many more. That's why it's so important to treat them with respect, care, and love. They deserve nothing less."

Cooper nodded, understanding the importance of the bond between dogs and humans.

Cooper's father's excitement was palpable as he continued to talk about the remarkable evolution of dogs. He explained that dogs had evolved to be incredibly attuned to human emotions through both selective breeding and natural selection. Certain breeds were bred to be more social and responsive to human cues, while others were selected for their ability to provide protection and security.

He went on to describe the many ways in which dogs have become more than just companions to humans. Studies have shown that owning a dog can have numerous physical and mental health benefits, from reducing stress and anxiety to improving cardiovascular health. Dogs can even be trained to assist individuals with disabilities, providing them with greater independence and a higher quality of life.

But perhaps the most incredible aspect of dogs' evolution, Cooper's father explained, was their ability to sense danger and protect their human companions. Dogs have an incredible sense of smell and hearing and are able to detect potential threats long before humans are aware of them. They can also be trained to protect their owners in dangerous situations, whether it be by alerting them to intruders or by providing physical protection.

"Dogs truly are amazing creatures," Cooper's father said, his voice full of admiration. "They have evolved to be the perfect companions for humans in so many ways. It's no wonder they are one of the most beloved animals in the world."

Cooper couldn't help but agree. As he listened to his father's words, he felt a renewed sense of respect and awe for these incredible animals. He knew that he wanted to find a dog who would not only be a loyal companion but who could also provide him with the many benefits that dogs were capable of offering.

Cooper smiled, feeling even more convinced that he wanted a dog. "So, can we get one?"

His father chuckled. "Well, let's talk more about it when we get home. There's a lot to consider before getting a dog. We need to make sure we're ready for the responsibility and commitment that comes with it. But I'm glad you're interested. Dogs can be wonderful additions to our lives."

As they walked back towards their house, Cooper's father began to elaborate on the many considerations that came with getting a dog. He talked about the importance of finding the right breed for their lifestyle and living situation and the responsibility of providing proper training, exercise, and healthcare for their new companion.

He stressed the need to make sure they were financially prepared for the costs associated with dog ownership, from food and supplies to veterinary care and potential unexpected expenses. He also mentioned the

7

importance of considering the time and energy required to care for a dog, from daily walks and playtime to grooming and training.

"It's important to remember that dogs are not just accessories," Cooper's father said, his tone serious. "They are living beings with their own needs and desires. It's our responsibility to ensure they have a happy and healthy life."

He went on to explain that owning a dog was a lifelong commitment and that they needed to be prepared for the long-term responsibility that came with it. He talked about the importance of socializing their dog and providing them with proper care throughout their entire life span.

Despite the seriousness of the discussion, Cooper could see the excitement in his father's eyes. He knew that his father was just as excited about the prospect of getting a dog as he was, but he wanted to make sure they approached it with the necessary thoughtfulness and consideration. But the answer was no. In my young mind, I thought that meant ever!

As they continued their walk, Cooper's father began to share more stories and information about his dogs. Cooper listened intently, taking mental notes and asking questions along the way. He was fascinated by the many different aspects of dog ownership, from training and exercise to nutrition. He knew that he had a lot to learn, but he was eager to soak up as much information as possible.

As they walked job sites, they encountered other dogs and their owners. Cooper couldn't help but observe the interactions between the dogs and their owners, noticing the different personalities and temperaments of each dog. He saw dogs who were excited and eager to meet new people and others who were more reserved and cautious. He saw dogs who were well-behaved and obedient and others who were still in need of more training and socialization.

Cooper's father used these encounters as teaching moments, pointing out the different behaviors and body language of the dogs and explaining what they meant. He talked about the importance of reading a dog's body language and understanding its needs and preferences.

As they approached their destination, Cooper felt a sense of excitement and anticipation. He knew that finding the perfect dog would take time and effort, but he was ready for the challenge. He was grateful for his father's guidance and knowledge and knew that he would continue to learn and grow as he embarked on this new journey. Yet the answer was still "NO."

"The greatest pleasure of a dog is that you may make a fool of yourself with him, and not only will he not scold you, but he will make a fool of himself, too."

- Samuel Butler

The Coon Hunt

Let's dive in. Writing a book about dogs brings up so many questions that never seem to have a clear answer. For my entire life, I've searched for answers to all the questions I have about dogs. Interestingly, when you start writing a book, you just have to begin somewhere.

This textbook is specifically designed for breeders, dog trainers, instructors, enthusiasts, teachers, professors, groomers, veterinarians, vet schools, and pet owners. I wrote this textbook because when I was in college, there was no comprehensive resource available for dog training, behavior, grooming, sciences, and sports involving dogs. NO Textbook.

There wasn't a single person who could provide all the information. Trainers were isolated in their own field, with their own techniques and methods. There were many egos that would say one technique was better than another or one trainer was better than another. However, what I found was that all trainers had the same goal: to have great dogs.

There was so much commonality between them, and I wanted to learn from them all. I didn't want to talk down about any of them because they all had a love of dogs and wanted to train them in their own way. There were differences in philosophy changes in the '80s and '90s, but the of dogs never changed. The philosophy of training changed because of human philosophy. Dog physiology has not and will never change because dogs are dogs, and humans are humans. The dog will never get the human memo.

Now, in 2023, there are so many new issues when it comes to dogs in people's households, thanks in part to the internet. Too many people lack the education to understand many of the dog training problems, and many things found on the internet are not fact-based. There are so many problematic situations provided. We now have more aggressive dogs and health issues from mixed breeds that veterinarians are capitalizing on. In the past, aggressive dogs were put down, and mixed breeds were not intentionally bred. Also, not everyone attempted to rescue everything.

My interest in dog training goes way back to watching stray dogs in my cousin's yard and observing how they ate and hunted. I also heard my dad's great dog stories about hunting dogs in the Arkansas bottoms and how the dogs helped put food on the table. Therefore, I'm going to begin this textbook with the story of driving down to Arkansas to see my Aunt and cousins.

We're going to start this book with a story, just like
my dad used to do on our road trips. This one begins on a 14-
hour drive, during which my dad would stop with in the first
3 hours for coffee and a snack. He would tell stories to pass
the time. I never wanted to miss anything, so I stayed awake
for the whole journey. In this book, I'm going to share some
of those stories.

The first one is about my dad's experience as a kid in
Arkansas. Dads nick name was Scoot, and he was about eight
years old when this happened. He was out in the field with
his dad and uncle, doing field stuff, when two white men
pulled up in a truck. Everyone in the area was usually
anxious or panicked when white men stopped to socialize,
but these two men walked up to Scoot's uncle and said,
Uncle, we heard that you have the best coon dogs in
Arkansas." Uncle replied, "I got a couple of dogs who will
put up a coon as they need."

The two men said, "Well, we'd like to challenge one
of your dogs with our dog to see who's got the best dog. We
brought our main dog, Spot. He's the best dog in Louisiana,
Texas, Florida, and Tennessee, but everybody in Louisiana
talks about Uncle's dogs in Arkansas, and you've never even

been to non of the national hunts or out of Arkansas for any to know you. So do so many know about you and your dogs.

Well, I've sold a few young dogs. You know ya can't keep em all," Uncle asked, "When would you like to go?" The men replied, "This evening if that works."

Uncle said, "Well, we need meat for dinner, so we can go out. Good weather tonight; good night to go." The two men left, and my father got all excited, ready to go hunting. Uncle instructed him to go up to the field and bugle in True Boy, who was out in the field earlier that day. Scoot was worried that True Boy might be tired, but Uncle insisted that he go ahead. Scoot went out, bugled in True Boy, put him on a lead, and brought him up to the house, tying him to the fence post. By the time field chores were done and all the animals were taken care of, it was time to go hunting.

The two men came back to the side road, this time with a judge in tow. Uncle asked who the new guy was, and they said he was there to witness the competition to see who had the best dog. Uncle wasn't too keen on the idea but agreed to the hunt under some land rules. The men agreed to follow Uncle's rules, and Scoot got the lanterns ready for the hunt.

They walked across the pasture and down the edge of
the peanut field, getting ready to turn the dogs loose. Uncle
instructed Scoot to hold on to True Boy and to let the white
men's dogs have a chance since they were not in their home
territory. The judge pointed out that this wouldn't be fair for
True Boy, as Spot would have a chance for the first strike
and probably the first tree.

Uncle didn't care about that and just wanted to give
the white man's dog an opportunity. The judge said they
could turn the dogs loose at any time, so they let Spot go first.
He ran around, peed on a bush or two, stuck his nose in the
air, and let out a long howl. The men said there was
something out there, and Spot let out another howl. He took
off like there was no tomorrow. One of the men said Spot
was about to tree and asked if they were going to turn True
Boy loose. Uncle replied that he wanted to make sure what
the other dog was doing before turning True Boy loose.

The men said their dog didn't run trash, and they
didn't want to win this way. Uncle just said coon ant been
seen yet. One of the men said Spot would be treed and locate
in a minute or two, they said, and if he didn't, they would bet
Uncle a brand new wagon. Uncle said he couldn't afford to
bet a new wagon! So the men asked if he had any sorghum.

Uncle said he had some from last year. Well, we will bet the sorghum against a new wagon.

Suddenly, Spot got into it and ran down the field and in to the bottom. Uncle said, "Oh Spot, he ain't treeing that one, white folks." The men asked why not, and Uncle replied that it was Old Nubby and he wouldn't go up. Spot would then come back down the peanut field and go quiet. The men said they would bet the sorghum for a wagon. The spot wasn't treed in two minutes. He's just trying to locate it.

Uncle agreed to the bet of two jars of sorghum against the white men's brand new wagon if Spot didn't tree, and Uncle gave them five minutes. Uncle said it wasn't a fair bet for them because Spot wasn't enough dog to put up Old Nubby. Spot went across the bottom and worked hard but then suddenly went quiet again. Seven minutes passed, and Uncle said Spot had lost him. The men said he couldn't have lost him because he was too hot and suggested giving him a minute to locate with no luck.

Uncle said he wasn't up because he was Old Nubby, and he knew how to fool and trick most any dog. Twenty minutes went by with nothing, and the judge said they would have to call a new first strike due to time. The men said if Spot couldn't tree Uncle's Bluetick dog had no chance as well. True Boy, he wouldn't have a chance in hell. Uncle said he would turn True Boy loose and give them two jars of sorghum if True Boy didn't tree in less than 15 minutes. The men said nobody beat Spot like that, and if True Boy put up that coon, they would give Uncle two mules with the wagon.

Uncle told Scoot to turn True Boy loose, and he quietly crossed the field. He got out into the woods and opened with a shot ball for the first strike. The judge wrote down the first strike, and the men said there was a spot with the second strike. The two dogs worked together, and there was no better music than two coon dogs working on a track, a beautiful song. Uncle said there he is. True Boy is treed. The judge said True Boy was treed, and within seconds, Spot opened up with a chop in the same area. One man said Spots treed. The judge wrote down the True Boy first and Spot second tree.

Uncle said they were going to go down and see the tree and the coon, but if it was Old Nubby, they wouldn't shoot him. That was the rule for Old Nubby. The group walked down to the bottom and found the tree with True Boy and Spot at the base. The two men except the loss

They then took the dogs to another field and let them loose. True Boy was the first to strike, and the first tree and

Spot was right there but second to the tree. The two men complemented True Boy on his speed and offered to bring their buddies for another competition. Uncle welcomed the idea as he loved the music of coon dogs. It was less than 10 days, and the two men were back with the young, broke mules and a brand new wagon!

Unit 2: Dog Breeds and Pedigrees

*"No matter how little money and how few
possessions you own, having a dog makes you rich."*

- Louis Sabin

Dogs have been an integral part of human history, serving various purposes such as hunting, herding, guarding, and companionship. As a result, numerous unique dog breeds have been developed, each with its distinct physical and behavioral traits. To understand their behavior, one needs a deeper knowledge of breeds and pedigrees, which can be fascinating for dog lovers.

This Unit explores the intriguing world of dog breeds and pedigrees, providing valuable insights into their behavior, from rolling in the snow to biting and roaming territories. We can better anticipate and understand our furry friend's behavior by delving deeper into each breed's original purpose and instincts, leading to a stronger bond and more effective training.

New dog owners often lack the knowledge and that's why they remain surrounded by questions and confusion. For example, one common question is why dogs roll in the snow. While there are many theories, it could be their way of cooling down or enjoying the sensation. Certain breeds, such as the Siberian Husky, were specifically bred for cold climates, which may explain why they have a natural affinity for colder temperatures and enjoy rolling in the snow because it allows air in the coat, which allows them to stay warm. These questions and answers may seem perplexing, but gaining a deeper understanding of dog behavior can help new owners provide better care for their furry friends.

Have you ever wondered why your dog barks? Let me tell you why. Barking is a mode of communication utilized by dogs to alert their owners and other dogs or merely express their emotions. Certain breeds, like the Beagle, tended to be vocal more than others, so the hunter knew where they were so they wouldn't shoot them. And were specially bred for their ability to alert their handlers during hunting, leading to a higher degree of unpredictability in dog behavior.

On the topic of dog bites, a common question among canine owners is why a canine companion may exhibit such behavior. I have to state all dogs bite, or they can't chew their food. Biting can be a defense mechanism, a response to fear or pain, or a sign of aggression. Certain breeds, such as the

German Shepherd, are actually bred for protection, but the protection is of the flock. The working world used this skill to their advantage, resulting in a stronger bite response. However, training and proper socialization can help mitigate biting incidents with most dogs.

Another very common question among dog owners is why their furry friend doesn't respond to their calls or whistles to come. There are numerous reasons that dogs may not come: distractions, fear, a lack of proper training, or common instincts. Some breeds, like the Border Collie, were bred to be independent and may require more consistent training to follow commands reliably, increasing the consistency of dog behavior. But the truth is the action of coming within a pack is different than how it's considered in the human world. The pack animal calls out, the receiving animal answers and the original caller goes to the one who answers. This is why when you call a dog, it stands their because it's waiting for you to come to it.

Dog breeds have been selectively bred over centuries to develop specific traits that make them suitable for different purposes. Whether it's for hunting, herding, guarding, or simply being a loving companion, there is a breed of dog out there for every lifestyle and personality.

There truly is no reason to mix new ones.

Toy breeds, as mentioned earlier, are small and often make great lap dogs. They're perfect for people who live in apartments or those who don't have alot of space. Despite their small size, toy breeds can be surprisingly stubborn and require consistent training. People often cause problems by picking them up.

Sporting breeds are perfect for people who enjoy an active lifestyle. These dogs need lots of exercise and thrive in homes with plenty of outdoor activities. Many sporting breeds are great for children and make excellent family pets.

Hound breeds are known for their exceptional sense of smell and are often used in law enforcement and search and rescue operations. They were bred to be independent, making them seem stubborn at times, but with consistent training, they can make wonderful pets.

Working breeds are often large and have a powerful build. They are intelligent, loyal, and protective of their families. These dogs require lots of exercise and need a job to do, whether pulling a sled, guarding livestock, or obedience competitions.

Terrier breeds may be small, but they have big personalities. They are often described as aggressive and energetic, with a strong prey drive. Terriers require lots of exercise and consistent training to curb their instinct to chase after small animals because their original jobs were to rid the farms and ships of vermin, this part of their behavior.

Non-sporting breeds are a diverse group of dogs that don't fit into any particular category. They vary in size, energy level, and temperament, making them a good option for people who want a unique and different dog.

Herding breeds are intelligent, active dogs that need lots of exercise and mental stimulation. They thrive in homes with lots of space and do well with families who have children or other pets. Because of their strong herding instincts, they may try to herd small children or other animals, so training and supervision are necessary.

Great Dogs Coming in all types

Valiant is one!

The American Kennel Club (AKC) has a long-standing history of over 135 years, dedicated to preserving the purity and health of purebred dogs. It has set the benchmark for breed standards and breed-specific training and is recognized worldwide as the largest and most respected purebred dog registry.

To ensure consistency and promote a clear understanding of each breed, the AKC has created seven distinct groups, each with a unique purpose. These groups provide a framework for breeders, judges, and enthusiasts to understand each breed's strengths, weaknesses, and characteristics. The AKC's dedication to preserving and protecting purebred dogs has made it an essential organization for breeders, owners, and enthusiasts alike.

Now that we have some understanding of dogs and their breeds let's move toward our next topic, which is pedigrees. What is this word, and why should anyone care about it? As a dog owner and enthusiast, I understand the importance of pedigrees and the wealth of information they provide. When I first started researching different dog breeds, I was fascinated by the concept of pedigrees and how the pedigree could help me predict what to expect from my new furry friend.

One of the things I love about pedigrees is that they tell a story about a dog's lineage. It's fascinating to see how a dog's traits and characteristics are passed down from generation to generation. For example, if a dog comes from a long line of champion show dogs, you can have a strong chance that it will likely have the same physical attributes and temperament that made its ancestors successful in the show ring. The hardest part today is how many don't truly research pedigrees.

But pedigrees aren't just useful for predicting physical traits. They can also be used to track potential health issues within a breed. By looking at a dog's pedigree, you can see if certain genetic diseases or health issues are common within its lineage. This knowledge can help you take proactive steps to prevent or manage these conditions with health testing.

A beautiful dog doesn't display its history!

Pedigree is a great way to visualize a dog's lineage and follow health records. I find it interesting the connections between different generations and how each ancestor contributes to a dog's genetic makeup. It's like piecing together a puzzle and discovering how all the pieces fit together. But with the other side with mixed breeds, they proclaim fewer health issues. But this claim is only made because they never test or track their pedigrees.

Reading a canine pedigree can be confusing if you are unfamiliar with the symbols and terminology used. Here are some basic steps to follow when reading a canine pedigree such as OFA, Ch, Gch, BIS, and FCGD

1. https://www.akc.org/sports/titles-andabbreviations/akc-titles-sorted-alphabetically/

Look for the dog's registered name at the top of the pedigree chart. This is the name that was officially registered with the kennel club.

2. Look for the dog's registration number, which is usually located near the dog's name.

3. Identify the dog's sire (father) and dam (mother). They will be located directly above and below the dog's name.

4. Look for the names and registration numbers of the grandparents, great-grandparents, and other ancestors. They will be listed in a hierarchical fashion, with the oldest generation at the top and the youngest at the bottom.

5. Pay attention to the symbols used in the pedigree. A square represents a male dog, while a circle represents a female dog. An "X" through a symbol indicates that the dog is deceased.

6. Look for titles and awards listed next to the dog's name, such as champion, obedience trial winner, or agility title.

7. Take note of any health information listed on the pedigree, such as hip and elbow scores or genetic tests for inherited diseases.

Reading a canine pedigree can provide valuable information about the dog's ancestry, health, and performance potential. It can also help breeders make informed decisions when selecting breeding pairs to improve the breed.

Reading the genetics of a canine pedigree can be complex and may require some basic knowledge of genetics. Here are some key concepts to keep in mind when reading the genetics of a canine pedigree:

1. Alleles: Alleles are different versions of a gene. For each gene, a dog inherits one allele from each parent.

2. Dominant and Recessive Traits: Some traits are dominant, which means that they will be expressed even if the dog has only one copy of the allele. Other traits are recessive, meaning that the dog must inherit two copies of the allele (one from each parent) to express the trait.

3. Genotypes: A genotype refers to the genetic makeup of an individual. It includes both alleles for each gene.

4. Phenotypes: A phenotype refers to an individual's physical appearance or traits. It is determined by the genotype, as well as environmental factors.

When reading the genetics of a canine pedigree, look for dogs that express certain traits or have a certain genotype. This can give you an idea of which alleles are present in the lineage and which traits may be passed on to future generations. For example, if you are interested in a specific coat color or pattern, look for dogs that express that trait and note their genotypes. If you are concerned about certain genetic disorders, look for dogs that are clear or carriers of the disorder and note their genotypes.

It's important to keep in mind that genetics can be complex and unpredictable, and the expression of certain traits or disorders can be influenced by many factors. Reading the genetics of a canine pedigree is just one tool in understanding a dog's genetics and potential health or behavioral issues. It is always recommended to consult with a canine consultant (Big D's Dog Training) for more information and guidance.

Tracking a genetic pattern or problem in a dog's pedigree can be a process made easy, but it typically involves the following steps:

1. Identify the trait or problem that you want to track, such as a certain health issue, behavioral trait, or physical characteristic.

2. Collect information on the dog's pedigree, including the names and registration numbers of the dog's ancestors, as well as any available health or behavioral information.

3. Construct a pedigree chart, which is a visual representation of the dog's lineage that shows the relationship between the dog and its ancestors.

4. Identify dogs in the pedigree that have expressed the trait or problem that you are tracking, as well as any closely related dogs that may carry the trait or problem.

5. Look for patterns in the occurrence of the trait or problem in the pedigree. Are certain lines or breeds more affected than others? Is the problem more common in certain generations?

6. Determine the mode of inheritance of the trait or problem. Is it dominant or recessive? Is it sex-linked or autosomal?

7. Make informed breeding decisions based on the information gathered from the pedigree. If a certain

trait or problem is a concern, it may be best to avoid breeding dogs that carry the trait or to select breeding partners that are clear of the trait.

8. Consider consulting with a veterinarian or genetic counselor for more information and guidance on tracking genetic patterns or problems.

It's important to keep in mind that tracking genetic patterns or problems is not an exact science, and other factors may contribute to the expression of certain traits or problems. However, tracking a dog's pedigree can provide valuable information for breeders and owners concerned about maintaining their dogs' health and well-being.

As a responsible dog owner, I always encourage and recommend people ask for a dog's pedigree when considering a new addition to my family. I try to know as much as possible about the dog's background and what I can expect from it in terms of temperament, health, and other important factors. Pedigrees, in this regard, are a valuable tool that can help one make informed decisions about pets.

Dogs come in all shapes, sizes, and personalities, and choosing the right one for you can be overwhelming. Now that we have read about breeds and pedigrees let's get into a more advanced topic: mixed or pure breeds. Which one should one get and why, and several other similar factors to consider. Each type of dog has its unique characteristics, and it's important to understand them to make an informed decision.

Let's start by discussing purebred dogs. These dogs are bred to conform to a specific breed standard and are registered with a breed club or registry, such as the American Kennel Club (AKC). Breed standards include physical and behavioral traits unique to the breed, which are carefully selected and maintained through generations of breeding.

Purebred dogs can be predictable in terms of temperament, size, coat type, and other characteristics. For example, a Labrador Retriever is known for its friendly and outgoing personality, love for the water, and desire to retrieve. On the other hand, the Great Dane is known for its strength, loyalty, and gentle nature.

Joy is really the friend.

Cooper & Spike

However, purebred dog breeders track certain genetic health issues because of the limited gene pool within a specific breed. Responsible breeders work hard to reduce the likelihood of genetic health issues by screening their breeding dogs for potential health problems and only breeding those that are healthy and free from genetic conditions.

Now, let's move on to mixed-breed dogs. These dogs are a combination of two or more different breeds and can vary widely in terms of physical and behavioral traits. Because of their mixed heritage, they can have unpredictable temperaments, sizes, coat types, health, and other characteristics.

One of the benefits of owning a mixed-breed dog is that it can be less prone to genetic health issues (THIS IS WHAT YOU SOLD, BUT ITS NOT TRUE) than purebred dogs. This is because they have a larger gene pool to draw from, which can help reduce the likelihood of inherited health issues. ALSO NOT TRUE. If so, all wolves and foxes would die of illnesses. Mixed-breed dogs can also be more unique and interesting, with different characteristics and personalities. THE ONLY TRUTH

However, it's important to note that because mixed breeders don't conform to a specific breed standard, predicting their temperament or physical traits will be more challenging. This means that it can be more difficult to find a specific breed mix that will meet your needs and preferences or, worse go aggressive at approximately 18 months.

Purebred dogs are bred with two parents of the same breed and meet a specific set of standards for that breed. They are often registered with a kennel club, which maintains the breed standards and keeps records of the dog's lineage.

On the other hand, mixed-breed dogs have parents of different breeds or whose ancestry is unknown. They do not meet any specific breed standards and may exhibit traits from multiple breeds.

Here are some key differences between purebred and mixed-breed dogs:

Predictability: Purebred dogs are more predictable in terms of their appearance, temperament, and behavior. This is because they are bred to meet specific standards for their breed, and their genetics are more consistent. On the other hand, mixed-breed dogs may exhibit a wide range of traits and characteristics from their various breeds, making predicting their behavior or appearance more difficult.

Health: Purebred dogs HAVE LESS certain health problems due to reputable genetic testing they do that helps safeguard new owners. On the other hand, mixed-breed dogs may have a high risk of genetic health and unknown problems due to their diverse genetic background.

Availability: Purebred dogs are often available through breeders or rescue organizations that specialize in a particular breed. Mixed-breed dogs are typically available through animal shelters or rescue organizations that take in dogs of various breeds and backgrounds.

Cost: Purebred dogs are often more expensive to purchase or adopt due to the demand for specific breeds and the cost of breeding and maintaining purebred lines. Mixed breed dogs are generally less expensive, and adoption fees are typically lower than those for purebred dogs.

Ultimately, the decision to adopt a purebred or mixed-breed dog depends on individual preferences and lifestyle. While purebred dogs may be more predictable in behavior and appearance, they may also be less susceptible to health problems and more expensive to obtain. On the other hand, mixed-breed dogs may have a wider range of traits and backgrounds but may also be less predictable in terms of behavior and appearance. Regardless of the breed, all dogs require proper care, attention, and love from their owners to live happy and healthy lives.

Understanding the nuances of different dog breeds and their behavior is crucial to building a strong relationship with your furry friend. By knowing a dog's breed and characteristics, you can better anticipate its needs, preferences, and potential health issues.

Similarly, being aware of pedigrees and your dog's lineage can help you make informed decisions about breeding and potential health issues. Conclusively, understanding dog breeds, behavior, pedigrees, and types of breeds is a must for any dog owner.

This knowledge helps you make informed decisions about your pet's health and well-being and enhances your relationship with your dog. Investing the time and effort to learn about your furry companion can create a happy, healthy, and fulfilling life together.

"The greatest pleasure of a dog is that you may make a fool of yourself with him, and not only will he not scold you, but he will make a fool of himself, too." - Samuel Butler

Discovering the Breeds

A Personal Story of Dog Enthusiasm

When you talk to people and ask how did you discover the breed that they were interested in. When. I remember back when I was a kid, For my self it was when I discovered the library in third grade, and I biked down to our local library because after hearing the dogs, hunting stories from my father went to the library to look up the Bluetick and all I found was ingomation on the black and tan Coonhounds, and no other Coonhounds. The Black and Tan was only dog I found represented in the Dog Book of the AKC was the Black and Tan. The others weren't accepted into the AKC all-breed book at that particular point in time. So, in talking to the librarian, she gave me a section of the books read, and I went back there and really just started looking at dog information. I then found the book.

"Where The Red Fern Grows". My love for Redbones came from Dan & Ann.

There was very little training. Richard Walters had a retriever training book, but I didn't want a retriever. I didn't know any about retrievers, but I grabbed that book and the dog encyclopedia. Threw those in my little bag, wiped them home, and started reading and paging through books about dogs, what dogs did and why dogs did certain things. My interest was finding out about the Bluetick, but I was reading about labs. The Blueticks I knew were True Boy, Old Bragg, and Old Mary, the dogs dad used to hunt over. But there was just no information about them. So, people, generally speaking, learn about dogs that they are exposed to. So I wanted a dog, a Bluetick and a Redbone.

At some point, my dad introduced me to a friend of his who had German Shorthaired Pointers, which had coloring like the Bluetick. So that struck my eye. Then, it was one of the dogs I read about in field magazines. They were exciting to read about. So, most of my information was from the magazines that I found. And from the stories my dad told and the friends he introduced me to, I wouldn't have known anything about German shorter if it had not been for Mr. Macmillan. I wouldn't have known anything about bird hunting. I had the joy of following the dog to training with Lori I Delany.

Information was not found walking down the street; back when I was a kid, all you saw was a German Shepherd and Labradors. Generally, all you saw. Back then, there was no such thing as dog parks; dogs wouldn't stay in a dog house. They were out in the backyard. Really, When you look back, many dogs that stayed out in the yard were often generally speaking healthier than some of the dogs of today. They did much more running around and exercising.

1. So, when you look at how I discovered the breeds that I was interested in, it was due to hunting with my father or working with my father's friend's dog when he got back from the trainer because he didn't have time to keep up with training, so I got to play with it. I got to take it out to the park, and I call it playing with it, but I was following some of the tips that I had found in some of the magazines about training for field dogs. When hunting season came along. Mr. McMillian realized the dog worked better for me, so I got to go hunting with him.

We got some birds; I think Mr McMillan got one, my dad got two. I wasn't old enough to carry a gun, so I just got to work the dog. But that's how you establish what you like via exposure. People don't know what they're buying often. Sometimes, it's based on color they like or cute. They're buying the dog from whom ever they can find, or the breed they like or for an activity such as hunting or showing. So, when you look at breeding or buying, more information should be considered and given when people research buying a dog. But most of them just buy a dog with minimal research.

The Science Of Why

In the world of dogs, so many questions go unanswered. Why does the dog roll in the snow? Why does a dog eat poop? Why does a dog bite? Why would the dog not come, it called? Why does the dog roam the territory? Why is the dog considered a pack animal? Why does training work? Why don't dogs speak the English language? How Can dogs have such endurance? All these statements are what many ask. Why does the dog lick my face? Why does the dog spin and be greedy? Why does the dog rub his body or glands on my legs? Why does the dog jump up on me? And all those things in different aspects have so many different answers. But in order to answer these questions, we have to look at the details. You have to look at the scientific makeup of what drives the animal from nutrition to survival, territorial, and breeding. Look at the Coyote, the wolf, the dingo, or the feral dog. All their actions are consistently similar to are dogs of today, so if you look at how the relationship between dogs and humans was developed via the domestication of the dog.

An example: An old feral dog injured started following some humans, gathering scraps that they were finding that the humans were leaving off. Then, humans started providing food and scraps. And captures that dog just like they captured horses. Most of the animals you looked at in the past had jobs of giving first warning, protecting humans from wolves, bears, and the things that could harm or injure them. But if you look at the overall history, you can go back into the Egypt drawings you see cats and dogs. Now, personally, I would love to go back in time and witness the domestication process. Now, over time, dogs have evolved into what they are now. Every dog known out there was bred for a use or a function. And that goes from a toy breed all the way up to the working breed. They were bred for a function. Some of the functions were similar. Now, to understand functions like a flushing dog versus a pointing dog. The difference between those two, for example, is the terrain in which they hunted. When you look at the hunting dog and harvesting, the farmer went out in the field and needed food. And it was the dog who helped obtain that. It goes back to the first story I told at the beginning of the book.

Lt Dan is Max!

My dad and his family were coon hunters and squirrel hunters; it was dinner, it was cooked up, and the meat was served. The woods were the grocery store. You didn't kill it you didn't eat. So, function handlers wanted a dog that worked fast to put that pray up the smallest tree because, on average, they had to chop trees down in order to harvest the game. Now, that chopped tree has become firewood for cooking and laundry. There was use for everything. So when you look at the overall science behind the dog, you have to understand that every single dog on the planet in the past had a function, whether it be sporting, which was a nice word for saying hunting, whether working, which was a nice term for gardening and protection. And you look at how chasing, smelling, and locating Terrier, cleaning up killing rats, getting rid of the secondary animals that would damage your food, waste your food, and get feces and stuff. And so you had the Terriers that would clean rats off of ships, clean rabbits out of barns, they were ratters. They were bred to kill. The non-sporting was a category created by breeders. Because the dogs were like the Dalmatians on the coaching side, which were protective animals and food. Now, the toys, contrary to popular belief, weren't toys. 90% of the toys were bred to be royalty animals.

That's why toy breeds are noisy; they were alarm systems. They were fail-safe to let the big dogs know where they needed to be. So, you look at the science behind it. It was more function than science.

There's a whole lot of detail in the selection of what to breed, setting standards, and setting groups by their jobs. We have now had over 100 years of development to help with their job. You had individuals who created dogs for this particular job and location. The original breeders created breeding roadmaps or breeding blueprints. And that breeding Blueprint was considered to be a standard. Now that standard was outlined, now the standard took into consideration what the animal looked like.

The modern-day standard spells out things like faults or flaws that would be problematic in the breeding program. While listing heights, weights, and overall sizes. That way, when an individual needed a carting dog, they would go to a carting type dog breeder. When they bought that dog from that breeder, they knew what they were going to get because the blueprint side of it was example, Bernese Mountain Dog.

If it's a German Shorthaired Pointer, it looks like a German Shorthaired Pointer and could do the job. If it's a Ridgeback, It looks like a Ridgeback and so on. The AKC as a registry help track fault or flaw. This information was important because faults took the working animal out of the working system, which wasn't cost-effective for replacement. So if your dog had hip dysplasia, and you ended up having to put it down in three years, now you're training another dog to try to do the job. And it's like being without a tractor; you have diminished your work cycle's ability. So tracking becomes important. You don't have the scientific. Now, they can pin hips, repair legs, decrease worm activity and provide health care. So it was extremely imperative that when you got a dog from a breeder, not for beauty but health. So you look at the jobs that a dog did. It was based on their abilities and on being able to do. So, we look at the genetic side or the genetics study in detail for health.

Quiz

1. What is a pedigree?

2. What information is included in a pedigree?

3. What is the purpose of reading a pedigree?

4. What is some health information that can be found on a pedigree?

5. What are some titles and awards that can be found on a pedigree?

6. What is the significance of symbols used in a pedigree?

7. What is the recommended age for puppies to be separated from their mother and littermates?

8. What is a genotype?

9. What is a phenotype?

10. What is an allele?

11. What is a dominant trait?

12. What is a recessive trait?

13. What is a fault?

14. How can faults be identified on a pedigree?

15. What should be considered when evaluating faults on a pedigree?

16. What is a carrier?

17. What is a clear dog?

18. What is linebreeding?

19. What is an outcross?

20. What is the goal of evaluating a pedigree?

Answers

1. A document that shows the lineage or ancestry of a dog.

2. The dog's registered name and registration number, the names and registration numbers of the dog's parents, grandparents, and other ancestors, titles and awards earned by the dog and its ancestors, and health information.

3. To gain insights into the dog's genetic background, temperament, and potential for certain health issues

4. Hip and elbow scores, genetic tests, and other health-related certifications.

5. Champion, obedience trial winner, agility title, etc.

6. A square represents a male dog, while a circle represents a female dog. An "X" through a symbol indicates that the dog is deceased.

7. 8 weeks.

8. An individual's genetic makeup includes both alleles for each gene.

9. Genotype and environmental factors determine an individual's physical appearance or traits.

10. Different versions of a gene. For each gene, a dog inherits one allele from each parent.

11. A trait that will be expressed even if the dog has only one copy of the allele.

12. A trait that requires the dog to inherit two copies of the allele (one from each parent) in order to express the trait.

13. An undesirable trait or characteristic in a dog's pedigree.

14. Looking for dogs in the lineage that have expressed the trait or characteristic, repeat occurrences of the trait in the lineage, and closely related dogs that may also carry the trait.

15. The prevalence of the trait in the breed as a whole and informed breeding decisions.

16. A dog has one copy of a recessive gene for a particular trait but does not express the trait.

17. What is a clear dog? Answer: A dog that does not carry any copies of a particular gene associated with a certain trait.

18. A breeding strategy involves mating dogs closely related to fixing certain desirable traits in the lineage.

19. A breeding strategy involving mating dogs that are not closely related to introducing new genetic material to the lineage.

20. To make informed decisions about breeding to improve the breed and promote healthy, happy dogs.

Unit 3: Basic Dog Care

"A dog will teach you unconditional love. If you can have that in your life, things won't be too bad."

- Robert Wagner

Dogs have been a part of human life for thousands of years, serving as protectors, hunters, and companions. They have earned their place in our hearts and homes as faithful, loving animals that offer unconditional love and loyalty. As a devoted dog lover, I understand the depth of emotion that they bring to our lives.

For me, dogs are not just pets but cherished members of the family. I believe that every dog deserves love, care, and attention, just like any other family member. Taking proper care of a dog's physical and emotional needs is essential to its overall health and well-being. From providing them with a nutritious diet and regular exercise to ensuring they have a comfortable place to sleep, everything we do for our furry friends contributes to their happiness.

When a dog is happy and healthy, it's an incredibly rewarding experience. Seeing them wag their tail in joy, playfully chase after a toy, or snuggle up beside you is one of life's greatest pleasures. And when a dog is sad or unwell, it's equally heartbreaking. That's why it's crucial to provide them with the love and care they deserve so they can live their best lives and bring us joy daily.

In addition to their physical needs, it's also important to address a dog's emotional needs. Dogs thrive on companionship and interaction with their human family members. They need socialization and positive reinforcement to develop good behavior and overcome any issues they may have. Providing them with plenty of affection, playtime, and training is essential to their emotional well-being.

In this Unit, we will explore some of the fundamental principles of dog care that every pet owner should know. From choosing the right dog food to understanding the importance of exercise, we will delve into the key factors contributing to a happy, healthy canine companion. Whether you're a seasoned dog owner or just getting started, the information in this Unit will help you provide the best possible care for your beloved pet.

Bringing a furry companion into your home is an exciting and life-changing decision. Dogs are loyal and loving and provide endless amounts of joy and companionship. However, it's important to remember that, as pet owners, we are responsible for providing our pets with the care and attention they need to thrive.

As a dog owner, I know how important it is to provide our furry friends with the right food and water. When I first brought home my dog, I was excited to go to the pet store and pick out his food. However, I was quickly overwhelmed by the number of options available. There were so many brands, types, and flavors to choose from that it was hard to know where to start.

After some research, I learned that choosing the right dog food is crucial for my dog's health and well-being. I discovered that high-quality dog food should contain a balanced protein, carbohydrate, and fat mix. The protein should come from sources like chicken, beef, or fish and be the main ingredient. Fruits and vegetables also provide essential vitamins and minerals that dogs need to stay healthy.

I also learned that I should avoid foods containing fillers like corn, wheat, and soy. These ingredients can be difficult for dogs to digest, leading to digestive issues or allergies. I needed to read the ingredients list carefully to ensure I was getting the best food for my dog.

Your dog's age and activity level are important considerations when choosing dog food. Puppies require more protein and calories than adult dogs, so choose a food that is specifically formulated for puppies if you have one. Similarly, highly active dogs require more food than sedentary dogs, so choose a food that meets the nutritional requirements of your dog's lifestyle.

Reading the ingredient label on a dog food bag can help you understand what is included in the food and whether it meets your dog's nutritional needs. Here are some tips on how to read a dog food bag:

1. Look for high-quality animal protein sources: The first few ingredients should include high-quality animal protein sources, such as chicken, beef, or lamb.

2. Avoid fillers: Avoid dog foods that include fillers, such as corn, wheat, and soy.

3. Check the fat content: Dogs need a certain amount of fat in their diet for energy and other essential functions. Look for dog food with appropriate fat content for your dog's age and activity level.

4. Look for essential vitamins and minerals: Dog food should include essential vitamins and minerals, such as vitamin E, vitamin C, and calcium, to support your dog's overall health and well-being.

5. Consider your dog's age and health needs: If your dog has specific health needs, such as joint problems or food sensitivities, look for a dog food that addresses those needs.

6. Check for preservatives and artificial ingredients: Look for dog foods that avoid artificial preservatives and ingredients, such as BHA, BHT, and ethoxyquin.

7. Look for feeding guidelines: The dog food bag should provide guidelines on how much to feed your dog based on their weight and activity level. But understand that the recommendations on the bag of food have the goal of feeding a bag a month.

When reading the dog food bag label, look for food that meets the minimum standards set by the Association of American Feed Control Officials (AAFCO). This information will give you an idea of the nutritional content of the food and whether it is appropriate for your dog's needs.

It's also important to consider your budget when choosing dog food. While high-quality dog food can be expensive, it's worth investing in a portion of food that fits within your budget. Investing in high-quality dog food can save you money in the long run by reducing the risk of costly health issues.

In addition to food, it's also important to ensure that your dog has access to fresh water at all times. Dogs need to stay hydrated, especially if they are active or spend a lot of time outdoors. I always fill my dog's water bowl a minimum of twice per day with fresh water and keep an eye on it to ensure it stays clean and full.

Although choosing a dog food that meets your dog's nutritional needs and supports its overall health and wellbeing is important, that's not all you have to do. There might be concerns even after that, and in that case, consulting with a veterinarian for guidance and advice should be the step you take.

Moreover, knowing basic first aid for a dog is important for every dog owner. Let's take a look at some of the must-know things if you are a dog owner:

1. Know your dog's normal vital signs: A dog's normal body temperature is 100.5-102.5°F, its heart rate should be between 60-140 beats per minute, and its breathing rate should be 10-30 breaths per minute. Knowing your dog's normal vital signs can help you recognize when something is wrong.

2. Be prepared: Have a basic first aid kit on hand that includes items such as bandages, gauze, antiseptic wipes, and tweezers.

3. Know how to handle injuries: If your dog is bleeding, apply direct pressure to the wound with a clean cloth or gauze. If your dog has a broken bone, keep it as still as possible and seek veterinary attention immediately.

4. Know how to handle choking: If your dog is choking, try to remove the object if possible, but be careful not to push it further down their throat. If you cannot remove the object, seek veterinary attention immediately.

5. Know how to perform CPR: If your dog is not breathing, perform CPR by giving them rescue breaths and chest compressions.

6. Know how to recognize signs of heatstroke: Symptoms of heatstroke in dogs include excessive panting, drooling, weakness, and vomiting. If your dog is exhibiting these symptoms, move them to a cool place and provide them with water. Seek veterinary attention immediately.

7. Know when to seek veterinary attention: If your dog has a serious injury or illness or if you are unsure of what to do, seek veterinary attention immediately.

Knowing basic first aid for a dog can help you provide immediate care in an emergency situation and may even save your dog's life. It's important to be prepared and know what to do in case of an emergency. Consider taking a pet first aid course or consulting with your veterinarian for more information on how to provide basic first aid for your dog.

But there are other important things, too, like providing your furry friend with a safe and comfortable shelter. Dogs, like humans, need a secure and cozy space to rest and relax in. A proper shelter can provide them with the necessary protection from the elements, such as rain, sun, or extreme temperatures. It can also give them a sense of security, which is crucial for their overall well-being.

The Bluetick Coonhound

When it comes to choosing a shelter for your dog, it's important to consider their specific needs. Different breeds may require different types of shelter based on their size, coat type, and activity level. For example, a larger breed like a Great Dane may need a larger crate or kennel to provide them with enough space to move around comfortably. A smaller breed, like a Chihuahua, may prefer a cozy dog bed in a quiet corner of your home. A dog truly doesn't want the space to be large.

However, when I first adopted my dog, I assumed that my couch was a good enough spot for him to sleep on. However, I quickly realized he needed his own space to feel secure and comfortable.

I then invested in a dog bed and crate and placed them in a quiet corner of my home. This allowed my dog to have a designated space to relax and rest. I made sure that the bed was soft and comfortable and that the crate was the appropriate size for my dog. It made a world of difference in his behavior and overall happiness.

In addition to providing a dog with an innocuous and comfy space, one should also ensure that their dog gets enough exercise. When the weather is nice, dogs can be taken for hikes and runs in the park.

Regular exercise is essential for dogs of all ages and breeds as it helps them maintain a healthy weight, prevents boredom and destructive behavior, and improves their overall physical and mental health. It's something that I learned soon after getting my own dog, as I realized how much energy she had and how important it was to ensure that she got enough exercise every day.

Take time to enjoy the weather.

When it comes to exercise, different breeds have different needs. It's important to research your specific breed to determine how much exercise they require. For instance, highly active breeds like Border Collies and German

Shepherds require a lot of exercise to keep them mentally and physically stimulated, while smaller breeds like Chihuahuas and Pomeranians require less exercise.

Regardless of your dog's breed, providing them with physical through exercise and playtime is essential. Activities such as walks, runs, hikes, and trips to the dog park are all great ways to provide your dog with physical exercise. Its also important to understand you may be walking, but your dog is hurting. These activities also help to strengthen the bond between you and your furry friend.

As a responsible dog owner, taking care of your pet's health is crucial for their overall well-being. While providing them with a healthy diet and regular exercise is important, regular veterinary check-ups are also crucial to ensure that any potential health issues are caught early.

Regular veterinary check-ups are essential in maintaining a dog's health. Like humans, dogs can experience various health problems, ranging from minor issues to serious conditions requiring immediate medical attention. A trusted veterinarian can diagnose and treat these problems and offer advice on how to care for your dog.

During a routine check-up, a veterinarian will typically perform a physical examination of your dog, checking their eyes, ears, nose, teeth, skin, and coat for any signs of abnormalities. They will also listen to your dog's heart and lungs and palpate its abdomen to check for any signs of pain or discomfort. Additionally, they may recommend additional tests, such as blood work or urine analysis, to detect any underlying health issues that may not be visible during the physical examination.

In addition to diagnosing and treating any health issues, regular veterinary check-ups also provide an opportunity to discuss any concerns or questions you may have about your dog's health. This could include questions about their diet, exercise routine, or behavioral issues. Your veterinarian can offer advice on how to address these concerns and provide recommendations for any necessary changes.

Establishing a relationship with a trusted veterinarian is crucial for your dog's health. A veterinarian familiar with your dog's medical history and personality can provide personalized care and make recommendations specific to your dog's needs. Additionally, a veterinarian who knows your dog well is better equipped to recognize any changes in their behavior or health that may indicate an underlying problem. The best care may not be received at a chain store.

While regular veterinary check-ups are important, some dog owners may be hesitant to take their pets to the vet due to fear of stress. However, it's important to note that a veterinarian can take steps to minimize stress during the appointment, such as using calming pheromones or offering treats. Additionally, the benefits of preventative care far outweigh the temporary stress that your dog may experience during the appointment.

It's also important to note that regular veterinary care can help save you money in the long run. Catching and treating health issues early can prevent them from becoming more serious and expensive to treat down the line.

In addition to physical exercise, mental stimulation is also crucial for a dog's overall health and well-being. Interactive toys, training sessions, and puzzle games are all great ways to provide mental stimulation for your dog. Mental exercise is also important for preventing behavioral issues like anxiety, boredom, and destructive behavior.

In conclusion, owning a dog comes with a big responsibility, but the love and companionship they provide are worth the effort. By providing your furry friend with the basic care they need, you can ensure that they live a long and healthy life. Remember that each dog is unique and may have individual needs, so always pay attention to their behavior and adjust their care accordingly.

"Dogs do speak, but only to those who know how to listen."

- Orhan Pamuk

Learning True Pet Care: My Experience Working at Brooklyn Pet Hospital

When it comes to your dogs, what is the first thing of importance? What's the first thing that comes to mind? When does someone suggest dog care? You know, the amount of detail that goes into taking care of one's dog really doesn't come to mind. The brushing, the grooming, the feeding, the watering. The vet visits, the cleaning up poop.

You know, so when my mom and dad found out that I had an interest in dog training or dogs in general, my dad was a contractor in the summer months, and he had built Dr. William Dudley Pet Hospital, Brooklyn Pet Hospital in Brooklyn Center, Minnesota. My mom, knowing that I had an interest, got together with Dr. Dudley and asked if I could do a little tag-along work for him at the pet hospital.

Well, it was a great opportunity to learn True Pet Care and all the details and all the interesting problems that people run into and the dangers that cause injury injuries, medications, surgeries, diagnostics and how to figure things out is what I actually learned.

The fun part about it is every Saturday. My mom

would drive me out to Brooklyn Pet Hospital and drop me off. And after a full day's work, she'd come back and pick me up, or my dad would come to pick me up from the time that they open at 730. From the morning until five six o'clock at night, I didn't think twice about it. I would just work mostly cleaning tables and kennels. I did whatever the doctor told me to.

Then, I graduated to look at slides for worm eggs, do a diagnostic stool, count medications, and assist in the surgery room. So, from a very young age, I got to learn the whole gamut. First Aid, the science, and many of the required medications.

Nowadays, kids don't have access to that kind of opportunity. So, Brooklyn Pet Hospital allowed me to learn every stage of the veterinary science industry. But still, my drive was to train dogs.

But if it wasn't for the vet care side, I wouldn't be as knowledgeable without having had my mini internship of 22 years with a pet hospital that went from the third grade to post-college.

A Dog is a dog first and a human never!

Quiz

1. What is the normal body temperature for a dog?

2. What is the normal heart rate for a dog?

3. What is the normal breathing rate for a dog?

4. What is the essential nutrient that dogs require in the highest amount?

5. What is a common sign of dental problems in dogs?

6. How often should you brush your dog's teeth?

7. What is a common cause of obesity in dogs?

8. What are the symptoms of heatstroke in dogs?

9. What is the first step in handling an injured dog?

10. What should you do if your dog is choking?

11. What should you do if your dog has a broken bone?

12. What is CPR?

13. What is a common cause of diarrhea in dogs?

14. What is a common symptom of food allergies in dogs?

15. What is a common symptom of arthritis in dogs?

16. What is a common symptom of ear infections in dogs?

17. What is the most common type of cancer in dogs?

18. What is a common symptom of heart disease in dogs?

19. What is the most common nutritional deficiency in dogs?

20. What is a common cause of urinary tract infections in dogs?

21. How often should you bathe your dog?

22. What should you do if your dog gets stung by a bee?

23. What is a common symptom of fleas in dogs?

24. What is a common symptom of ticks in dogs?

25. What is a common symptom of heartworm disease in dogs?

26. What is a common symptom of anxiety in dogs?

27. What is the essential nutrient that dogs require in the second-highest amount?

28. What is the essential nutrient that dogs require in the third-highest amount?

29. What should you do if your dog ingests something toxic?

30. What is a common symptom of kennel cough in dogs?

Answers

1. Answer: 100.5-102.5°F.

2. Answer: 60-140 beats per minute.

3. Answer: 10-30 breaths per minute.

4. Answer: Protein.

5. Answer: Bad breath.

6. Answer: At least once a day.

7. Answer: Overfeeding and lack of exercise.

8. Answer: Excessive panting, drooling, weakness, and vomiting.

9. Answer: Secure the dog to prevent it from moving and causing further injury.

10. Answer: Try to remove the object if possible, but be careful not to push it further down their throat. If you cannot remove the object, seek veterinary attention immediately.

11. Answer: Keep them as still as possible and seek veterinary attention immediately.

12. Answer: Cardiopulmonary resuscitation is a procedure used to restore the heartbeat and breathing

in an unconscious or unresponsive dog.

13. Answer: Dietary indiscretion, such as eating something they shouldn't have.

14. Answer: Itching and skin irritation.

15. Answer: Stiffness and difficulty moving.

16. Answer: Head shaking and scratching at the ears.

17. Answer: Skin cancer.

18. Answer: Coughing.

19. Answer: Vitamin E deficiency.

20. Answer: Bacterial infections.

21. Answer: It depends on the dog's activity level and coat type, but generally, no more than once a month.

22. Answer: Remove the stinger if possible and apply a cold compress to the affected area.

23. Answer: Excessive scratching and biting at the skin.

24. Answer: A small bump or swelling at the site of the tick bite.

25. Answer: Coughing and difficulty breathing.

26. Answer: Excessive barking, whining, or pacing.

27. Answer: Fat.

28. Answer: Carbohydrates.

29. Answer: Seek veterinary attention immediately.

30. Answer: Coughing and hacking.

Unit 4:

Canine Health and Nutrition

Canine health and nutrition are essential aspects of a dog's well-being. Proper nutrition ensures that dogs get the necessary nutrients to maintain healthy skin, coats, and overall body condition. Dogs require a balanced diet that includes high-quality protein, carbohydrates, fats, vitamins, and minerals. Feeding dogs a complete and balanced diet based on their life stage and activity level is crucial for optimal health.

Regular veterinary checkups and preventative care, such as vaccinations and parasite control, are also vital components of canine health. Monitoring your dog's weight, body condition, and eating habits is essential. Any appetite, energy level, or behavior changes are to be addressed promptly. Let's take a look at each of these points in detail and try to understand their significance in your furry friend's life.

The Importance of Proper Hydration for Dogs

Proper hydration is crucial to a dog's overall health, and it is essential to provide them with the right amount of water to keep them healthy and happy. One of the main functions of water in a dog's body is to regulate its body temperature. Dogs release heat through panting and sweating, and if they do not have enough water, their body temperature can rise rapidly, leading to heat exhaustion or heatstroke.

Additionally, water helps to maintain a dog's joint health, as it acts as a lubricant and keeps their joints from becoming stiff or sore. It also aids digestion and helps flush out toxins from the body.

To ensure your dog is properly hydrated, you should always provide them with clean, fresh water. Change the water in their bowl frequently and clean their bowl regularly to prevent the growth of harmful bacteria. If your dog is reluctant to drink water, you can try adding flavorings or even ice cubes to make it more appealing.

It's important to monitor your dog's water intake, especially during hot weather or when they are engaging in physical activity. Ensure they have water access during walks, runs, or any other form of exercise. You can also monitor their hydration levels by checking their skin elasticity - gently pinch their skin and release it. It may be a sign of dehydration if it takes a long time to return to its original position.

The Role of Protein, Carbohydrates, and Fats in a Dog's Diet

Protein, carbohydrates, and fats are the three macronutrients that are essential for a dog's health. Protein is necessary for building and repairing tissues and plays a vital role in producing hormones and enzymes. Carbohydrates provide energy, while fats are important for maintaining healthy skin and coat and supporting organ function.

When choosing dog food, it's important to consider the quality and quantity of each nutrient. High-quality protein sources include chicken, beef, lamb, and fish. Carbohydrates can come from sources such as brown rice, sweet potatoes, and peas. Fats can be obtained from chicken fat, fish oil, and flaxseed sources.

It's important to note that the nutritional requirements of dogs can vary depending on their age, size, and activity level. Puppies require more protein and calories than adult dogs, while senior dogs may need less protein and fewer calories. Active dogs may require more protein and carbohydrates to support their energy needs.

In addition to protein, carbohydrates, and fats, dogs require essential vitamins and minerals to maintain overall health and prevent disease. These nutrients are necessary for maintaining healthy bones, teeth, and muscles, supporting the immune system, and aiding in the absorption of other nutrients.

Some common vitamins and minerals that dogs need include vitamins A, D, and E, calcium, phosphorus, and iron. When selecting dog food, it's important to choose a formula that is appropriate for your dog's specific needs. For example, large-breed puppies require diets with lower levels of calcium and phosphorus to prevent bone disorders, while small-breed dogs may benefit from diets that are higher in fat and protein to maintain their energy levels.

It's also important to avoid certain ingredients that can harm dogs, such as artificial preservatives, colors, and flavors. Some dogs may also have allergies or sensitivities to certain ingredients, such as grains or chicken, and may require a special diet to avoid adverse reactions.

Common Allergens in Dog Food

Dogs, like humans, can suffer from food allergies or food sensitivities, which can cause a range of symptoms. The most common allergens found in dog food include beef, chicken, dairy, eggs, soy, and wheat. Some dogs may also be allergic to certain additives or preservatives commonly found in commercial dog food.

What such allergies do in dogs is that they can manifest skin irritation, itchiness, hives, ear infections, gastrointestinal issues, and, in some cases, respiratory problems. This is why one must develop a habit of observing their dog's actions, as they may indicate an allergic reaction.

If you suspect that your dog has a food allergy, the foremost step should be to consult with your veterinarian. Your vet can help you identify the allergen and recommend a suitable diet for your dog. In some cases, a hypoallergenic diet may be necessary. This type of diet typically involves feeding your dog a novel protein, such as venison or duck, and a novel carbohydrate, such as sweet potato or pea, to avoid triggering their allergy.

It's worth noting that food sensitivities and allergies can develop at any time in a dog's life, even if they've been eating the same food for years. Therefore, it's crucial to monitor your dog's behavior and symptoms and make changes to its diet as needed. A balanced and nutritious diet is essential for your dog's overall health and well-being.

The Benefits and Drawbacks of Different Types of Dog Food

Dogs are an important part of our lives, and we want to make sure they are healthy and happy. Providing the right type of food is how one can ensure their dog gets the nutrition it needs. Besides, dry kibble, wet food, and homemade diets, which are the most common options, other types of dog food are also available, such as freeze-dried or dehydrated food. Though these options are convenient and have a long shelf life, they can be more expensive. Let's discuss some benefits and drawbacks of each type of dog food:

Dry kibble is the most common type of dog food and comes in a wide range of flavors and formulas. Some brands are specially formulated for certain breeds, ages, or health conditions. Dry kibble is easy to measure and feed, making it a convenient option for busy pet owners. However, it's important to note that not all dry kibble is created equal. Some may contain low-quality ingredients or fillers, which can lead to nutritional deficiencies and health problems in dogs. Choosing a high-quality brand that meets your dog's nutritional needs and preferences is essential.

Wet food is another popular option that comes in

canned or pouch form. This type of food has a higher moisture content than dry kibble, making it a good choice for dogs who need additional hydration in their diet. Wet food can also be more palatable for picky eaters or dogs who have trouble chewing. However, checking the ingredients to ensure they meet your dog's nutritional requirements is crucial. Wet food can spoil quickly, so storing it properly and discarding any uneaten portions is important.

Homemade diets are an alternative option for dogs who have specific dietary requirements or allergies. A homemade diet can be tailored to your dog's individual needs and preferences, but it's important to ensure that it's nutritionally balanced and meets all of your dog's dietary needs. Consulting with a veterinarian or canine nutritionist can be helpful in creating a homemade diet for your dog. It's essential to use high-quality ingredients and follow a balanced recipe to avoid nutritional deficiencies.

Freeze-dried and dehydrated food is a relatively new option that is becoming more popular. These types of food are convenient and have a long shelf life, making them a good choice for busy pet owners. Freeze-dried and dehydrated food is made by removing moisture from raw or cooked ingredients, preserving the nutrients and flavor. They can be rehydrated with water before serving and are available in a range of flavors and formulas.

The Impact of a Dog's Age, Size, and Activity Level on their Nutritional Needs

A dog's nutritional needs can vary depending on its age, size, and activity level. Puppies need more protein and calories to support their growth and development, while senior dogs may require less. Similarly, larger breeds may need more food to maintain their weight, while smaller breeds may need less. Owners must also consider their dog's activity level when determining their nutritional requirements. Active dogs require more protein and carbohydrates to support their energy needs, while less active dogs may require fewer calories. It's crucial to monitor your dog's weight and adjust its food intake as necessary to maintain optimal health.

The Potential Dangers of Certain Human Foods for Dogs

There are a number of human foods that can be harmful to dogs and should be avoided at all costs. For instance, chocolate contains caffeine and theobromine, which can cause a range of symptoms in dogs, including vomiting, diarrhea, seizures, and even death. Grapes and onions can also cause severe health issues, such as kidney failure and damage to red blood cells. As such, it's vital to keep all human foods out of reach of your dog and educate yourself about potential dangers. If you suspect that your dog has ingested something toxic, seek veterinary care immediately.

The Warning Signs of Potential Health Issues in Dogs

As a responsible dog owner, it's important to be aware of potential health issues that your dog may face. Changes in appetite, energy levels, or behavior could be warning signs of a health problem. Vomiting, diarrhea, coughing, sneezing, and lethargy are also symptoms to look out for. If you observe any of these changes in your dog, it's crucial to consult with your veterinarian promptly. Early detection and treatment can prevent serious health problems from developing.

The Importance of Good Dental Hygiene and Oral Health in Dogs

Good dental hygiene and oral health are crucial to your dog's overall well-being. Poor dental hygiene can lead to dental disease, which can cause pain, infection, and other health issues. Bad breath, swollen or bleeding gums, loose teeth, and difficulty chewing are some signs of dental disease in dogs. Scheduling regular dental cleanings with your veterinarian, providing dental chews or toys, and regularly brushing your dog's teeth is important for maintaining good dental health in your dog. These measures can help prevent dental disease and ensure your dog's optimal health.

In conclusion, ensuring the health and well-being of our canine companions involves a multifaceted approach that encompasses proper nutrition, hydration, exercise, preventative care, and dental hygiene. As responsible pet owners, we must provide our dogs with the necessary care and attention they need to live happy, healthy lives. By educating ourselves on their nutritional needs, being vigilant about potential health issues, and establishing a strong relationship with a trusted veterinarian, we can help our dogs live their best lives possible. So, let's continue to prioritize their health and well-being and give our faithful companions the love and care they deserve.

Quiz

1. How much water should a dog drink per day?
2. What are the signs of dehydration in dogs?
3. How can I keep my dog hydrated?
4. Can dogs drink milk?
5. What is the role of protein in a dog's diet?
6. How much protein does a dog need in its diet?
7. Can dogs be vegetarian?
8. What is the role of carbohydrates in a dog's diet?
9. How many carbohydrates does a dog need in its diet?
10. What are some common sources of protein for dogs?
11. What are some common sources of carbohydrates for dogs?
12. What are some common dog food allergens?
13. How can I tell if my dog has a food allergy?
14. How can I find out what my dog is allergic to?
15. What are some hypoallergenic dog food options?
16. Can dogs eat grains?
17. Can I give my dog human food?
18. How many times a day should I feed my dog?
19. Can I give my dog treats?
20. Can I give my dog bones?

Answers

1. Dogs should drink about 1 ounce of water per pound of body weight each day.

2. Dry nose, sunken eyes, lethargy, loss of skin elasticity, and dry gums.

3. Always provide fresh, clean water, and make sure your dog has access to it at all times. You can also give your dog water-rich foods like fruits and vegetables.

4. It is not recommended to give dogs milk as many dogs are lactose intolerant, which can cause digestive upset.

5. Protein is essential for building and repairing tissues in a dog's body, including muscles, organs, and bones.

6. The amount of protein a dog needs depends on its age, size, and activity level, but generally, dogs need a minimum of 18-25% protein in their diet.

7. While dogs can survive on a vegetarian diet, it is not recommended as meat provides essential nutrients that dogs require.

8. Carbohydrates provide energy for a dog's body and brain.

9. The amount of carbohydrates a dog needs depends on its age, size, and activity level, but generally, dogs need a minimum of 30-50% carbohydrates in their diet.

10. Meat, poultry, fish, eggs, and dairy products.

11. Rice, potatoes, sweet potatoes, peas, and beans.

12. Beef, chicken, dairy, wheat, and soy.

13. Common symptoms of food allergies in dogs include itching, vomiting, diarrhea, and skin rashes.

14. A veterinarian can perform a food allergy test to determine what your dog is allergic to.

15. Lamb, venison, duck, and salmon are often used in hypoallergenic dog food.

16. Yes, dogs can eat grains, but some dogs are sensitive to certain grains like wheat and corn.

17. Some human foods are safe for dogs in moderation, but many are not, so it's best to consult with your veterinarian before giving your dog any human food.

18. It depends on your dog's age and activity level, but most adult dogs do well with two meals per day.

19. Yes, but treats should be given in moderation and should not make up more than 10% of your dog's daily caloric intake.

20. Cooked bones can splinter and cause serious health issues for dogs, so it's best to avoid giving them to your dog. Instead, give your dog a safe, chewable toy to play with.

Unit 5

Understanding Dog Behavior

Have you ever looked into the eyes of a dog and felt an unbreakable bond, a connection that transcends language and species? Dogs have been earning their title as "man's best friend" for centuries, not just for their wagging tails and slobbery kisses but for their unwavering loyalty, unconditional love, and fierce protectiveness. Yet, as with any relationship, owning a dog is not always a walk in the park. From chewing up your favorite shoes to barking at strangers, these furry friends can exhibit some puzzling and occasionally aggravating behaviors. But hey, isn't that part of what makes them so endearing?

But let's say your dog constantly barks. It can be a nuisance to the neighbors, while a dog that is aggressive towards other dogs or humans can be a liability and may even pose a danger to you or others.

This is why dog owners need to understand dog behavior and be able to recognize the signs that indicate their pet's emotional state. By doing so, they can take steps to address any issues or potential problems before they escalate. Or just be smarter than the people you are around.

The Importance of Understanding Dog Behavior

Understanding dog behavior is important for several reasons. Here are a few:

Better Communication

Dogs use body language to communicate their thoughts and feelings. As a dog owner, understanding your pet's body language can help you communicate better with your furry friend. You will be able to recognize when your dog is happy, sad, scared, or angry and respond accordingly. This can help strengthen the bond between you and your pet and create a better relationship.

Preventing Behavior Problems

Behavior problems in dogs are common and can be caused by various factors, including lack of socialization, fear, anxiety, and frustration. By understanding your dog's behavior, you can identify potential problems early and take steps to prevent them from developing into more serious issues. Suppose your dog is showing signs of fear or anxiety around strangers. In that case, you can work on desensitizing them to the stimulus and teaching them that there is nothing to fear.

Ensuring the Safety of Your Dog

Understanding dog behavior can also help keep your pet safe. For example, if you know that your dog is prone to chasing cars or bikes, you can keep them on a leash or in a fenced area to prevent them from running into traffic. Similarly, suppose your dog is aggressive toward other dogs. In such cases, you can take steps to keep them away from situations where they may encounter other dogs.

Big D's Training Rally

Provides Balance

Promoting Good Health

Behavior problems in dogs can also be a sign of underlying health issues. For example, if your dog suddenly starts showing signs of aggression or fear, it could be a sign of pain or illness. By understanding your dog's behavior, you can recognize when something is not right and seek medical attention if necessary.

Building a Stronger Bond

Finally, understanding your dog's behavior can help you build a stronger bond with your pet. Dogs are social animals and thrive on positive social interactions with their owners. By understanding your dog's behavior, you can provide them with the socialization and attention they need to be happy and healthy.

Common Dog Behaviors

There are several common dog behaviors that every dog owner should be aware of. Here are a few:

• **Barking**

Barking is a natural behavior in dogs, and they use it to communicate a variety of things, including excitement, fear, or warning. However, excessive barking can be a problem and may indicate that your dog is bored, anxious, or in need of attention.

• **Chewing**

Chewing is also a natural behavior in dogs; they use it to explore their environment and relieve stress. However, destructive chewing can be a problem and may indicate that your dog is bored or not getting enough exercise.

• **Social Behaviors**

Socialization is a critical aspect of a dog's life. It helps dogs develop healthy relationships with other dogs and humans, preventing aggressive behavior towards other dogs or strangers. Proper socialization involves exposing them to different environments, people, and situations to help them learn how to behave appropriately. It also teaches them how to communicate and interpret the body language of other dogs.

- **Digging**

  Digging is another natural behavior in dogs, and they use it to create a comfortable spot or to bury their toys or bones. However, excessive digging can be a problem and may indicate that your dog is bored or anxious.

- **Jumping**

  Jumping is common in dogs, especially when they are excited or want attention. However, it can be a problem when your dog jumps on people, particularly children or elderly individuals, who may be knocked over or injured.

- **Territorial Behaviors**

  Dogs are territorial creatures by nature and have a strong instinct to mark and guard their territory. Marking involves urinating on objects to leave a scent, while guarding involves protecting their territory from intruders. Understanding these behaviors is crucial for preventing unwanted marking and guarding. Unaddressed territorial behavior may lead to aggression towards other dogs or people who approach their territory.

• **Aggression**

Aggression is a serious problem in dogs and can be caused by various factors, including fear, anxiety, lack of socialization, or past traumas. Aggressive behavior can include growling, barking, snapping, or biting and can be dangerous for both your dog and others around them.

• **Separation Anxiety**

Separation anxiety is a common problem in dogs and can be caused by a variety of factors, including lack of socialization, past traumas, or changes in their routine or environment. Signs of separation anxiety may include excessive barking or howling, destructive behavior, or toileting inside the house.

Understanding your dog's behavior and recognizing any changes or issues early on can help you address these behaviors and prevent them from escalating into more serious problems.

Understanding the Dog's Body Language

Dogs are social animals, and they communicate through various means, including body language.

Understanding a dog's body language can be essential in forming a strong bond with your pet and can help you identify when your dog is happy, scared, or aggressive. Here are some key components of a dog's body language and how to interpret them:

- **Ear Position**

   A dog's ears can indicate its emotional state. When a dog's ears are relaxed and in their natural position, the dog is generally calm and content. However, if the ears are erect and pointing forward, the dog may be alert or curious. If the ears are pinned back against the head, the dog may be scared, anxious, or submissive.

- **Tail Position**

   The position of a dog's tail can provide valuable information about its mood. A wagging tail typically indicates that the dog is happy or excited, but the speed and direction of the wag can also be important. A tail held high and stiff could indicate that the dog is alert or on guard, while a tail tucked between the legs suggests fear or submission.

• **Posture**

A dog's overall posture can convey its level of confidence, aggression, or submission. A confident dog will stand tall with their head held high and its weight evenly distributed, while a submissive dog may lower their head and cower down. An aggressive dog may stand stiffly with its hackles raised and weight forward.

• **Other signs**

A dog's body language is not limited to just its ears, tail, and posture. Other indicators of their emotional state can include facial expressions, such as bared teeth or a relaxed mouth, and body movements, such as pacing, panting, or jumping.

To accurately interpret a dog's body language, it's essential to consider their behavior as a whole rather than relying on just one indicator. Additionally, understanding a dog's body language can take time and practice, so it's essential to observe your dog and learn their unique cues. Finally, if you are unsure of a dog's behavior or if you feel uncomfortable around a dog, it's best to seek the advice of a professional trainer or veterinarian.

Taking Inspiration from Mother Dog Regarding Pup Training

Mother dogs play a crucial role in their puppies' early development by providing them with warmth, nourishment, and protection. In addition, they also teach important social skills and behaviors that are essential for the puppies to survive and thrive.

Mother Dog's Teaching of Important Life Skills to Puppies

Mother dogs teach their puppies important life skills such as communication, socialization, and hierarchy. They also teach them how to control their biting, chewing, and play behaviors, which are important for developing healthy relationships with humans and other animals.

Application of Mother Dog Training Techniques in Puppy Training

Dog trainers can learn a lot from observing mother dogs and applying their training techniques to puppies. This includes positive reinforcement, socialization, and using body language to communicate with the puppies. Trainers can also use games and play to teach puppies important skills.

Benefits of Mother Dog Training Techniques for Puppies' Long-term Behavior

By using mother dog training techniques, puppies can develop good behavior habits that will last a lifetime. This includes proper socialization, communication, and the ability to control their behavior. Puppies that receive proper training are more likely to become well-behaved adult dogs that are a joy to be around.

Understanding Dog Behavior for Veterinarians and Dog Trainers

Understanding dog behavior is crucial for veterinarians and dog trainers to provide dogs with the best care and training. This includes understanding how dogs communicate, how they learn, and how their environment influences their behavior.

Dog behavior has a significant impact on owners' lives and the community. Poorly trained dogs can cause various problems, including aggressive behavior, excessive barking, and destructive behavior. By understanding dog behavior, trainers and veterinarians can help prevent these issues and promote safe and happy communities.

The field of dog behavior is constantly evolving, and there is always new research and studies being conducted.

Staying up-to-date on the latest research, which includes studies on dog cognition, communication, and behavior modification, can help trainers and veterinarians provide the best care for their clients.

Moreover, personal anecdotes and experiences of dog owners and trainers can also provide valuable insights into dog behavior. This includes stories about successful training techniques, difficult behavior issues, and the joys and challenges of owning and training dogs. Sharing these stories can help build a community of dog lovers who can learn from and support each other.

In conclusion, the importance of continued learning and understanding of dog behavior cannot be overstated for dog owners and trainers. A deeper knowledge of canine behavior allows for better communication with dogs, leading to more effective training and a stronger bond between humans and their canine companions.

With education, one can prevent behavioral issues and misunderstandings that may arise between dogs and their owners, resulting in a happier and safer living environment for both parties. Therefore, it is crucial for dog owners and trainers to constantly educate themselves on dog behavior and seek professional help when necessary to ensure the well-being of their furry friends.

Unit 6:
Training a New Dog

Imagine the joy of bringing home a new furry companion, a loyal friend who will share your life's adventures and bring endless moments of happiness. The moment you set eyes on your new four-legged friend, your heart fills with warmth and anticipation, knowing that this special bond will create memories that will last a lifetime. Whether you've decided to add a playful puppy to your family or give a loving home to an older dog, embarking on training a new canine companion is exciting and rewarding.

Becoming a search dog

As you welcome your new furry family member into your home, a sense of anticipation fills the air. You can envision the days ahead filled with playful romps in the park, peaceful walks by the beach, and cozy cuddles on lazy afternoons. This new addition to your household brings fresh energy and a renewed sense of purpose.

Training your new canine companion is essential to ensuring a harmonious and fulfilling relationship. It allows for clear communication, mutual respect, and trust. You can shape your dog's behavior through training, help them understand their role in the family, and set them up for a lifetime of good manners and socialization.

The training journey begins with patience and consistency. Like humans, dogs have unique personalities, temperaments, and learning styles. Some may be eager to please and quick to pick up commands, while others may require more time and repetition. But every step forward, no matter how small, brings a sense of accomplishment and strengthens the bond between you and your furry companion.

With each training session, you discover dogs' remarkable intelligence and adaptability. You witness their eagerness to learn, ability to understand cues and gestures, and unwavering loyalty. Training becomes more than just a means to an end; it becomes a shared experience that deepens your connection and builds a foundation of trust.

But training a dog is not just about obedience; it's also about nurturing a loving and nurturing environment. You learn to understand their needs, listen to their nonverbal cues, and provide them with the care and attention they require. In return, your furry friend showers you with unconditional love, unwavering loyalty, and a boundless capacity for joy.

The journey of training a new canine companion is not without its challenges. There may be moments of frustration, setbacks, and even the occasional chewed-up shoe. However, the rewards far outweigh the difficulties. The bond you forge, the memories you create, and the love you share make it all worthwhile.

Training a New Dog

Training a new dog is a fundamental and educational process that sets the stage for a harmonious relationship and a well-mannered pet. By following proven techniques and strategies, you can effectively train your new furry companion and foster a strong bond that will last a lifetime.

One of the primary considerations when training a new dog is establishing a consistent routine. Dogs thrive on structure, so developing a daily schedule for feeding, exercise, and training sessions is crucial. This helps your dog anticipate and understand their daily activities and aids in potty training by establishing regular bathroom breaks.

Fundamental obedience commands should be a top priority during training. Teaching your dog commands like "sit," "stay," "come," and "lie down" provides them with a solid foundation for good behavior and ensures that you have control in various situations. Direction reinforcement techniques, such as presentation, praise, and affection, play a pivotal role in reinforcing desired behaviors and motivating your dog to learn and obey. Consistency and repetition are key elements of this process. Commands build a line of communication.

Socialization is another vital aspect of training that should not be overlooked. Exposing your dog to various people, animals, and environments from an early age helps prevent fear, aggression, and anxiety issues. Organizing playdates with other dogs, visits to parks, and encounters with different sights and sounds help your dog become comfortable and well-adjusted in a wide range of social settings.

Addressing behavioral issues promptly is crucial to preventing them from becoming ingrained habits. Common problems such as chewing, jumping, or excessive barking can be redirected through positive reinforcement and providing appropriate alternatives. For example, redirect your dog's chewing behavior to chew toys or discourage jumping by teaching them to sit and greet people calmly.

It is important to remember that dog training is an ongoing process. Dogs continue to learn and adapt throughout their lives, so consistent reinforcement and occasional refresher training sessions are necessary to maintain good behavior. Seeking the assistance of professional dog trainers or enrolling in obedience classes can offer valuable guidance, specialized techniques, and personalized solutions for any training challenges you may encounter.

Understanding Birth to Maturity

Understanding what happens when a dog comes into the world is a fascinating journey that sheds light on its development and behavior. From birth to maturity, dogs undergo significant transformations that shape their abilities and interactions with humans and their environment. Additionally, comparing the training methods employed by K9 pack training and human understanding of training can provide valuable insights into the most effective approaches for teaching and communicating with dogs.

Lt. Dan

When a dog is born, they enter the world as a helpless and dependent creature. During the first few weeks of life, they rely entirely on their mother for nourishment, warmth, and protection. During this critical period, puppies begin to develop their senses, motor skills, and social behavior. They learn to communicate with their littermates through body language, vocalizations, and play, laying the groundwork for future interactions with other dogs and humans. Dogs never receive a manual on how to live in the human world.

As the puppies grow, they go through a phase known

as the socialization period. This is a crucial stage where they become more receptive to new experiences, people, and environments. Proper socialization during this period greatly influences their temperament, confidence, and ability to adapt to various situations. Positive interactions and exposure to different stimuli can shape a well-rounded and sociable adult dog during this time.

Contrasting K9 Pack Training and Human Understanding

When it comes to training methods, there are distinct differences between K9 pack training and human understanding of training. K9 pack training, often observed in wild or feral dog groups, relies on natural pack dynamics and hierarchy. Dogs in a pack learn from their interactions with other pack members, primarily through observation and imitation. Dominance and submission play key roles in their social structure, and training occurs through correction and reinforcement from the alpha dog or leader.

On the other hand, human understanding of training incorporates various techniques based on positive reinforcement, consistency, and communication. Modern dog training emphasizes building a bond between the dog and its human companion, using rewards such as treats, praise, and play to reinforce desired behaviors. Training methods focus on teaching dogs to understand cues, commands, and boundaries, promoting cooperation and obedience through mutual understanding.

While both approaches have their merits, the human understanding of training has gained prominence due to their emphasis on positive reinforcement, respect for the dog's well-being, and the establishment of a cooperative relationship. It recognizes the importance of clear communication, consistency, and patience in helping dogs learn and adapt to human expectations.

Training is not jail!

Understanding the Training Process

Training a dog is a multi-faceted process that goes beyond teaching basic commands. It involves fostering a deep understanding of a dog's behavior, motivations, and learning capabilities. By gaining insight into the training process, both dogs and owners can embark on a transformative journey of growth and cooperation.

At its core, the training process is about effective communication between humans and dogs. Dogs primarily communicate through body language, vocalizations, and instinctual behaviors. As owners, learning how to interpret and respond to these signals is essential, creating a bridge of understanding between species. Owners can tailor their training methods to meet their pet's needs by observing and understanding their dog's unique communication style.

Positive reinforcement lies at the heart of successful training. It involves rewarding desired behaviors to encourage their repetition. This method strengthens the bond between dog and owner, as it associates training with positive experiences. Whether it's using treats, praise, or play, the key is to provide immediate and consistent rewards that motivate the dog to continue learning and behaving appropriately.

Consistency and clear communication are vital elements in the training process. Dogs thrive on routine, so it is essential to establish consistent rules and expectations. Training cues and commands should be clear, concise, and consistent across all training sessions. Dogs quickly pick up on patterns and respond better to a predictable, structured training environment.

Understanding the learning capabilities of dogs is crucial for successful training. Dogs learn through repetition and association, so breaking down complex tasks into smaller, manageable steps is key.

Gradually increasing difficulty levels and providing ample opportunities for practice ensures a steady learning curve. It is essential to recognize that each dog is unique and may learn at their own pace. Patience and persistence are vital qualities for owners to possess throughout the training journey.

Training should be a positive and enjoyable experience for both dogs and owners. Incorporating a variety and incorporating fun activities during training sessions can keep dogs engaged and motivated. Interactive toys, games, and challenges can add an element of excitement and make learning a rewarding experience.

Preparing for a New Dog

Preparing for a new dog involves several essential steps to ensure a smooth transition and a harmonious living environment. Firstly, conduct thorough research to choose a breed that aligns with your lifestyle and preferences. Next, dog-proof your home by removing potential hazards and creating a safe space for your new companion.

Acquire essential supplies such as food bowls, a comfortable bed, toys, and a leash. Establish a consistent routine for feeding, exercise, and potty breaks to provide structure and stability. Select a reputable veterinarian and schedule an initial check-up to address health and vaccination needs.

Finally, prepare for training by familiarizing yourself with positive reinforcement techniques and creating a designated training area. By following these steps, you can set the groundwork for a successful and fulfilling journey with your new furry friend.

Basic Training Techniques

Basic training techniques lay the groundwork for a well-behaved and obedient dog. These techniques focus on teaching essential commands and behaviors that ensure safety, promote good manners, and strengthen the bond between dog and owner. Here are a few key techniques to get you started:

Positive Reinforcement

- Use rewards such as treats, praise, and play to reinforce desired behaviors.
- Reward your dog immediately after it performs the desired behavior to associate it with positive outcomes.
- Avoid punishment-based methods, as they can damage the trust and relationship with your dog.

Start with Basic Commands

- Begin with fundamental commands like "sit," "stay," "come," and "lie down."

- Use clear and consistent verbal cues and hand signals to accompany each command.
- Break down each command into small steps and gradually increase the difficulty as your dog progresses.

Consistency and Repetition

- Practice training sessions regularly to reinforce learned behaviors and establish consistency.
- Keep training sessions short and frequent to maintain focus and prevent boredom.
- Incorporate training into daily routines and activities to generalize learned behaviors.

Leash Training

- Teach your dog to walk calmly on a leash without pulling.
- Use positive reinforcement to reward loose leash walking and redirect undesirable behaviors.
- Gradually introduce distractions and different environments to reinforce leash manners.

Socialization

- Expose your dog to various people, animals, and environments to promote sociability and reduce fear or aggression.

- Arrange controlled and positive interactions with other dogs and individuals of different ages and backgrounds.

- Reward your dog for calm and appropriate behavior during socialization experiences.

Patience and Persistence

- Understand that training takes time and that dogs learn at their own pace.

- Be patient with your dog's progress and avoid getting frustrated.

- Celebrate small successes and remain consistent in your training efforts.

By implementing these basic training techniques, you can establish a solid foundation for your dog's behavior and create a positive and cooperative relationship. Remember to make training sessions enjoyable and rewarding for you and your dog, as this will enhance the learning experience and strengthen your bond.

Training a new dog is a transformative journey that requires understanding, preparation, and effective techniques. By recognizing the developmental stages of dogs, appreciating the differences between training approaches, and following basic training techniques, owners can create a solid foundation for a well-behaved and happy canine companion. Through patience, consistency, and positive reinforcement, the training process builds a strong bond between owner and dog, resulting in a harmonious and fulfilling relationship that lasts a lifetime.

Training Humans versus Training Dogs: Exploring the Dynamics

Training is crucial for shaping behavior and developing skills involving humans or dogs. While humans possess complex cognitive abilities, dogs rely on their instinctual learning capabilities. Let's delve into the dynamics of training humans and dogs, understanding the underlying principles, techniques, and challenges involved.

Human Training:

With their advanced cognitive abilities, humans present unique characteristics that influence training.

Cognitive Abilities: Humans possess abstract reasoning, language acquisition skills, and problem solving capabilities. These abilities enable diverse forms of training, as humans can grasp complex concepts and apply them in various contexts. Additionally, humans have the capacity for self-directed learning, actively seeking knowledge, setting goals, and monitoring progress.

Techniques: Human training encompasses a combination of cognitive and behavioral approaches. Cognitive techniques focus on critical thinking, conceptual understanding, and knowledge transfer. Behavioral approaches employ behavior modification techniques like positive reinforcement and punishment to shape human behavior and achieve desired outcomes.

Challenges: Human training introduces specific challenges. Motivation plays a crucial role, influenced by factors like intrinsic and extrinsic motivation, personal interest, and individual goals. Resistance to change is also common, necessitating strategies to overcome obstacles and foster openness to new ideas or behavior changes.

Dog Training:

Dogs possess their own cognitive abilities and communication methods, requiring unique approaches for effective training.

Cognitive Abilities: Dogs learn through association, repetition, and reinforcement. While their abstract reasoning is limited, they excel at understanding and responding to their environment. Dogs have a natural inclination towards social hierarchies, routines, and cues, facilitating their learning process.

Techniques: Dog training relies on techniques such as operant conditioning and classical conditioning. Positive reinforcement, involving treats, praise, and rewards, proves highly effective in shaping desired behaviors. Classical conditioning techniques, like clicker training or associating specific cues with actions, help dogs establish conditioned responses.

Challenges: Communication poses a significant challenge in dog training. Dogs heavily rely on nonverbal cues and body language, requiring clear and consistent communication from trainers. Additionally, each dog possesses a unique temperament, personality, and learning pace, necessitating tailored training approaches that accommodate individual differences.

Comparisons and Distinctions:

Motivation and Reinforcement: Both humans and dogs respond well to direction reinforcement, which encourages desired behaviors and motivates learning. Rewards and consistent reinforcement contribute to successful training outcomes in both species.

Communication and Understanding: Humans rely on verbal language, while dogs rely on non-verbal cues and body language for communication. Trainers must adapt their communication methods to suit the different communication styles of humans and dogs.

Complexity and Adaptability: Human training involves complex cognitive processes, including abstract reasoning and problem-solving, whereas dog training focuses on simpler associations and responses. Humans possess the ability for self-directed learning, while dogs rely on guidance from trainers for their learning process.

In conclusion, while fundamental principles and techniques are shared between training humans and dogs, differences in cognitive abilities and communication methods result in distinct approaches and challenges. Recognizing these distinctions allows trainers to develop effective techniques tailored to each species, ultimately leading to successful learning experiences for both humans and dogs.

Preparing to Bring a Dog Home: A Comprehensive Guide

Bringing a dog into your home is an exciting and fulfilling experience. However, it also comes with responsibilities and requires careful preparation to ensure a smooth transition for both you and your new furry friend. This paper aims to provide a comprehensive guide on how to prepare for bringing a dog home, covering important aspects such as research, home preparation, acquiring supplies, establishing routines, and ensuring a safe environment.

Research and Choosing the Right Dog:

- Understanding different breeds and their characteristics
- Assessing your lifestyle and finding a compatible breed or mix
- Considering adoption options and reputable breeders
- Conducting interviews or visits to ensure compatibility **Home Preparation:**
- Designating a suitable space for the dog

- Securing hazardous areas and eliminating potential dangers
- Ensuring proper fencing and gating
- Creating a comfortable sleeping area
- Puppy-proofing the house Acquiring Essential Supplies:

- Food and water bowls
- High-quality dog food
- Collar, leash, and identification tags
- Dog bed or crate
- Toys, treats, and chews
- Grooming supplies
- Dog waste disposal equipment

Establishing Routines:

- Designing a feeding schedule
- Establishing a bathroom routine and training plan
- Setting exercise and playtime routines
- Organizing a regular grooming schedule
- Planning for socialization and training activities

Ensuring a Safe Environment:

- Checking for toxic plants and household chemicals
- Safely storing medications and hazardous substances
  - Securing loose cables and cords

- Identifying and eliminating potential choking hazards
- Implementing a safe outdoor space or supervised play area

Preparing to bring a dog home involves a variety of considerations to ensure a smooth transition and a safe, happy environment for your new companion. By conducting thorough research, preparing your home adequately, acquiring necessary supplies, establishing routines, and ensuring a safe environment, you set the stage for a successful dog adoption experience. Proper preparation is key to building a strong foundation for a lifelong bond between you and your new furry friend.

Exploring Dog Training Techniques: Unveiling the Alpha Bitch's Approach

Dog training is an essential aspect of responsible pet ownership. It establishes a bond between dogs and their human companions while promoting obedience, good behavior, and overall well-being. Over the years, various training techniques have emerged, each with its own philosophy and methodology. In this article, we will explore some of the many different dog training techniques and shed light on the unique approach of the Alpha Bitch.

Additionally, we will explore why dog training is effective and beneficial for dogs and their owners.

Direction Reinforcement Training:

One popular approach to dog training is a direction reinforcement. This technique focuses on rewarding desired behaviors to encourage their repetition. Treats, praise, and playtime serve as direction enforcement tools. Positive reinforcement training creates a positive association in dogs' minds, making them more likely to engage in behaviors that result in positive outcomes.

Clicker Training:

Clicker training is another technique that relies on positive reinforcement. It involves using a handheld clicker to signal desired behaviors, followed by a treat or reward. The clicker serves as a distinct sound marker that communicates to the dog when it correctly performs the desired action. Through consistent repetition, dogs learn to associate the clicker sound with a reward, making the training process more efficient.

Alpha Bitch Training:

The Alpha Bitch approach is based on the concept of establishing a clear hierarchy within the human-dog relationship. This technique emphasizes the dog's natural pack instinct and relies on the owner taking on the role of the alpha or pack leader. The Alpha Bitch is assertive, confident, and consistent in their interactions with the dog.

Dircction Reinforcement (The Best Training Option)

The training begins with setting boundaries and rules, establishing that the owner is the one in control. The Alpha Bitch uses assertive body language, clear vocal cues, and appropriate physical touch to communicate expectations. Use a little of all Training techniques! This approach emphasizes consistency, patience, and repetition to reinforce desired behaviors and discourage unwanted ones.

Why Training Works:

Dog training, regardless of the technique used, works due to several key factors:

Communication: Dogs are highly perceptive and responsive to human communication cues. Training provides a structured way to communicate expectations and reinforce appropriate behaviors.

Mental Stimulation: Training engages dogs' minds and provides mental stimulation, preventing boredom and the development of destructive behaviors.

Bonding and Trust: The training process strengthens the bond between dogs and their owners. Consistent positive interactions build trust and enhance the human-dog relationship.

Problem Prevention: Training addresses potential behavioral issues before they become problematic. Training minimizes the likelihood of future conflicts or undesirable habits by teaching dogs appropriate behaviors.

Quiz: Dog Training Techniques

Questions

1. What is positive reinforcement training?
2. What is the purpose of clicker training?
3. What is the concept behind Alpha Bitch training?
4. What is one key factor why training works?
5. How does positive reinforcement training work?
6. How does clicker training work?
7. What is the role of the Alpha Bitch in training?
8. What is positive reinforcement in dog training?
9. What is clicker training?
10. How does lure training work?
11. What is compulsion training?
12. What is relationship-based training?
13. How does the Alpha Bitch approach training?
14. What role does consistency play in dog training?
15. How does socialization benefit dog training?
16. What are the benefits of effective dog training?
17. Why is a strong bond important in dog training?

Answers

1. Positive reinforcement training focuses on rewarding desired behaviors to encourage their repetition.

2. Clicker training uses a distinct sound marker to signal desired behaviors, followed by a treat or reward.

3. Alpha Bitch training emphasizes establishing a clear hierarchy and the owner taking on the role of the pack leader.

4. Communication - training provides a structured way to communicate expectations and reinforce appropriate behaviors.

5. Positive reinforcement training rewards desired behaviors to encourage their repetition.

6. Clicker training uses a distinct sound marker to signal desired behaviors, followed by a treat or reward.

7. The Alpha Bitch establishes boundaries, sets rules, and communicates expectations with assertiveness and consistency.

8. Positive reinforcement is a technique that involves rewarding desired behaviors to reinforce their occurrence.

9. Clicker training uses a clicker device to mark desired behaviors, followed by a reward, to help dogs associate the sound with positive reinforcement.

10. Lure training involves using treats or toys to guide the dog into desired positions, gradually shaping their behavior through repetitive actions.

11. Compulsion training, also known as dominance-based training, emphasizes correction and punishment for an unwanted behavior, often utilizing tools like choke chains or shock collars.

12. Relationship-based training focuses on building a strong bond between the dog and the owner, relying on clear communication, trust, and mutual respect.

13. The Alpha Bitch utilizes a combination of techniques, including consistency, body language, assertiveness, positive reinforcement, exercise, mental stimulation, and socialization.

14. Consistency helps dogs understand and adhere to the rules and expectations set by the owner, facilitating effective training.

15. Socialization exposes dogs to various environments, people, and animals, promoting well-rounded behavior and preventing issues related to fear or aggression.

16. Effective dog training improves communication, modifies behavior, ensures safety, provides mental stimulation, and reduces stress for both the dog and the owner.

17. A strong bond between a dog and its owner enhances trust, cooperation, and understanding, facilitating successful training outcomes.

Unit 7 Advanced Training Techniques

Advanced dog training encompasses a wide range of specialized skills that enable dogs to perform specific tasks and fulfill important roles in various fields. This chapter will explore the training techniques and capabilities of service dogs, search dogs, detector dogs, and protection dogs. These highly trained canines contribute significantly to human welfare and safety, and their expertise is achieved through rigorous training and dedication.

Service Dogs

Service dogs are trained to assist individuals with disabilities, providing invaluable support and enhancing their independence. These dogs can aid people with physical disabilities, hearing impairments, visual impairments, and even those with psychiatric conditions such as PTSD. The training process for service dogs is meticulous and involves teaching them specific tasks tailored to the needs of their handler. Some common tasks service dogs perform include retrieving objects, opening doors, guiding the visually impaired, and alerting their handlers to sounds or alarms. The dogs must also exhibit exceptional behavior in public, remaining calm and focused in various environments.

Search Dogs

Search dogs play a vital role in locating missing persons or detecting specific items. These highly skilled canines are commonly used in search and rescue operations, law enforcement efforts, and disaster response teams. Search dogs are trained to follow scent trails, track human scents over long distances, and detect scents trapped under debris or water. They undergo extensive training in scent discrimination and obedience, allowing them to work effectively in challenging environments. Handlers utilize a variety of training methods, such as reward-based training and scent recognition exercises, to develop the dogs' search capabilities.

Merkel the Bulldog "Nosework"

Action Dog Association

Detector Dogs

Detector dogs possess an exceptional sense of smell, allowing them to detect a wide range of substances, including narcotics, explosives, firearms, or even agricultural products. Law enforcement agencies, border patrol units, and security firms employ these dogs to identify illegal substances or potential threats. Training detector dogs involves imprinting specific odors and teaching them to indicate the presence of the targeted substance. Positive reinforcement techniques are utilized to reward accurate detections, ensuring that the dogs maintain high accuracy and reliability in their work.

Protection Dogs

Protection dogs, also known as guard dogs, are trained to provide security and protection to individuals or properties. These dogs possess a strong sense of loyalty, an instinct to defend, and the ability to assess potentially threatening situations. Training protection dogs involves a combination of obedience training, specialized guarding techniques, and controlled aggression. Protection dogs must receive training from experienced professionals to ensure their behavior is predictable and well-controlled. Law enforcement agencies, security firms, or even individuals seeking personal protection can employ protection dogs.

Advanced dog training is a specialized field that enables dogs to perform essential roles in various sectors. Service dogs enhance the lives of individuals with disabilities, search dogs assist in locating missing persons, detector dogs help identify illicit substances, and protection dogs provide security and peace of mind. These remarkable animals exemplify the incredible bond between humans and dogs, and their training showcases the intelligence, dedication, and skills that dogs possess. Through rigorous training and expert guidance, these dogs become highly proficient in their respective roles, positively impacting society and helping to ensure our safety and well-being.

Course Unit: *Uses of Service Dogs, Service Dog Training, Service Dog Requirements*

Introduction:

Service dogs are highly trained animals that assist and support individuals with disabilities. They are trained to perform specific tasks that help their handlers navigate their daily lives. This course unit will provide an overview of the various uses of service dogs, the training they undergo, and the requirements for both the dogs and their handlers.

Uses of Service Dogs:

1. Guide Dogs: Guide dogs are trained to assist individuals with visual impairments or blindness by navigating obstacles and guiding them safely.

2. Hearing Dogs: Hearing dogs are trained to alert individuals with hearing impairments or deafness to important sounds, such as alarms, doorbells, or approaching vehicles.

3. Mobility Assistance Dogs: These dogs help individuals with physical disabilities by performing tasks such as retrieving objects, opening doors, or providing balance and stability.

4. Medical Alert Dogs: Medical alert dogs are trained to detect changes in their handler's body odor or behavior that indicate an upcoming medical episode, such as a seizure or diabetic episode.

5. Psychiatric Service Dogs: These dogs provide support to individuals with psychiatric or mental health conditions, such as anxiety, depression, or

post-traumatic stress disorder (PTSD), by providing comfort, grounding, and assistance during crisis situations.

Service Dog Training:

1. Basic Obedience Training: Service dogs undergo rigorous obedience training to ensure they respond reliably to commands and maintain good behavior in various environments.

2. Task Training: Service dogs are trained to perform specific tasks that assist their handlers with their disabilities. This training is tailored to the individual's needs and can include tasks such as retrieving medication, alerting to sounds, or providing deep pressure therapy.

3. Public Access Training: Service dogs must be trained to behave appropriately in public settings, including restaurants, stores, and public transportation. They should be able to remain calm and focused, ignore distractions, and maintain good manners.

4. Socialization: Service dogs undergo extensive socialization to ensure they are comfortable and well-behaved in various social situations. They are

exposed to different people, animals, environments, and stimuli to build their confidence and adaptability.

5. Handler Training: Service dog training often includes training the handler on effectively working with and managing their service dog. This training helps create a strong bond and promotes successful teamwork.

Service Dog Requirements:

1. Handler's Disability: To qualify for a service dog, individuals must have a disability recognized under the Americans with Disabilities Act (ADA) or similar legislation in their country.

2. Recommendation from a Healthcare Professional: In most cases, individuals need a recommendation from a healthcare professional, such as a doctor or therapist, stating that a service dog would be beneficial for their disability.

3. Commitment to Care: Service dog handlers must be capable of providing proper care, including food, grooming, veterinary care, and exercise, to ensure the well-being of the dog.

4. Training and Certification: While certification is not required by law in many places, it is recommended to ensure that the dog has undergone appropriate training and meets the necessary standards for public access.

5. Compliance with Regulations: Handlers must adhere to local laws and regulations regarding service dogs, including keeping their dog under control, cleaning up after them, and ensuring their behavior does not pose a threat to public safety.

Course Unit Duration: 4 weeks (8 sessions)

Learning Outcomes:

By the end of this course unit, participants will be able to:

- Understand the principles and benefits of dog agility training.

- Identify and utilize appropriate equipment for agility exercises.

- Implement positive reinforcement techniques to train dogs for agility.

- Teach their dogs a variety of tricks using effective training methods.

- Recognize safety considerations when engaging in agility activities with their dogs.

- Strengthen the bond with their canine companion through training and play.

Session 1: Introduction to Dog Agility Training

- Importance and benefits of dog agility training

- Overview of agility equipment and its uses

- Safety Considerations and Precautions for Agility Training

- Setting training goals and developing a training plan

Session 2: Foundation Skills for Agility

- Introduction to basic obedience commands

- Building focus and attention through positive reinforcement

- Teaching the "touch" and "target" commands

- Introducing dogs to agility obstacles (e.g., tunnels, jumps)

Session 3: Intermediate Agility Training

- Training dogs to navigate weave poles

- Teaching the "pause table" command

- Introducing contact obstacles (e.g., A-frame, dog walk)

- Implementing handling techniques (e.g., front cross, rear cross)

Session 4: Advanced Agility Techniques

- Perfecting obstacle performance and speed

- Advanced weave pole training methods

- Sequencing obstacles to create courses
- Introduction to agility trials and competitions

Session 5: Introduction to Dog Trick Training

- Understanding the benefits of trick training for dogs

- Selecting appropriate tricks based on the dog's abilities and interests

- Basic training techniques for teaching tricks

- Teaching foundational tricks such as sitting, staying, and rolling over

Session 6: Intermediate Trick Training

- Expanding the trick repertoire with more complex tricks (e.g., spin, shake hands)

- Shaping behaviors through capturing and shaping techniques

- Incorporating props and cues into trick training

- Troubleshooting common challenges during trick training

Session 7: Advanced Trick Training

- Teaching advanced tricks such as playing dead, jumping through hoops, and crawling

- Combining tricks to create impressive sequences

- Incorporating verbal and visual cues for complex tricks

- Developing a routine for performances or demonstrations

Session 8: Strengthening the Human-Canine Bond through Training and Play

- Importance of positive reinforcement in training

- Engaging in interactive play with dogs to enhance training and bonding

- Incorporating training exercises into daily routines

- Strategies for ongoing training and 44 beyond the course

Assessment:

Participants will be assessed through practical demonstrations of training exercises, trick performances, and a written reflection on their training journey. Additionally, active participation in discussions and group activities will contribute to the overall assessment.

Note: This course unit is designed to provide a foundation in dog agility and trick training. Further courses or workshops may be beneficial for more advanced training and specialized areas.

1. What is dog agility training?
2. Which piece of agility equipment requires dogs to climb up and down?
3. What is the purpose of using positive reinforcement in dog training?
4. What is the command used to teach dogs to touch an object with their nose?
5. Which agility obstacle requires dogs to weave in and out of a series of poles?

6. Which command is used to teach dogs to stay in a designated spot for a period of time?

7. What is the purpose of incorporating handling techniques in agility training?

8. What is the key to successful trick training?

9. What is the first trick often taught to dogs?

10. What technique involves capturing and reinforcing behaviors gradually to shape a trick?

11. Which trick involves the dog rolling over onto its back?

12. What is the purpose of incorporating props in trick training?

13. What trick involves the dog spinning around in a circle?

14. Which trick requires the dog to lift its paw and touch the owner's hand?

15. What is the term for combining multiple tricks to create a sequence of behaviors?

16. What command is used to teach dogs to lie flat on the ground?

17. Which trick involves the dog jumping through a hoop?

18. How can play be incorporated into training to enhance the human-canine bond?

19. What is the purpose of ongoing training and enrichment for dogs?

20. What is the most important aspect of dog training?

Answers

- Dog agility training is a sport that involves teaching dogs to navigate through a variety of obstacles and perform tasks within a set course.

- A-frame.

- Positive reinforcement helps to encourage desired behaviors by rewarding the dog with treats, praise, or play.

- "Touch" command.

- Weave poles.

- "Stay" command.

- Handling techniques help guide the dog through the course efficiently and effectively.

- Patience and consistency.

- "Sit" command.

- Shaping.

- "Roll over" trick.

- Props can add novelty and visual interest to the trick, making it more engaging for the dog and the audience.

- "Spin" trick.
- "Shake hands" trick.
- Chaining.
- "Down" command.
- "Jump through hoop" trick.
- Play can be used as a reward during training sessions and can also be a fun bonding activity outside of formal training.
- Ongoing training and enrichment help keep dogs mentally stimulated, prevent boredom, and reinforce learned behaviors.
- Building a strong and trusting bond between the owner and the dog.

Quiz:

- What is the purpose of a guide dog?
- What is the main role of a hearing dog?
- What tasks do mobility assistance dogs perform?

Answers

- To assist individuals with visual impairments or blindness by navigating obstacles and guiding them safely.
- To alert individuals with hearing impairments or deafness to important sounds, such as alarms or doorbells.
- They help individuals with physical disabilities by performing.

Unit 8 Canine First Aid

Knowing how to administer first aid to your beloved canine companion in emergencies can significantly improve their well-being and save their lives. This unit will provide you with a comprehensive guide to understanding and applying basic first-aid techniques for dogs. From recognizing normal behavior to performing CPR, we will cover essential skills that every dog owner should know. Additionally, we will discuss the importance of preparation, safety precautions, and the significance of training and certifications in canine first aid.

In Memory of Jim Couch

A great Search & Rescue Handler

Certified by

Big D's Dog Training

Understanding the Importance of Canine First Aid

Before delving into the specific techniques, it is crucial to grasp the importance of canine first aid. Dogs, like humans, are susceptible to accidents, injuries, and sudden illnesses. Being able to provide immediate care can prevent further harm, alleviate pain, and increase the chances of a successful recovery. Canine first aid is not a substitute for professional veterinary care, but it serves as a vital bridge between an emergency situation and veterinary assistance.

Preparation and Approach

1. Recognizing Normal Dog Behavior:
   To effectively administer first aid, it is crucial to understand what constitutes normal behavior in dogs. By becoming familiar with your dog's typical actions, body language, and vital signs, you can quickly identify when something is amiss and respond promptly.

2. Safety Precautions When Giving First Aid to Dogs: Before initiating any first aid procedures, ensuring your and your dog's safety is paramount. Remember that injured or ill dogs may be scared, confused, or in pain, which can affect their behavior. Taking precautions such as using a muzzle if necessary, approaching slowly, and avoiding sudden movements will help minimize the risk of bites or further injuries.

3. Approach During Emergencies:

During emergencies, it is crucial to stay calm and composed. Assess the situation and prioritize your safety before approaching the injured dog. Call for help or ask someone to assist you while you tend to the dog. Always remember that providing first aid is essential, but you should also seek veterinary care as soon as possible.

Basic First Aid Skills

1. Assessing the Situation:

   The first step in providing first aid to your dog is to assess the situation and ensure your own safety. Be cautious, as injured dogs may behave unpredictably due to fear or pain. Approach your dog slowly, and speak calmly and soothingly to avoid escalating the situation. Observe your dog's breathing, behavior, and the extent of the injury to determine the severity of the situation.

2. Muzzling:

   Injured or scared dogs may bite out of fear or pain. Suppose your dog shows signs of aggression or discomfort. In that case, it is essential to muzzle them before proceeding with any first aid. Use a soft cloth, gauze, or a commercially available dog muzzle to ensure it is properly secured while allowing your dog to breathe comfortably.

3. Bleeding:

In the case of bleeding, apply direct pressure to the wound using a clean cloth or sterile dressing. Maintain pressure until the bleeding stops or until you can seek veterinary assistance. Elevating the injured area above the heart level can help slow down the bleeding. If the bleeding is severe or arterial, apply a tourniquet between the wound and the heart, but only as a last resort. Remember to release the tourniquet every 10 to 15 minutes to prevent further damage.

4. Wounds and Cuts:

Clean minor wounds and cuts by gently rinsing them with a mild antiseptic solution or clean water. Avoid using hydrogen peroxide, as it can be harmful to healthy tissues. Apply an antibiotic ointment and cover the wound with a clean dressing or sterile gauze. Seek veterinary attention if the wound is deep or gaping or if there are signs of infection such as redness, swelling, or discharge.

5. Fractures and Sprains:

If you suspect your dog has a fracture or sprain, it's essential to immobilize the injured limb to prevent further damage. Use a makeshift splint by securing a rigid object (such as a rolled-up newspaper or a sturdy stick) on either side of the injured limb. Carefully wrap the splint and limb with a bandage, ensuring it is snug but not too tight. Transport your dog to the vet immediately for further evaluation and treatment.

6. Choking:

If your dog is choking, it's crucial to act quickly. Check their mouth and remove any visible obstructions if you can do so safely. Perform the Heimlich maneuver by standing behind your dog, placing your hands just below the ribcage, and applying firm upward pressure. For larger dogs, lift their back legs off the ground while applying the maneuver. If the obstruction persists, transport your dog to the nearest veterinary clinic immediately.

7. Heatstroke:

Heatstroke can be life-threatening for dogs, especially in hot weather. If you suspect your dog is suffering from heatstroke, move them to a cool, shaded area and provide them with fresh water. Use cool (not cold) water or wet towels to cool their body gradually. Do not use ice or cold water, as it can constrict blood vessels and impede cooling. Seek immediate veterinary attention, as heatstroke requires prompt, professional treatment.

Being knowledgeable about basic first aid techniques for dogs can make a significant difference in ensuring the well-being of your furry companion in an emergency. However, it is important to remember that first.

Training and Certifications for Canine First Aid

Obtaining proper training and certifications in canine first aid can greatly enhance your ability to respond effectively during emergencies. Look for reputable organizations or courses that provide comprehensive training, practical exercises, and hands-on experience. These certifications equip you with the necessary skills and give you the confidence to handle various emergency situations with competence.

Common Medical Emergencies for Dogs

Digestive Problems

1. Bloat/Gastric Dilatation-Volvulus (GDV): Bloat is a life-threatening condition where a dog's stomach fills with gas and becomes twisted. Recognizing the symptoms, such as a distended abdomen, restlessness, or unproductive vomiting, is crucial. Immediate veterinary attention is required to alleviate the pressure and restore blood flow to the affected organs.

2. Foreign Body Ingestion: Dogs are curious creatures and may swallow objects that can cause intestinal blockages. Signs of foreign body ingestion include vomiting, diarrhea, abdominal pain, or refusal to eat. Depending on the severity, veterinary intervention may be necessary to remove the foreign object.

Respiratory Issues

1. Allergic Reactions: Dogs, like humans, can experience allergic reactions to various substances, including food, medications, or environmental allergens. Signs may include itching, swelling, difficulty breathing, or hives. Removing the allergen if possible and seeking veterinary assistance if the reaction worsens is important.

2. Breathing Difficulties: Respiratory distress in dogs can occur due to various reasons, such as choking, respiratory infections, or heart problems. Immediate veterinary attention is crucial if your dog displays signs of difficulty breathing, such as rapid or labored breaths, coughing, or bluish gums.

Poisoning

1. Identifying Common Canine Poisons: Numerous substances can be toxic to dogs, including certain foods, plants, household chemicals, and medications. Familiarize yourself with common canine poisons and be cautious to prevent accidental ingestion.

2. Initial Steps in Case of Poisoning: If you suspect your dog has been poisoned, immediately contact a veterinarian or pet poison helpline. They can provide guidance on inducing vomiting (if appropriate) or other initial measures while you transport your dog to a veterinary facility.

Seizures

1. Recognizing Seizure Symptoms: Seizures can manifest differently in dogs, ranging from mild tremors to full-body convulsions. Common signs

include uncontrolled shaking, loss of consciousness, drooling, or loss of bowel or bladder control. Note the duration and details of the seizure for the veterinarian's evaluation.

2. What to Do During a Scizure Event: During a seizure, it is crucial to ensure your dog's safety. Move away any objects that could harm them and refrain from restraining or placing objects in their mouth. Time the seizure and contact your veterinarian for further guidance and potential treatment options.

Trauma and Accidents

1. Hit by Vehicle: If your dog is hit by a vehicle, approach them cautiously and prioritize their safety and yours. Stabilize any bleeding wounds, minimize movement of the injured areas, and seek immediate veterinary attention for a thorough assessment and treatment.

2. Falls and Injuries: Accidental falls or injuries can lead to fractures, sprains, or internal injuries. Assess the situation, keep your dog calm, and carefully transport them for veterinary evaluation. Avoid manipulating any suspected broken bones.

Urgent Medical Conditions

1. Urinary Obstructions: Male dogs, especially those prone to urinary issues, can develop obstructions in their urinary tract, leading to difficulty or inability to urinate. This medical emergency requires immediate veterinary attention to relieve the obstruction and prevent further complications.

2. Sudden Blindness: The sudden onset of blindness in dogs can indicate underlying medical conditions, such as retinal detachment or glaucoma. Keep your dog calm, avoid moving furniture, and seek veterinary assistance to determine the cause and explore potential treatment options.

How to Prepare a First Aid Kit for Your Dog?

Essential Items for Canine First Aid Kit

1. Bandages and Dressings: Include a variety of bandages, gauze pads, adhesive tape, and self-adhesive bandages for wound care and stabilization.

2. Antiseptics and Ointments: Include antiseptic solutions, hydrogen peroxide, and topical ointments to clean wounds and prevent infection.

3. Medical Tools: Include a rectal thermometer, tweezers for splinter or tick removal, blunt-ended scissors, and a syringe for administering medication or flushing wounds.

4. Emergency Contact Information: Keep a list of emergency contact numbers, including your veterinarian's office, local emergency veterinary clinics, and poison control helpline.

Adding Specific Items for Your Dog's Needs

Consider any specific medical conditions or medications your dog requires and add them to the kit. For example, if your dog has a history of allergies, include antihistamines recommended by your veterinarian.

Storing and Maintaining the First Aid Kit

Keep the first aid kit in a readily accessible location, such as a cupboard or a designated spot in your home. Ensure that all items are in good condition within their expiration dates, and replace any used or expired items promptly.

Training on Using the First Aid Kit

Acquire proper training on how to use the items in the first aid kit effectively. Attend a canine first aid course or consult with your veterinarian to learn how to handle emergencies and utilize the supplies in your kit.

Being prepared and knowledgeable about basic first aid techniques for dog medical emergencies can help save your pet's life. However, it is essential to remember that first-aid measures are temporary solutions, and professional veterinary care should always be sought as soon as possible.

By having a solid understanding of common emergencies and appropriate first aid measures, you can provide immediate care and support to your dog during critical situations.

Evaluation of Veterinary Services

Importance of Veterinary Care for Dogs

Understanding the importance of veterinary care is crucial for ensuring your dog's overall health and well-being. Regular check-ups, preventive care, and timely medical intervention play vital roles in maintaining your dog's health, detecting potential issues early on, and providing appropriate treatments when necessary.

Choosing a Veterinary Clinic

When it comes to selecting a veterinary clinic for your dog, several factors should be considered:

1. Location and Accessibility: Choose a clinic that is conveniently located and easily accessible in case of emergencies or routine visits.

2. Staff and Vet Experience and Qualifications: Evaluate the expertise and qualifications of the veterinary staff, including the veterinarians, veterinary technicians, and support personnel. Look for clinics with a team that has experience and knowledge in various areas of veterinary medicine.

3. Clinic Facilities and Services: Assess the clinic's facilities and available services. A well-equipped clinic with diagnostic capabilities, surgical facilities, and access to specialized treatments can provide comprehensive care for your dog's needs.

Evaluation of Veterinary Services

1. Regular Check-ups and Preventive Care: Evaluate the clinic's approach to preventive care, such as vaccinations, parasite control, and wellness exams. Regular check-ups are crucial for early detection of

health issues and preventive measures to ensure your dog's well-being.

2. Emergency Services Availability: Find out if the clinic provides emergency services or has a network of trusted emergency facilities. Knowing that you can rely on immediate veterinary care during emergencies is essential for your peace of mind.

3. Medical and Surgical Capabilities: Assess the clinic's medical and surgical capabilities. Look for clinics offering a wide range of medical treatments, diagnostic tools, and surgical procedures to address various health conditions in your dog's lifetime.

4. Communication and Client Service: Evaluate the clinic's communication methods and client service. A veterinary clinic that maintains open and effective communication with clients, provides clear explanations and promptly addresses concerns contributes to a positive experience for you and your dog.

Other Veterinary Services

1. Rehabilitation and Physiotherapy: Consider if the clinic offers rehabilitation and physiotherapy

services. These services can be beneficial for dogs recovering from injuries, undergoing post-surgical rehabilitation, or managing chronic conditions.

2. Specialist Referrals (e.g., Dermatology, Neurology): Evaluate if the clinic has the ability to provide specialist referrals when needed. Some health conditions may require the expertise of veterinary specialists in fields such as dermatology, neurology, or cardiology. Having access to a network of specialists ensures your dog receives optimal care.

Veterinary Ethics and Legal Aspects

Understanding veterinary ethics and the legal aspects of veterinary care is important. Veterinarians are expected to adhere to ethical standards, such as providing honest and transparent information, respecting client confidentiality, and maintaining the highest level of professionalism.

The Role of Veterinary in Public Health

Recognize the role of veterinarians in public health. Veterinarians contribute to the health and well-being of individual animals and the larger community. They play a crucial role in disease prevention, zoonotic disease control, and public health education.

Training clinic

Understanding Dog Insurance

What is Dog Insurance?

Dog insurance is a type of coverage that aims to protect pet owners from unexpected veterinary expenses. It provides financial support by reimbursing a portion of the costs associated with medical treatment for dogs. The purpose of dog insurance is to offer peace of mind to owners, knowing that they can provide necessary care for their pets without worrying about the expense.

Dog insurance works by requiring pet owners to pay a monthly or annual premium to an insurance provider. When the dog requires medical attention, the owner pays the veterinary bill upfront. The owner then submits a claim to the insurance company, including the necessary documentation, such as receipts and invoices. The insurance company reviews the claim and reimburses the owner for the eligible expenses according to the policy's terms and conditions.

There are different types of dog insurance policies available. Accident coverage focuses on covering costs related to accidents, such as injuries from car accidents or ingesting harmful substances. Illness coverage, on the other hand, covers veterinary expenses for diagnosed illnesses, including infections, diseases, and chronic conditions. Wellness coverage is designed to cover routine preventive care, such as vaccinations, annual exams, and flea/tick prevention. Additionally, there are additional coverage options that may include coverage for hereditary and congenital conditions, behavioral treatments, alternative therapies, and prescription medications.

Benefits of Dog Insurance

Dog insurance offers several benefits to pet owners. Firstly, it provides financial protection by covering unexpected veterinary costs. This can be particularly beneficial in cases of emergencies or serious illnesses that require expensive treatments or surgeries. Dog insurance also provides peace of mind to owners, knowing that they can provide necessary care for their pets without worrying about the financial burden.

Furthermore, dog insurance grants access to a wide range of veterinary services. Owners can seek appropriate medical care for their dogs without financial restrictions, allowing them to make decisions based on their pet's health needs rather than financial constraints. Some policies may even provide additional coverage options, such as assistance in finding lost pets or potential savings on routine preventive care through wellness plans.

Coverage Options

Accident Coverage

Accident coverage within dog insurance focuses on protecting owners from costs resulting from unexpected accidents. This may include injuries from accidents or falls, poisoning or ingestion of harmful substances, burns, lacerations, or broken bones. Accident coverage aims to alleviate the financial burden of emergency veterinary care in the event of accidents.

However, it's important to be aware of the limitations and exclusions associated with accident coverage.

Preexisting conditions are generally not covered, meaning injuries or conditions that were present before the insurance policy's start date. Additionally, some policies may have waiting periods before accident coverage becomes effective, meaning the coverage may not apply immediately after purchasing the policy.

Illness Coverage

Illness coverage provides financial support for veterinary expenses related to diagnosed illnesses. This includes infections, such as urinary tract infections or respiratory infections, as well as chronic conditions like allergies, diabetes, or cancer. Illness coverage helps owners manage the costs of medical treatment for their dogs when they fall ill.

Similar to accident coverage, it's important to understand the limitations and exclusions of illness coverage. Pre-existing conditions are typically not covered, and waiting periods may apply before the coverage takes effect.

Wellness Coverage

Wellness coverage focuses on routine preventive care for dogs. This includes vaccinations, annual exams, dental cleanings, routine bloodwork, and preventive treatments for fleas, ticks, and heartworms. Wellness coverage aims to help owners manage the costs of regular veterinary care and maintain their dog's overall health.

When considering wellness coverage, it's essential to evaluate the specific routine care needs of your dog and compare the cost of the plan to the potential savings on preventive treatments. Some owners may find that the coverage provided by wellness plans aligns well with their dog's healthcare requirements.

Additional Coverage Options

In addition to accident, illness, and wellness coverage, some dog insurance policies offer additional coverage options. These options may include coverage for hereditary and congenital conditions, such as breed-specific genetic conditions or birth defects. Behavioral treatments and therapy coverage can assist owners in seeking consultations and treatments for behavioral issues. Some policies may also provide coverage for alternative therapies and holistic care, including acupuncture, chiropractic care, or herbal remedies. Furthermore, certain policies include coverage for prescription medications, which can help manage ongoing treatment costs.

171

It's important to review the additional coverage options offered by different insurance providers to determine which options align with your dog's specific needs and potential future requirements.

Our canine companions depend on us for their safety and well-being. Through the understanding of basic first aid techniques and common medical emergencies, you can provide immediate help for your dog when it's most needed.

Equipping yourself with a well-prepared first aid kit acts as a safety net during critical moments. Nonetheless, these preparations and knowledge are not replacements for professional veterinary care.

Regular evaluations of veterinary services and cultivating a trusted relationship with a vet are integral to securing the best health outcomes for our dogs. Ultimately, this blend of proactive care, first aid knowledge, and professional veterinary assistance enables us to be responsible and responsive caregivers to our loyal companions.

Quiz

Instructions: Choose the correct answer for each question. At the end of the quiz, the correct answers will be provided.

1. What is the first step you should take when providing first aid to an injured dog?

   a) Assess the dog's vital signs

   b) Administer CPR immediately

   c) Apply a tourniquet to control bleeding

   d) Call a veterinarian

2. Which of the following signs may indicate that a dog is experiencing heatstroke?

   a) Shivering and trembling

   b) Rapid breathing and panting

   c) Limping and favoring a leg

   d) Coughing and wheezing

3. True or False: You can induce vomiting in a dog by giving them hydrogen peroxide.

   a) True

   b) False

4. What should you do if a dog is choking and unable to breathe?

   a) Reach into their throat and attempt to remove the obstruction

   b) Offer them water to try and dislodge the object

   c) Perform the Heimlich maneuver

   d) Leave them alone and hope the obstruction resolves on its own

5. Why is it important to have dog insurance?

   a) It covers routine veterinary check-ups.

   b) It provides financial assistance in case of unexpected medical expenses

   c) It guarantees that your dog will receive priority treatment at the vet

   d) It allows you to skip vaccination appointments

6. What is one common item that can be toxic to dogs if ingested?

   a) Apples

   b) Peanut butter

   c) Chocolate

   d) Carrots

7. True or False: Applying a cold compress to a dog's injury can help reduce swelling.

a) True

b) False

8. Which of the following is a potential sign of poisoning in dogs?

a) Excessive thirst

b) Dilated pupils

c) Lethargy

d) All of the above

9. When should you seek immediate veterinary care for your dog?

a) If they have a minor cut or scrape

b) If they vomit once after eating

c) If they show signs of extreme pain or distress

d) If they have a mild case of diarrhea

10. What is the purpose of the Good Samaritan laws in relation to providing first aid to dogs?

a) To protect individuals from legal liability when providing reasonable assistance to injured dogs

b) To require mandatory first aid training for all dog owners

175

c) To encourage bystanders to ignore injured dogs and not intervene

d) To ensure that injured dogs are taken directly to a veterinarian's office

Answers

1. d) Call a veterinarian

2. b) Rapid breathing and panting

3. a) True

4. c) Perform the Heimlich maneuver

5. b) It provides financial assistance in case of unexpected medical expenses

6. c) Chocolate

7. a) True

8. d) All of the above

9. c) If they show signs of extreme pain or distress

10. a) To protect individuals from legal liability when providing reasonable assistance to injured dogs

Unit 9 Grooming and Hygiene

It was a typical Saturday evening, and the atmosphere was exciting as the crowd danced and celebrated at a lively event. Cooper, a passionate DJ with a love for music and a soft spot for animals, was in his element, spinning tunes and keeping the energy high. Little did he know that this evening would present him with a challenge that would test his compassion and quick thinking.

As the music filled the air, a sudden commotion erupted on the outskirts of the event. Startled attendees turned their heads towards the source of the chaos, only to witness a dog chasing a 4x4 recklessly down the driveway, dangerously close to the vehicles. Panic spread through the crowd as it became apparent that the poor dog was in imminent danger from injuries.

Cooper, known for his strong sense of empathy and a heart full of kindness, didn't hesitate for a moment. He swiftly set his DJ equipment aside and sprinted toward the dog, his adrenaline kicking in as he assessed the severity of the situation. The dog had cut his nose chasing a 4x4, leaving a deep, gruesome wound on its nose. Blood gushed from the injured area, causing the dog to yelp in pain.

Despite the panic and chaos around him, Cooper maintained his composure. Drawing upon his knowledge of first aid, he quickly assessed the situation. Aware that time was of the essence, he remembered the importance of controlling bleeding. Taking off his jacket, he gently pressed it against the dog's nose, applying firm yet gentle pressure.

Game Fair Open winner

Anna & Panda

Cooper's swift actions caught the attention of a few compassionate individuals nearby. They sprang into action, assisting him by creating a makeshift stretcher using a discarded piece of plywood they found nearby. Carefully and delicately, they lifted the injured dog onto the makeshift stretcher, ensuring it was stable and comfortable.

Cooper directed the group toward the host car with the dog now secure. Aware that rushing the injured animal to the U of M Veterinarian emergency.

During the car journey, Cooper watched the injured dog, continuously applying pressure to control the bleeding.

The dog, though visibly in pain, seemed to sense the compassion and care being extended to it

Arriving at the veterinary clinic, the team sprang into action. The veterinarian and his team swiftly assessed the dog's injuries and began the necessary treatment. Cooper stayed by the dog's side, offering comfort and reassurance as the medical professionals worked diligently to save its life.

Hours passed, and Cooper anxiously awaited news of the dog's condition. Finally, the veterinarian emerged from the treatment room, a smile tugging at the corners of his lips. Their combined efforts successfully stabilized the dog's condition and saved its life.

This story is a reminder of how dogs, too, feel immeasurable pain but are often disregarded as they have no way of asking for help or sympathy from others. We must know how to care for our dogs; hence, below are tips and tricks that will help you to do so;

Keeping your dog's coat clean and well-maintained is essential to their health and happiness. Regular brushing helps remove dirt and tangles and promotes healthy skin and a shiny coat. This chapter will explore different ways to brush a dog's coat, including stripping and line brushing techniques. By understanding these methods, you'll be better equipped to keep your furry friend looking and feeling their best.

Zarf Best In Show

Brushing Techniques

Bristle Brushing:

Bristle brushing is one of the most common and basic techniques for brushing dogs with short, smooth coats. This brush has soft, natural bristles that help remove loose hair and debris while stimulating the skin. Regular bristle brushing can enhance your dog's coat's shine and overall appearance.

Bristle brushing is a gentle method that can be used on most dogs, regardless of their coat type. It is particularly effective in distributing natural oils throughout the coat, which helps keep the skin moisturized and healthy. To perform bristle brushing, start at the head and work your way down the body, brushing in the direction of hair growth. Pay extra attention to areas prone to tangles, such as behind the ears and under the armpits.

Slicker Brushing:

Slicker brushes are an excellent choice for dogs with medium to long coats. They have fine, short wires on a flat or curved base. The wires penetrate through the topcoat and gently remove tangles and mats. Slicker brushes also help to remove loose hair and distribute natural oils, promoting a healthier coat.

To use a slicker brush, start at the head and work your way down the body, brushing in the direction of hair growth. Use gentle, sweeping motions, and be careful not to apply too much pressure, as it can cause discomfort to your dog.

Pay close attention to areas where tangles and mats are likely to occur, such as the chest, belly, and tail. If you encounter any tangles or mats, use the slicker brush to gently work through them, starting from the ends of the hair and working your way up.

Undercoat Raking:

Undercoat raking is particularly useful for double-coated breeds that shed heavily. This technique involves using a specialized rake brush with long, wide-spaced teeth to penetrate through the topcoat and remove loose, dead undercoat hair. It helps reduce shedding, prevents matting, and allows air circulation to reach the skin.

To perform undercoat raking, start at the head and work your way down the body, focusing on the areas where the undercoat is the thickest, such as the neck, chest, and hindquarters. Hold the rake brush at a slight angle and comb through the coat, making sure to reach the undercoat. Be gentle to avoid causing any discomfort or pulling on the hair. Regular undercoat raking can help keep your dog's coat healthy and reduce shedding.

Stripping the Coat

Understanding Stripping:

Stripping means removing dead hair from a dog's coat by hand or stripping a knife. This technique is commonly used on wire-haired breeds or those with a harsh outer coat. The goal of stripping is to maintain the natural texture and color of the coat while promoting healthy hair growth.

Hand Stripping:

Hand stripping involves using your fingers or a specialized stripping knife to pluck out the dead hairs from the coat. This technique is done by grasping a small section of hair at the base and pulling it toward growth. Hand stripping is time-consuming but helps maintain the coat's desired texture and color.

Hand stripping is typically performed on wire-haired breeds, such as terriers, to preserve their characteristic wiry coat. It is important to properly understand the breed's coat type and the appropriate technique for hand stripping. Some owners choose to learn hand stripping themselves, while others prefer to seek the assistance of professional groomers who specialize in this technique.

Knife Stripping:

Knife stripping utilizes a stripping knife, a specialized tool with a serrated edge, to remove dead hair from the coat. The knife is carefully used to cut and pull out the hairs. It requires skill and should be done cautiously to avoid injuring the dog. Knife stripping is commonly used for terrier breeds with wiry coats.

Knife stripping should only be performed by individuals with experience and knowledge. It is crucial to understand the specific requirements of your dog's coat type and seek guidance from professional groomers if necessary. Improper use of a stripping knife can cause harm to the dog or damage the coat, so it is essential to exercise caution and practice this technique with care.

Line Brushing

Understanding Line Brushing:

Line brushing is a technique used to remove tangles and mats from the coat while ensuring each section is thoroughly brushed. It involves systematically dividing the coat into smaller sections and brushing them one at a time.

Line brushing is particularly beneficial for dogs with long, flowing coats prone to tangles.

Line brushing helps prevent mats from forming by ensuring that every part of the coat is properly brushed and tangle-free. By dividing the coat into sections, you can focus on one area at a time and give it the attention it needs. This technique is especially useful for breeds such as Golden Retrievers, Afghan Hounds, and Yorkshire Terriers.

Steps for Line Brushing:

Step 1: Start at the neck and work down the back, dividing the coat into small sections using your fingers or a comb. This helps ensure you don't miss any areas and allows you to work methodically through the entire coat.

Step 2: Brush each section using a slicker brush or a combination of slicker and bristle brushes, depending on your dog's coat type. Begin at the roots of the hair and work your way towards the ends, using gentle, sweeping motions. Be thorough and ensure that you reach the undercoat if necessary.

Step 3: Pay special attention to areas prone to tangles, such as behind the ears, under the armpits, and around the tail. These areas tend to mat easily and require extra care. Use your fingers or a comb to work through any tangles or mats, starting from the ends of the hair and working your way up to avoid causing discomfort to your dog.

Step 4: Once a section is brushed thoroughly, move on to the next until the entire coat has been attended to. Take your time and be patient, especially if your dog has a long or dense coat.

Step 5: If you encounter any difficult tangles or mats to remove, you can use a detangling spray or a wide-toothed comb to help loosen them. Apply the detangling spray to the affected area and gently work through the tangles using the comb. Be careful not to pull or tug too hard, as this can cause discomfort or pain to your dog.

Step 6: After line brushing the entire coat, give your dog a final once-over with a soft bristle brush to smooth the hair and remove any remaining loose hairs. This will leave the coat looking polished and well-groomed.

Step 7: If your dog has a particularly dense or long coat, you may consider using a grooming rake or de-matting tool to address stubborn tangles or mats. These tools should be used carefully, avoiding the skin and sensitive areas. Use them sparingly and only when necessary to avoid causing discomfort or harm to your dog.

Step 8: Regular line brushing helps to prevent mats from forming and keeps your dog's coat healthy and tanglefree. Aim to brush your dog's coat at least once or

187

twice a week or more frequently for breeds with high-maintenance coats. This regular grooming routine will keep your dog looking its best and promote a healthy coat and skin.

Grooming your dog's coat is essential to their overall care and well-being. Regular brushing and maintenance help keep the coat clean, healthy, and free from tangles and mats. You can effectively remove loose hair, distribute natural oils, and prevent tangles by understanding different brushing techniques, such as bristle brushing, slicker brushing, and undercoat raking. Additionally, for wire-haired breeds, hand stripping and knife stripping techniques can help maintain the desired texture and appearance of their coat. Finally, line brushing is a systematic approach to thoroughly brush each coat section, reducing the risk of matting. Proper grooming techniques and regular maintenance can keep your dog's coat looking beautiful and promote their overall comfort and well-being.

Quiz

Instructions: Choose the correct answer for each question. At the end of the quiz, the correct answers will be provided.

PAWSITIVELY PAWESOME: THE ULTIMATE DOG LOVER'S HANDBOOK

1. What first step should you take when providing first aid to an injured dog?

   a) Assess the dog's vital signs

   b) Administer CPR immediately

   c) Apply a tourniquet to control bleeding

   d) Call a veterinarian

2. Which of the following signs may indicate that a dog is experiencing heatstroke? a) Shivering and trembling

   b) Rapid breathing and panting

   c) Limping and favoring a leg

   d) Coughing and wheezing

3. True or False: You can induce vomiting in a dog by giving them hydrogen peroxide. a) True

   b) False

4. What should you do if a dog is choking and unable to breathe?

   a) Reach into their throat and attempt to remove the obstruction

   b) Offer them water to try and dislodge the object

   c) Perform the Heimlich maneuver

   d) Leave them alone and hope the obstruction resolves on its own

5. Why is it important to have dog insurance?

   a) It covers routine veterinary check-ups.

   b) It provides financial assistance in case of unexpected medical expenses

   c) It guarantees that your dog will receive priority treatment at the vet

   d) It allows you to skip vaccination appointments

6. What is one common item that can be toxic to dogs if ingested? a) Apples

   b) Peanut butter

   c) Chocolate

   d) Carrots

7. True or False: Applying a cold compress to a dog's injury can help reduce swelling. a) True

   b) False

8. Which of the following is a potential sign of poisoning in dogs? a) Excessive thirst

   b) Dilated pupils

   c) Lethargy

   d) All of the above

9. When should you seek immediate veterinary care for your dog?

   a) If they have a minor cut or scrape,

b) If they vomit once after eating,

c) If they show signs of extreme pain or distress

d) If they have a mild case of diarrhea

10. What is the purpose of the Good Samaritan laws concerning providing first aid to dogs?

a)   To protect individuals from legal liability when providing reasonable assistance to injured dogs

b)   To require mandatory first aid training for all dog owners

c)   To encourage bystanders to ignore injured dogs and not intervene

d)   To ensure that injured dogs are taken directly to a veterinarian's office

Answers:

1. d) Call a veterinarian

2. b) Rapid breathing and panting

3. a) True

4. c) Perform the Heimlich maneuver

5. b) It provides financial assistance in case of unexpected medical expenses

6. c) Chocolate

7. a) True

8. d) All of the above

9. c) If they show signs of extreme pain or distress

10. a) To protect individuals from legal liability when providing reasonable assistance to injured dogs

Unit 10: Understanding Canine Cognition Insights into the Mind of a Dog

Introduction:

Dogs have long been regarded as man's best friend, but how do they perceive the world around them? What goes on in a dog's mind when they interact with their environment and their human companions? This chapter explores the fascinating topic of canine cognition, shedding light on how dogs think, learn, and perceive the world. By understanding their cognitive processes, we can deepen our bond with these beloved companions and enhance their overall well-being.

Sensory Perception in Dogs:

Dogs rely on their senses to navigate and make sense of the world. While their senses may not be as sharp as some other animals, they excel in specific areas. Their sense of smell, for instance, is incredibly powerful, allowing them to detect scents that are undetectable to humans. Additionally, their hearing is sensitive to a broader range of frequencies than ours. By appreciating these differences, we can better understand the unique perspective from which dogs experience the world.

Social Cognition:

Dogs are highly social animals with a remarkable ability to understand and communicate with humans and other dogs. They can read human body language and facial expressions, recognize familiar people, and respond to their emotions. Dogs also exhibit a sense of empathy, offering comfort and companionship during times of distress. Their social cognition allows them to form strong emotional bonds with humans, making them excellent companions and even service animals.

Author awarded publication

Learning and Problem-Solving:

Dogs are intelligent animals capable of learning and problem-solving. They can be trained to perform a wide range of tasks and respond to various commands. Through positive reinforcement training methods, dogs learn to associate certain behaviors with rewards, allowing them to acquire new skills and modify their behavior accordingly. Understanding the principles of dog training and utilizing positive reinforcement techniques can help foster a harmonious and cooperative relationship with our canine friends.

Memory and Recall:

Like humans, dogs possess memory capabilities that allow them to remember past experiences and learn from them. They can recall associations between events, places, and people, which helps shape their behavior. Dogs have been shown to remember specific commands, recognize familiar faces, and recall certain scents for extended periods. Their memory skills contribute to their ability to learn and adapt to their environment.

Emotional Intelligence:

Dogs experience a wide range of emotions, including joy, fear, anger, and sadness. They can perceive and respond to human emotions, often providing comfort and support when needed. Research suggests that dogs may even experience a rudimentary form of empathy, being able to detect and respond to the emotional state of their human companions. Their emotional intelligence allows them to form deep emotional bonds with humans and exhibit behaviors that reflect their understanding of our emotions.

While we cannot fully know what goes on inside a dog's mind, studying canine cognition provides valuable insights into how they perceive and interact with the world. Dogs possess unique sensory abilities, exhibit social cognition, and demonstrate learning and problem-solving capabilities. By appreciating their cognitive processes, we can build stronger bonds with our four-legged friends, train them effectively, and ensure their overall well-being. Embracing a deeper understanding of how dogs think enhances our ability to provide them with the love, care, and enrichment they need to lead happy and fulfilling lives.

Communication Among Canids

Introduction:

Canids, a family of carnivorous mammals, encompass a diverse range of species, including dogs, coyotes, foxes, wolves, and Dingo's. These fascinating creatures have developed unique ways to communicate with one another, allowing them to coordinate group activities, establish territories, and maintain social bonds. This chapter unit explores the communication methods employed by canids, focusing on dogs, coyotes, foxes, wolves, and Dingo's. By delving into their vocalizations, body language, and scent marking, we can gain a deeper understanding of the intricate communication systems that exist within this family of animals.

Vocalizations:

Dogs:

- Barking: Dogs use various types of barks to communicate different messages, such as alerting to danger, expressing playfulness, or seeking attention.

- Howling: While domesticated dogs don't howl as much as their wild counterparts, howling can still serve as a form of communication, expressing loneliness or joining in group howling sessions.

- Whining and whimpering: Dogs whine and whimper to convey emotions like fear, anxiety, or a desire for something, such as food, affection, or to go outside.

Coyotes:

- Howling: Coyotes use distinctive howling as a means of communication, coordinating group activities, and establishing territorial boundaries.

- Yipping and barking: Yipping and barking are social interactions among coyotes, used during play, hunting, or as alarm calls to warn others of potential threats.

- Growling and snarling: Coyotes growl and snarl to express aggression, assert dominance, and as warning signals to deter intruders.

Foxes:

- Barking and yapping: Foxes use barking and yapping to communicate with other foxes, indicating territorial boundaries, mating calls, or expressing excitement or agitation.

- Screaming and screeching: These vocalizations are often distress calls used by foxes when threatened or injured. Screeching can also serve as a mating vocalization.

Wolves:

- Howling: Wolves use howling extensively as a complex communication tool within their packs, coordinating activities, locating pack members, and reinforcing social bonds.

- Growling and snarling: Growling and snarling are displays of dominance and aggression among wolves, used during conflicts or to warn intruders.

- Whining and whimpering: Whining and whimpering are social interactions among wolves expressing submission, reassurance, or a need for attention.

Dingo's:

- Vocal repertoire: Dingo's have a unique set of sounds for communication, including barks, hoots, grunts, and whines.

- Hooting and barking: Dingo's hoot and bark to communicate with other pack members, signaling their presence and location or alerting them to potential dangers.

- Grunting and whining: Grunting can indicate contentment or serve as a greeting while whining may express discomfort, pain, or a desire for attention or social interaction.

Body Language

Dogs:

1. Tail wagging: The speed and direction of tail wagging in dogs can convey different meanings,

such as happiness, excitement, friendliness, or caution.

2. Ear position: Dogs' ear position can indicate their mood and level of alertness. Erect ears often signal attentiveness, while flattened ears may suggest fear or submission.

3. Posture and stance: Dogs use their posture and stance to assert dominance (standing tall and erect) or display submission (crouching or rolling onto their back).

Coyotes:

1. Tail position and movement: Coyotes communicate aggression by holding their tails high and stiff, while a tucked tail indicates submission or fear.

2. Ear position and facial expressions: Coyotes use ear positions and facial expressions to convey their emotions and intentions, such as raised ears indicating attentiveness or forward-facing ears signaling aggression.

3. Body posture: Coyotes establish dominance and convey social status through their body posture, including arching their backs, stiffening their bodies, and puffing up their fur.

Foxes:

1. Tail movements: Foxes use tail movements to display their emotions and signal their intentions. A relaxed, wagging tail may indicate friendliness, while a bushy and puffed-up tail signifies fear or aggression.

2. Ear positions and facial expressions: Foxes communicate fear, aggression, or submission through their ear positions and facial expressions, such as flattened ears indicating fear and bared teeth signaling aggression.

3. Play behavior: Foxes engage in non-aggressive play behavior, such as chasing, pouncing, and mock fighting, which helps build social bonds and establish hierarchies.

Wolves:

1. Tail positions and movements: Wolves use their tails to express emotions and signal their hierarchy. A high, stiff tail denotes dominance, while a lowered tail indicates submission or fear.

2. Eye contact: Wolves establish dominance and convey their intentions through direct eye contact.

   Alpha wolves often maintain prolonged eye contact to assert their authority.

3. Aggressive displays: Wolves display aggression through behaviors like baring their teeth, growling, snarling, and snapping, indicating a warning to potential threats or intruders.

Dingo's:

1. Tail and ear positions: Dingo's communicate their emotions and intentions through the positions of their tails and ears. A high, erect tail often indicates confidence or dominance, while flattened ears suggest fear or submission.

2. Facial expressions: dingos use facial expressions, such as bared teeth or wrinkled noses, to signal threat or submission to other individuals.

3. Play behavior: Dingo's engage in play behavior, including chasing, wrestling, and mock-fighting, which helps strengthen social bonds, establish hierarchies, and relieve stress within the pack.

Scent Marking:

Dogs:

1. Urine marking: Dogs use urine to mark their territory, establish boundaries, and communicate their presence to other dogs.

2. Anal gland secretions: Dogs have scent glands near their anus that release secretions, which can convey emotional states and social status to other dogs.

3. Pheromones: Dogs also communicate through pheromones, which are chemical substances released through glands in their bodies, aiding in social bonding and communication.

Coyotes:

1. Urine marking: Coyotes mark their territory by urinating on objects or specific locations, defining

boundaries, and advertising their presence to other coyotes.

2. Fecal deposits and scent posts: Coyotes use fecal deposits and scent posts to communicate important social information to other members of their species, such as reproductive status, dominance, or territorial claims. These markers can be found along trails, rocks, or vegetation.

Foxes:

1. Urine marking: Foxes use urine to mark their territories, leaving scent trails and communicating their presence to other foxes.

2. Scent gland secretions: Foxes possess scent glands on various parts of their bodies, such as the feet and tail, which they use to leave scent markings on objects and communicate social and reproductive information.

3. Fecal deposits: Foxes may leave fecal deposits in specific locations to mark territory or communicate with other foxes.

Wolves:

1. Urine marking: Wolves use urine to mark their territories, often done by alpha individuals, to communicate their presence and assert dominance within the pack.

2. Scent glands: Wolves have scent glands on their paws and other body parts, which they use to leave scent markings on objects, trails, and other members of the pack. These scent markings convey information about pack identity and territory ownership.

3. Fecal deposits: Wolves may strategically place fecal deposits in certain areas as a means of communication, such as marking territorial boundaries or providing information about pack activities.

Dingo's

1. Urine marking: Dingos use urine to mark their territories, leaving scent trails to communicate their presence and assert ownership of an area.

2. Scent glands: Dingos possess scent glands on various parts of their bodies, including the anal region, which they use to release scent markings to convey information about their social status, reproductive readiness, or territory boundaries.

3. Rubbing and scratching: dingos may engage in rubbing or scratching behaviors on trees, rocks, or other surfaces, leaving their scent and visual markings as a way of communication and territorial marking.

Dog Psychology

Introduction:

In this chapter, we will explore the fascinating world of dog psychology. Dogs have been domesticated for thousands of years and have become integral parts of our lives. Understanding their psychology is crucial for effective training, communication, and building strong bonds with our canine companions. In this unit, we will delve into the unique characteristics of dog psychology and highlight the key differences between dog and human psychology.

The Canine Mind

Instincts and Drives:

Dogs possess a set of innate instincts and drives that influence their behavior. These include pack dynamics, hunting instincts, territoriality, and social hierarchy. Understanding these primal instincts helps us comprehend and address certain behaviors exhibited by dogs.

Sensory Perception:

Dogs rely heavily on their senses, particularly their sense of smell and hearing. Their olfactory capabilities far surpass those of humans, enabling them to detect subtle scents and even diseases. Additionally, their acute hearing allows them to pick up high-frequency sounds imperceptible to humans.

Communication:

Dogs have a unique system of communication involving body language, vocalizations, and scent marking. Tail wagging, ear positions, and postures convey a range of emotions and intentions. Exploring the nuances of canine communication enhances our ability to interpret and respond appropriately to their signals. **Social Behavior**

Pack Mentality:

Dogs are descendants of social pack animals, and their social structure reflects this heritage. Understanding pack dynamics, including the roles of alpha, beta, and omega, helps us establish leadership and maintain a harmonious household.

Socialization:

Proper socialization is crucial for dogs to develop healthy relationships with other animals and humans. We will explore the critical socialization periods in a dog's life and the impact they have on their long-term behavior.

Separation Anxiety:

Dogs are highly social creatures and can experience distress when separated from their owners. We will delve into the causes, signs, and effective strategies for managing separation anxiety in dogs. **Learning and Training**

Learning Styles:

Dogs learn primarily through association and consequence. We will explore their capacity for associative learning, including classical and operant conditioning, and how to leverage these techniques for effective training.

Canine Cognition:

While dogs may not possess the same cognitive abilities as humans, they exhibit remarkable problem-solving skills, memory, and a capacity for learning complex tasks. Understanding their cognitive abilities enables us to develop tailored training methods.

Direction Reinforcement:

Direction reinforcement is a highly effective training method for dogs. We will discuss its benefits, the importance of timing and consistency, and how it influences a dog's behavior and emotional well-being.

Understanding dog psychology is key to building a strong bond with our canine companions and addressing their behavioral needs. While there are fundamental differences between dog and human psychology, grasping the unique aspects of the canine mind allows us to provide appropriate care, training, and enriching experiences for our four-legged friends. By respecting their instincts, communication style, and social needs, we can nurture happy and well-adjusted dogs.

Canine Communication: Understanding the Language of Dogs and Humans

Introduction:

Communication is a fundamental aspect of our daily lives, allowing us to connect, share information, and understand each other's needs and emotions. This chapter explores the intriguing world of communication between dogs and humans. Despite being different species, dogs and humans have developed a remarkable ability to understand and communicate with each other. In this chapter, we will delve into the unique ways dogs and humans interact, including their body language, vocalizations, and non-verbal cues. By gaining insights into canine communication, we can strengthen our bond with our furry companions and build a deeper understanding of their needs and emotions.

The Importance of Communication:

The Role of Communication in Human-Dog Relationships:

- Effective communication plays a crucial role in fostering strong bonds between humans and dogs. It allows for understanding, trust, and cooperation, enhancing the overall relationship between the two.

- The benefits of effective communication extend to various aspects of dog ownership, including training and behavior management. Clear and consistent communication helps dogs learn desired behaviors and understand expectations, leading to better obedience and improved behavior.

- Furthermore, communication promotes the overall well-being of dogs. It allows owners to understand their dogs' needs, emotions, and physical state, enabling them to provide appropriate care, comfort, and medical attention when necessary.

Canine Communication in the Wild:

- Wild canids, such as wolves, rely on complex communication systems to survive and thrive in their natural habitats. They use vocalizations, body language, and scent marking to convey information within their packs, coordinate hunting, establish hierarchies, and defend territories.
- Dog communication has its evolutionary roots in the communication systems of their wild counterparts. Over time, as dogs adapted to living alongside humans, their communication skills have evolved and adjusted to meet the demands of coexistence.

Body Language:

Understanding Dog Body Language:

- Recognizing and interpreting canine body language is essential for dog owners. Key elements to observe include posture, facial expressions, tail movements, ear positions, and overall body posture. Each of these communicates specific messages about a dog's emotional state, intentions, and level of comfort.

- By understanding dog body language, owners can recognize signs of relaxation, fear, aggression, playfulness, and other emotional states. This knowledge enables them to respond appropriately to their dogs' needs and prevent misunderstandings or potential conflicts.

Human Body Language and Its Impact on Dogs:

- Human body language also has a significant impact on dog behavior. Dogs are highly attuned to human cues and can pick up on subtle changes in body language, tone of voice, and facial expressions. They often mirror and respond to human cues, making it important for owners to be mindful of their own body language. It is also important to understand actions with tones.

- Using clear, calm, and consistent body language can help convey messages to dogs effectively. It can aid in training, reinforce desired behaviors, and establish trust and confidence between humans and dogs.

- Overall, understanding and utilizing both canine and human body language can greatly enhance communication in human-dog relationships, leading to a stronger bond, improved training outcomes, and better overall well-being for dogs.

Vocalizations and Verbal Cues:

Dog Vocalizations:

- Exploring the range of vocalizations dogs use to express themselves, such as barking, growling, whimpering, and howling.

- Understanding the various meanings behind different vocalizations.

Human Verbal Cues and Commands:

- Investigating the role of verbal cues and commands in dog training and communication.

- Exploring effective techniques for teaching dogs to understand and respond to human speech.

Non-Verbal Cues and Signals:

Canine Scent Communication:

- Shedding light on the importance of scent in dog communication.

- Understanding how dogs use scent marking, sniffing, and pheromones to convey information.

Human Non-Verbal Cues:

- Discussing the impact of human gestures, eye contact, and physical touch on dog behavior and communication.

- Identifying appropriate and inappropriate human behaviors when interacting with dogs.

Cultural Differences in Communication:

Cultural Variations in Human-Dog Communication:

- Recognizing how cultural differences can affect communication between humans and dogs.

- Exploring examples of cultural practices and beliefs that influence canine communication.

Cross-Species Communication Challenges:

- Addressing common misunderstandings and challenges that arise when humans and dogs attempt to communicate.

- Strategies for overcoming communication barriers and fostering effective cross-species communication.

In this chapter, we have explored the fascinating ways dogs and humans communicate with each other. From body language and vocalizations to non-verbal cues and cultural influences, understanding canine communication enhances our ability to connect with dogs on a deeper level. By becoming more proficient in interpreting their needs, emotions, and intentions, we can strengthen the bond we share with our canine companions. Effective communication is the cornerstone of a harmonious and fulfilling human-dog relationship, enabling us to build trust, empathy, and mutual understanding.

Unit 10 Quiz

Understanding Dog Psychology and Communication

Question 1: What is the primary sense that dogs rely on for gathering information about their surroundings?

 a) Smell

 b) Sight

 c) Hearing

 d) Taste

Answer: a) Smell

Question 2: What is the term used to describe the process of dogs forming associations between a specific behavior and a consequence?

 a) Conditioning

 b) Habituation

 c) Socialization

 d) Imprinting

Answer: a) Conditioning

Question 3: Which of the following behaviors can be

an indication of fear or anxiety in dogs?

    a) Tail wagging

    b) Relaxed body posture

    c) Yawning or lip-licking

    d) Eagerly approaching unfamiliar people

Answer: c) Yawning or lip licking

Question 4: What is the average lifespan of a dog?

    a) 5-8 years

    b) 10-12 years

    c) 15-18 years

    d) 20-25 years

Answer: b) 10-12 years

Question 5: Which of the following is an essential component of effective dog training?

    a) Punishment

    b) Isolation

    c) Positive reinforcement

    d) Verbal commands only

Answer: c) Positive reinforcement

Question 6: What is the term for a dog's tendency to follow its instincts and take independent actions without waiting for commands from its owner?

a) Pack mentality

b) Alpha behavior

c) Self-reliance

d) Prey drive

Answer: a) Pack mentality

Question 7: Which of the following is a common sign of aggression in dogs?

a) Ears pulled back

b) Tail wagging vigorously

c) Relaxed facial expression

d) Play bowing

Answer: a) Ears pulled back

Question 8: What does it mean when a dog's tail is held high and wagging slowly?

a)   Aggression

b)   Happiness and excitement

c)   Fear or submission

d)   Alertness Answer: d) Alertness

Question 9:

Which of the following is an effective way to communicate with a dog?

a) Using complex verbal commands

b) Staring directly into their eyes

c) Using clear body language and signals

d) Raising your voice to assert dominance

Answer: c) Using clear body language and signals

Question 10: What is the term for a dog's repetitive, rhythmic behavior, such as pacing or tail chasing, often caused by stress or boredom?

a) Obsessive-compulsive disorder

b)

c)

Hyperactivity disorder

Schizophrenia

d) Epilepsy

Answer: a) Obsessive-compulsive disorder

Question 11: True or False: Dogs are pack animals and have an instinctual need for social interaction and companionship.

Answer: True

Question 12: What is the term for the process of gradually introducing a dog to new experiences in a controlled and positive manner to help reduce fear and anxiety?

a) Desensitization
b) Isolation
c) Obedience training
d) Reinforcement

Answer: a) Desensitization

b)

c)

Question 13: Which of the following behaviors can indicate a dog is feeling threatened or defensive?

a) Tail wagging

b) Ears pinned back

c) Relaxed posture

d) Playful jumping

Answer: b) Ears pinned back

Question 14: What is the purpose of crate training a dog?

a) To punish the dog for misbehavior

b) To provide a safe and secure space for the dog

c) To limit the dog's movement and freedom

d) To prevent the dog from bonding with its owner

Answer: b) To provide a safe and secure space for the dog

Question 15: Which of the following is an example of a calming signal used by dogs to communicate their desire to avoid conflict or diffuse tension?

a) Barking loudly

Tail wagging

Snarling

d) Turning their head away

Answer: d) Turning their head away

Question 16: What is the primary hormone associated with bonding and attachment between dogs and their owners?

a) Dopamine

b) Serotonin

c) Oxytocin

d) Cortisol

Answer: c) Oxytocin

b)

c)

Question 17: What is the term for a dog's ability to understand and respond to human gestures and cues?

a) Instinctual behavior
b) Pack mentality
c) Socialization
d) Canine cognitive skills

Answer: d) Canine cognitive skills

Question 18: *True or False:* Dogs rely heavily on vocalization to communicate with humans.

Answer: False

Question 19: Which of the following is an important aspect of establishing leadership and a positive relationship with a dog?

a) Using physical force and dominance-based techniques
b) Consistency in training and expectations
c) Allowing the dog to roam freely without boundaries

d) Avoiding any form of discipline or correction

Answer: b) Consistency in training and

expectations

Question 20: What is the significance of a dog's tail
position in relation to its body?

a) It indicates the dog's breed and ancestry.

It reflects the dog's level of intelligence.

It provides information about the dog's
emotions and intentions.

d) It has no particular meaning or significance.

Answer: c) It provides information about the dog's
emotions and intentions.

b)

c)

Unit 11 The
Importance of Exercise

Regular exercise is crucial for the overall health and well-being of dogs. It provides numerous physical and mental benefits, contributing to a happy and balanced life for your canine companion.

Benefits of exercise for dogs:

*   *Physical fitness:* Exercise helps dogs maintain a healthy weight, build strong muscles and bones, and improve cardiovascular health. It increases endurance, agility, and overall physical capabilities.

*   *Mental stimulation*: Engaging in physical activity stimulates a dog's mind. It provides an outlet for mental energy and prevents boredom. Dogs that receive regular exercise are less likely to engage in destructive behaviors or develop behavioral problems associated with frustration or pent-up energy

Stress and anxiety reduction: Exercise releases endorphins, known as "feel-good" hormones, in dogs. These hormones help alleviate stress and anxiety, promoting a calm and relaxed state of mind.

Behavior management: Dogs that receive adequate exercise are generally better behaved. Regular physical activity helps reduce hyperactivity, restlessness, and excessive energy. It promotes mental and physical balance, making it easier for dogs to focus, listen to commands, and exhibit appropriate behavior.

- *Bonding and socialization*: Exercise provides opportunities for dogs to interact with their owners and other dogs. This promotes socialization skills, strengthens the human-dog bond, and enhances overall social well-being.

Types of exercise for dogs:

- *Walking and jogging:* Regular walks or jogs are fundamental forms of exercise for dogs. They provide cardiovascular benefits, help maintain joint health, and offer mental stimulation through exposure to different environments and scents.

- *Playtime:* Interactive play with toys, such as fetch, tug-of-war, or chasing games, is an excellent way to engage dogs physically and mentally. It encourages natural instincts, improves coordination, and strengthens the bond between dogs and their owners.

- *Agility training:* Activities like agility courses or obstacle courses challenge a dog's physical abilities and provide mental stimulation. They involve navigating through various obstacles, including jumps, tunnels, and weave poles, promoting balance, coordination, and problem-solving skills.

- *Swimming:* Swimming is a low-impact exercise that is gentle on a dog's joints. It provides a full-body workout and is especially beneficial for dogs with arthritis, joint issues, or those recovering from injuries.

- *Dog sports:* Engaging in dog sports like obedience trials, flyball, disc dog, or dock diving offers structured exercise and promotes teamwork between dogs and their owners. These activities provide mental and physical challenges, enhance obedience and focus, and can be highly rewarding for dogs.

How much exercise your dog needs: The amount of exercise required varies depending on factors such as breed, age, health, and individual energy levels. As a general guideline, most dogs benefit from at least 30 minutes to 2 hours of exercise each day. However, it's essential to consider your dog's specific needs and characteristics. Highenergy breeds or working dogs may require more exercise to stay mentally and physically satisfied. On the other hand, senior dogs or dogs with health issues may need modified or lower-impact exercise routines.

It's important to assess your dog's overall health, consult with your veterinarian, and tailor the exercise routine accordingly. Gradually increase the intensity and duration of exercise over time to avoid overexertion or injury. Remember to provide a balanced approach that combines physical exercise with mental stimulation, and always consider your dog's individual needs and limitations.

Regular exercise should be a part of your dog's daily routine to keep them physically fit, mentally stimulated, and happy. It not only promotes their overall health but also enhances their quality of life and strengthens the bond between you and your furry friend.

The Health Benefits of Exercising with Your Dog

Exercising with your dog offers numerous health benefits for both humans and our furry companions. Let's discuss the importance of exercise and explore the different ways it positively impacts our physical fitness, mental well-being, and bonding with our dogs.

Hunting Lt Dan is a great form of exercise!

Physical Fitness

Regular exercise with your dog provides a range of physical fitness benefits. By engaging in activities like walking, jogging, or playing fetch, you increase your

231

cardiovascular health. Elevating your heart rate through exercise improves your cardiovascular fitness, reducing the risk of heart disease, high blood pressure, and other cardiovascular conditions.

Furthermore, exercising with your dog contributes to weight management. Both you and your furry friend burn calories during physical activities, helping to maintain a healthy weight. This, in turn, reduces the risk of obesity-related health issues such as diabetes and joint problems.

Additionally, participating in activities like hiking or agility training with your dog enhances your strength and endurance. Pushing yourself physically during these exercises improves muscular strength and endurance, making everyday tasks easier and enhancing overall physical performance.

Mental Well-being

Exercising with your dog has significant mental health benefits as well. Spending time with your dog and engaging in physical activities reduces stress levels and promotes relaxation. Interacting with dogs has been shown to lower cortisol levels, the hormone associated with stress, leading to improved mental well-being.

Moreover, exercise stimulates the release of endorphins, often referred to as "feel-good" hormones. These endorphins boost your mood and overall happiness, contributing to improved mental well-being. Additionally, the companionship and unconditional love provided by your dog further elevate your mood and reduce feelings of loneliness or depression.

Exercising with your dog also increases social interaction. When you walk or participate in dog-related activities, you often come across other dog owners or enthusiasts. Building connections with like-minded individuals expands your social support network, improves your sense of community, and enhances overall well-being.

Bonding and Motivation

Exercising with your dog strengthens the bond between you and your furry companion. The shared experiences and quality time spent during physical activities create a deeper connection. The trust and companionship built through exercising together enhance the overall relationship and communication with your dog.

Additionally, owning a dog provides the necessary motivation and accountability to maintain a regular exercise routine. Dogs thrive on routine and eagerly look forward to physical activities. Their enthusiasm and energy can serve as a motivating factor, helping you establish a consistent exercise schedule for both you and your pet.

In conclusion, exercising with your dog has significant health benefits. It improves physical fitness, promotes mental well-being, strengthens the human-dog bond, and provides motivation and accountability for maintaining an active lifestyle. By engaging in regular exercise with your furry friend, you both can enjoy a happier, healthier life together.

Conditioning a Dog for Events, Field Trials, Agility, Pulling, Carting, Skijoring, and Mushing

Now that we have discussed fitness and exercise of our furry partners, let's explore the process of conditioning them for various activities such as events, field trials, agility, pulling, carting, skijoring, and mushing. Each of these activities requires a different set of skills, and it's crucial to prepare your dog physically and mentally to ensure its success and safety. Conditioning involves a systematic approach that gradually builds your dog's stamina, strength, and focus. Let's dive into the specifics of conditioning for each activity.

Events and Field Trials:

Events and field trials often require dogs to showcase their natural instincts and abilities, such as hunting, retrieving, or herding. Conditioning for these activities should focus on building endurance, stamina, and agility. Start with regular exercise routines, gradually increasing the duration and intensity. Incorporate specific training exercises that mimic the challenges your dog will face during the event or trial. For example, if your dog will be retrieving, work on distance retrieves and multiple retrieves to improve their endurance and focus.

Agility:

Agility requires dogs to navigate through a course, overcoming obstacles such as jumps, tunnels, and weave poles. Conditioning for agility involves a combination of cardiovascular fitness, strength, and flexibility. Regular aerobic exercises like jogging or swimming can improve overall fitness. Focus on exercises that enhance core strength, such as balance boards or stability balls. Introduce obstacle training gradually, starting with low jumps and simple tasks and progressively advancing to more challenging courses.

Pulling:

Pulling sports like weight pulling or sled pulling requires a dog to pull a heavy load over a set distance. Conditioning for pulling activities involves building muscle strength and endurance. Incorporate exercises that target the muscles used for pulling, such as weight-pulling exercises or sled training. Begin with light loads and gradually increase the weight as your dog becomes stronger. It's essential to pay attention to proper form and ensure your dog doesn't overexert themselves.

Carting:

Carting involves dogs pulling a cart or wagon, often used for transportation or light work. Conditioning for carting requires strength, endurance, and obedience. Begin by getting your dog accustomed to the cart and gradually increase the weight they pull. Focus on exercises that improve pulling power, such as uphill pulls or resistance training with a weighted sled. Obedience training is crucial to ensure your dog responds to commands during carting activities.

Skijoring:

Skijoring is a winter sport where dogs pull a skier through snow-covered trails. Conditioning for skijoring involves building endurance, strength, and the ability to work in tandem with the skier. Start with regular leash training and basic obedience commands. Gradually introduce skis and equipment while training on flat surfaces. As your dog becomes more comfortable, progress to pulling a skier on snow-covered trails, gradually increasing the distance and intensity.

Mushing:

Mushing involves dogs pulling a sled over long distances, often in cold and harsh conditions. Conditioning for mushing requires exceptional endurance, strength, and mental focus. Begin with foundational training, including obedience, teamwork, and basic commands. Gradually increase the mileage while pulling a sled, ensuring your dog is comfortable and well-conditioned for longer distances. Training should also include exposure to different weather conditions to prepare for the challenges encountered during mushing events.

Conditioning a dog for various activities requires a tailored approach that considers the specific demands of each activity. Always prioritize your dog's safety, starting with foundational training and gradually increasing the intensity and difficulty. Regular exercise, obedience training, and incremental challenges will help your dog build the physical and mental capabilities needed to excel in events, field trials, agility, pulling,

Unit 11 Quiz

Benefits of Exercising Dogs

Instructions: Choose the correct answer from the options provided.

1. Exercise helps maintain a healthy weight in dogs and prevents obesity, which can lead to various health issues. True or False?

Answer: True

2. Regular exercise improves cardiovascular health in dogs. Which of the following is a benefit of improved cardiovascular health?

a) Increased risk of heart disease

b) Lower blood pressure

c) Decreased energy levels

d) Weaker muscles

Answer: b) Lower blood pressure

3. Exercise helps reduce behavioral problems in dogs. Which of the following behaviors can be improved through exercise?

a) Aggression

b) Anxiety

c) Destructive chewing

d) All of the above

Answer: d) All of the above

4. What type of exercise is especially beneficial for dogs with high energy levels and a need for mental stimulation?

a) Short walks

b) Obedience training

c) Agility training

d) Resting

Answer: c) Agility training

5. Regular exercise promotes better joint health in dogs. Which of the following is a benefit of maintaining healthy joints?

   a) Increased risk of arthritis
   b) Improved mobility
   c) Higher likelihood of injuries
   d) Reduced lifespan

   Answer: b) Improved mobility

6. Exercise enhances the bond between dogs and their owners. Which of the following activities can strengthen this bond?

   a) Playing fetch
   b) Grooming sessions
   c) Training sessions
   d) All of the above

   Answer: d) All of the above

7. Exercise helps prevent boredom in dogs. Which of the following can be a consequence of boredom in dogs?

    a) Excessive barking

    b) Destructive behavior

    c) Obesity

    d) All of the above

    Answer: d) All of the above

8. Regular exercise improves digestive health in dogs. True or False?

    Answer: True

9. Exercise stimulates the release of endorphins in dogs, leading to which of the following?

    a) Increased anxiety

    b) Elevated mood

    c) Decreased energy levels

    d) Weaker immune system Answer: b) Elevated

    mood

10. Exercise helps to prevent the development of which common medical condition in dogs?

 a) Diabetes
 b) Allergies
 c) Blindness
 d) Hearing loss

Answer: a) Diabetes

11. Which of the following is NOT a benefit of exercising dogs?

 a) Improved cognitive function
 b) Enhanced socialization skills
 c) Increased risk of injury
 d) Weight management

Answer: c) Increased risk of injury

12. Exercise promotes better sleep in dogs. True or False?

Answer: True

13. Which of the following factors should be considered
when determining the appropriate exercise routine
for a dog?

    a) Age
    b) Breed
    c) Health condition
    d) All of the above

    Answer: d) All of the above

14. Exercise helps to prevent the development of which
common behavioral issue in dogs?

    a) Excessive licking
    b) Aggression
    c) Excessive sleeping
    d) Separation anxiety

    Answer: b) Aggression

15. Regular exercise increases the lifespan of dogs. True
or False?

    Answer: True

16. What is an example of a low-impact exercise suitable
for senior dogs or those with joint issues?

a) Swimming

b) Tug-of-war

c) High jumps

d) Sprints

Answer: a) Swimming

17. Exercise improves mental stimulation in dogs, reducing the risk of which of the following?

a) Depression

b) Hyperactivity

c) Cognitive decline

d) Allergies

Answer: c) Cognitive decline

18. Which of the following is a benefit of exercising dogs in outdoor environments?

a) Exposure to different smells and stimuli

b) Increased risk of tick and flea infestation

c) Reduced socialization opportunities

d) Limited sensory experiences

Answer: a) Exposure to different smells and stimuli

19. Exercise helps to strengthen muscles and improve overall physical fitness in dogs. True or False?

Answer: True

20. What is an appropriate warm-up activity to include before exercising a dog?

   a) Stretching exercises
   b) Immediately engaging in vigorous activity
   c) Skipping warm-up and starting exercise directly
   d) Offering treats as a warm-up

   Answer: a) Stretching exercises

Congratulations on completing the quiz! Remember, exercising dogs provides numerous benefits for their physical health, mental well-being, and the bond between dogs and their owners.

Unit 12 Teaching Kids to Respect Dogs and Understand Boundaries

Teaching children how to respect dogs and understand that not all dogs will be their friends is crucial for their safety and the well-being of the dogs themselves. Dogs, as living beings, have their own personalities, emotions, and boundaries, and it's essential to educate children about these aspects to foster positive and safe interactions. DON'T PET THE DOG – MEANS – DON'T PET THE DOG!

One key concept to emphasize is that dogs have different temperaments and preferences, just like humans do. Some dogs may be friendly and sociable, while others may be more reserved or even fearful. Teaching children that not all dogs will necessarily want to be petted or approached can help them understand and respect the individuality of each dog they encounter.

Guidelines for interacting with dogs should include teaching children to always ask for permission from the dog's owner before approaching or petting a dog. This respect for the dog's owner is important, as they know their pet's behavior and can provide guidance on the appropriate way to interact with them. Additionally, children should learn to approach dogs calmly and avoid sudden movements or loud noises that may startle or agitate them.

Children should also be taught how to recognize signs of discomfort or aggression in dogs. These signs may include growling, barking, showing teeth, stiff body posture, or attempting to move away. Understanding these signals can help children identify when a dog is feeling uneasy or threatened, and it's crucial to emphasize that in such situations, they should give the dog space and not try to force interaction.

Activities can be incorporated to reinforce these lessons. For example, children can learn about different dog body language through pictures or videos, allowing them to practice identifying various cues and interpreting the dog's emotional state. Role-playing exercises can also be helpful, where children take turns pretending to be dogs and practice appropriate and respectful behavior.

Chapter Objectives:

- Introduce the concept of dog respect and the importance of understanding dogs' boundaries.

- Teach children how to approach dogs safely and appropriately.

- Help children recognize and interpret dog body language and behavioral cues.

- Raise awareness about the diversity of dog temperaments and the need for individualized approaches.

- Provide practical tips for children to interact safely and respectfully with dogs.

Introduction to Dog Respect

Dogs are living creatures that deserve to be treated with respect. They possess emotions and experiences similar to humans, such as joy, fear, pain, and love. It is crucial to recognize that dogs are not inanimate objects to be mistreated but rather companions and cherished members of our families.

To ensure the safety of both dogs and children, understanding and respecting dogs' boundaries is essential. Teaching children to recognize and honor these boundaries can help prevent accidents and encourage positive interactions. Dogs, like humans, have personal space preferences and specific behaviors that should be acknowledged and respected.

Positive interactions with dogs offer valuable life lessons for children. By engaging with dogs in a respectful and caring manner, children can learn empathy, responsibility, and compassion. Dogs provide comfort, companionship, and opportunities for play and exercise. Building a healthy relationship with dogs from a young age fosters a lifelong love and respect for animals.

Moreover, this respect extends beyond our immediate interactions with dogs. It also involves advocating for their welfare and ensuring they are treated ethically and responsibly in all aspects of life. This means promoting initiatives that prevent animal cruelty, supporting adoption and rescue efforts, and encouraging responsible pet ownership.

Approaching Dogs Safely and Appropriately

The "Ask First" rule is crucial for approaching dogs. Children should always ask the owner's permission before approaching a dog, even if the dog seems friendly. Not all dogs are comfortable with strangers, and it's important to respect the owner's judgment. This simple act of asking for permission shows respect for both the dog and its owner.

Dogs should be allowed to approach children. Approaching dogs head-on can be intimidating and may trigger a defensive response. Teach children to stand still and wait for the dog to approach them if the dog seems interested and friendly. This allows the dog to approach at its own comfort level, promoting a positive and relaxed interaction.

Approaching dogs calmly is vital. Sudden movements or loud noises can startle dogs, potentially leading to fear or aggression. Children should approach slowly, use gentle voices, and avoid making sudden gestures. By demonstrating calm and non-threatening behavior, children can help create a relaxed environment for both themselves and the dog.

Teach children not to disturb dogs that are eating, sleeping, or caring for puppies. These activities are essential for a dog's well-being, and interrupting them can cause stress or protective behavior. It is important to give dogs their space and allow them to engage in these activities undisturbed. Respecting a dog's need for privacy and rest reinforces the concept of boundaries and empathy towards animals.

Interpreting Dog Body Language

Introduce children to common dog body language signals and their meanings. For example, teach them that a wagging tail can indicate both happiness and stress, depending on other accompanying cues. Raised hackles, lip licking, and other body language signals convey a dog's emotional state. By understanding these cues, children can better assess a dog's feelings and respond accordingly.

Use visual aids or videos to help children understand dog expressions and postures. Show them examples of relaxed, happy dogs, as well as dogs displaying signs of discomfort or fear. This visual understanding can enhance their ability to interpret dog body language in real-life situations. It helps children develop observational skills and empathy toward the needs and emotions of animals.

Teach children to recognize signs of dog discomfort or stress, such as growling or bared teeth. These signs indicate that a dog feels threatened and may act defensively. Children should understand these signals and know how to react appropriately to ensure their safety. This knowledge empowers children to make informed decisions and avoid potentially dangerous situations.

Encourage children to give dogs space if they show signs of discomfort or fear. This includes backing away slowly, avoiding direct eye contact, and seeking adult

251

assistance if necessary. It is crucial for children to understand not to push a dog beyond its limits and to respect the dog's need for space. Respecting a dog's boundaries promotes a safe and mutually respectful interaction.

By educating children on dog respect, safe approaches, and understanding body language, we promote compassion and responsible interactions with dogs. These lessons keep children safe and foster harmonious relationships between humans and dogs, ensuring a positive and mutually beneficial coexistence. Through knowledge and respect, we can create a world where both humans and dogs thrive together.

Understanding Individual Dog Temperaments

Dogs are incredible animals with their own unique personalities, much like humans. It's important for children to understand that dogs have individual temperaments and behaviors, just like people do. Some dogs may be full of energy and outgoing, while others may be more reserved and shy. This understanding helps children recognize that not all dogs will behave the same way.

When discussing dog temperaments with children, it's important to talk about different breeds and their general temperaments. However, it's crucial to emphasize that there can be variation within each breed. While certain breeds may have specific traits and tendencies, it's essential to remember that every dog is an individual. For example, Labrador Retrievers are generally known to be friendly and sociable, but there can be variations within the breed where some may be more independent.

Children should be encouraged to approach each dog as an individual. They should avoid making assumptions or judgments based solely on a dog's breed. Instead, they should assess the dog's behavior, body language, and individual cues to understand its comfort level. This approach helps children treat each dog as a unique being and learn to respect their boundaries.

Patience is crucial when interacting with dogs. Children should be taught to give dogs time to warm up and become comfortable. Some dogs may initially appear aloof or shy, but it's essential to give them space and time to relax. Forcing interactions or overwhelming dogs with sudden gestures or loud noises can be stressful for them. By being

253

patient and using gentle approaches, children can help dogs feel at ease and build trust.

Interacting Safely and Respectfully with Dogs

When it comes to interacting with dogs, it's essential to prioritize safety and respect. Teaching children how to engage with dogs in a responsible manner can help prevent any potential harm or discomfort. Here are some important guidelines to emphasize:

Children should be taught to avoid actions that may provoke or frighten dogs. Pulling a dog's ears or tail, for example, can cause pain or distress. It's crucial to instill in children the understanding that dogs should be treated with care and kindness, just like any other living being.

Discussing appropriate ways to pet a dog is essential. Children should be taught to use gentle strokes and avoid sensitive areas such as the face, tail, or paws. It's important to encourage them to always ask for permission from the dog's owner before approaching and petting a dog they are unfamiliar with.

To create a safe environment, children should be encouraged to avoid engaging in rough play, screaming, or running around dogs. Loud noises and sudden movements can startle or agitate dogs, potentially leading to undesirable reactions. Teaching children to remain calm and composed in the presence of dogs helps create a peaceful atmosphere for both the child and the dog.

Highlighting the importance of not bothering service dogs or dogs wearing identification vests is crucial. Children need to understand that service dogs are working animals and must focus on their tasks. It's essential to instruct them not to distract or interact with service dogs unless given permission by the dog's handler. Dogs wearing identification vests may have specific roles or training, and it's important to respect their responsibilities.

Activities to Reinforce Learning

To reinforce the concepts of dog safety and respect, engaging children in interactive activities can be both fun and educational. Here are some activity ideas:

Role-playing scenarios where children practice approaching dogs safely and responding to different cues can be beneficial. Set up simulated situations where children can learn to interpret a dog's body language and respond appropriately. This hands-on approach allows them to apply their knowledge in a safe and controlled environment.

Engage children in drawing or coloring activities that depict appropriate interactions with dogs. Provide coloring sheets or art materials for children to express their understanding of dog safety and respect. This activity encourages creativity while reinforcing the key concepts they have learned.

Watching educational videos or reading books that emphasize dog safety and respect can be insightful. Utilize age-appropriate videos or books that focus on teaching children about dog behavior, body language, and responsible pet ownership. These resources can enhance their knowledge and further reinforce the importance of interacting safely with dogs.

Organize a visit from a trained therapy dog or a responsible dog owner who can share experiences and answer questions. Arrange for a responsible dog owner or a therapy dog team to visit the children. This interactive experience allows children to observe and interact with a well-behaved dog while the owner or team can provide valuable insights, answer questions, and reinforce the lessons on dog safety and respect.

DON'T PET THE DOG – MEANS – LEAVE THE DOG ALONE!

Conclusion

In conclusion, teaching children to respect dogs and understand their boundaries is crucial for creating a positive and safe environment. By educating children about dog body language, individual temperament differences, and appropriate interaction guidelines, they develop empathy, compassion, and responsible behavior. This ensures the well-being of dogs and reduces the risk of accidents or negative experiences.

Understanding dog body language helps children interpret signals like wagging tails or flattened ears, enabling them to assess a dog's mood and intentions. Recognizing individual temperament differences teaches children to approach dogs with caution, respect, and sensitivity to their needs. Teaching safe interaction guidelines, such as avoiding dogs that are eating or sleeping and demonstrating gentle and appropriate petting techniques, fosters positive experiences for both children and dogs.

By instilling these values, we cultivate empathy, compassion, and responsible behavior in children, creating a harmonious coexistence with dogs. This promotes a safe and enjoyable environment for everyone involved.

Unit 13 Socialization for Dogs

Socialization plays a crucial role in the development of a well-rounded and balanced dog. Proper socialization helps prevent environmental temperament problems by exposing dogs to various people, animals, and environments from a young age. This chapter will provide you with essential guidelines and techniques for socializing both puppies and adult dogs effectively.

Understanding the Importance of Socialization

The Critical Socialization Period

During the critical socialization period, which typically occurs between 3 and 14 weeks of age, a dog's experiences have a significant impact on its lifelong behavior and temperament. This period is crucial for exposing puppies to positive and diverse experiences to shape their social skills and reduce the likelihood of developing behavior problems later in life. YOU ARE HELPING THE DOG LIVE IN THE HUMAN WORLD.

Lifelong Socialization

While the critical socialization period is vital, socialization should continue beyond that time frame. Lifelong socialization ensures that a dog remains well-adjusted and adaptable throughout their life. Ongoing socialization provides benefits such as increased confidence, reduced fearfulness, and improved ability to handle new situations, ultimately preventing environmental temperament problems.

LT Dan Best In Specialty

Nico Reserve Best In Specialty

With Cooper & Spike

Socializing Puppies

Controlled Exposure

Controlled exposure is a key concept in puppy socialization. It involves gradually introducing the puppy to different stimuli and environments to prevent overwhelming or traumatic experiences. Essential experiences to expose puppies to include various surfaces (e.g., grass, carpet, tiles), noises (e.g., vacuum cleaner, thunder), objects (e.g., toys, different types of equipment), and people of different ages, genders, and appearances.

Reinforcement

Positive reinforcement techniques are highly effective during puppy socialization. By rewarding desirable behavior with treats, praise, or play, you create positive associations with new experiences. This approach encourages puppies to feel confident and relaxed in different situations, reducing the likelihood of developing fear or aggression towards unfamiliar people, animals, or environments.

Puppy Classes

Enrolling puppies in puppy socialization classes is highly recommended. These classes provide supervised play and interaction with other puppies in a controlled environment. Puppy classes offer a structured setting where puppies can learn appropriate social skills, develop bite inhibition, and gain exposure to various dogs, people, and training exercises.

Handling and Gentle Touch

Getting puppies accustomed to being handled is essential for their overall socialization. Puppies should feel comfortable with human touch, including being touched on various body parts, having their paws, ears, and tails handled, and being gently restrained. Regular handling exercises help prevent fear or aggression towards handling activities, making grooming, veterinary visits, and everyday interactions more pleasant for both the dog and the owner.

Socializing Adult Dogs

Individual Assessment

Before socializing adult dogs, it is crucial to assess their previous socialization experiences and temperament. Understanding their background can help tailor the socialization process to suit their specific needs. Some adult dogs may have had limited socialization or negative experiences, requiring extra care and patience during the socialization process. Keep in mind a dog doesn't always need or want to go everywhere you do.

262

Desensitization and Counterconditioning

Desensitization and counterconditioning are effective techniques for socializing adult dogs. The principles involve gradually exposing the dog to new stimuli or experiences at a comfortable distance and pairing them with positive associations. Step-by-step instructions should be followed to ensure gradual and positive exposure to new situations, helping the dog build confidence and overcome any fears or anxieties.

Controlled Socialization

Controlled socialization is essential when introducing adult dogs to unfamiliar dogs or people. It is important to manage interactions carefully and gradually increase exposure over time. Controlled environments, such as structured playgroups or supervised meet-and-greets, can be beneficial for helping adult dogs develop appropriate social skills and positive associations with new individuals or dogs.

Building Positive Associations

Creating positive associations with new experiences is crucial for adult dogs. Using treats, praise, and play to reinforce positive behavior during socialization can help the dog associate new situations with positive outcomes. By focusing on positive reinforcement, adult dogs can develop confidence and learn that new experiences are enjoyable and rewarding.

Overcoming Challenges in Socialization

Fear and Anxiety

During the socialization process, dogs may exhibit fears and anxieties. Common fears can include loud noises, crowded environments, or specific objects. To help dogs overcome their fears, techniques such as desensitization and gradual exposure can be employed. By gradually introducing the feared stimuli in a controlled manner and pairing them with positive associations, dogs can learn to feel more comfortable and less anxious in those situations.

Aggression

Aggression can be a challenging issue during socialization. If aggression problems arise, it is essential to seek professional help from a qualified dog trainer or behaviorist. They can assess the underlying causes of aggression and provide guidance on managing and preventing aggressive behaviors. General tips for managing aggression include avoiding situations that trigger aggression, using positive

reinforcement techniques, and ensuring the dog feels safe
and secure during socialization experiences.

Socializing puppies and adult dogs is a proactive
approach to preventing environmental temperament
problems. By following the guidelines and techniques
outlined in this chapter, you can help your canine companion
develop into a confident and well-socialized member of
society. Remember, patience, consistency, and positive
reinforcement are key to successful socialization.

Stages of Fear in a Puppy or Dog

The Startle Response

During the startle response, the dog's senses become
heightened, and its body prepares for potential danger. The
sudden or unexpected stimulus triggers an immediate
physiological and behavioral reaction. The dog's heart rate
may increase, its muscles tense up, and its senses become
more alert. They may exhibit a startled expression, with
widened eyes and raised ears. The startle response is an
innate survival mechanism that allows the dog to quickly
assess the situation and determine if further action is
necessary.

Defensive Aggression

Defensive aggression is a natural progression from the startle response when the perceived threat continues or escalates. At this stage, the dog perceives a real danger and feels the need to protect themselves. Their body language becomes more overtly aggressive as they attempt to intimidate the threat and establish boundaries. They may bare their teeth, growl deeply, and display piloerection (raising of the fur) to appear larger and more intimidating. Biting may occur as a last resort if the dog feels their safety is compromised. It is important to note that it's the dog's proceeded threats, not the humans.

Avoidance and Escape

When the dog's initial response and defensive aggression fail to resolve the perceived threat, it may enter the stage of avoidance and escape. At this point, the dog recognizes that confronting the threat directly is not feasible or safe. They shift their focus to removing themselves from the situation entirely. The dog may display submissive behaviors such as crouching or tucking their tail between their legs. They may try to hide behind objects or seek shelter in a safe area. If given the opportunity, the dog will attempt to flee or retreat to a place where they feel secure.

Learned Fear

If a dog experiences repeated or prolonged exposure to fearful stimuli, it can develop learned fear. In this stage, the dog associates specific triggers or situations with the experience of fear, even if the threat is not immediately present. The learned fear response becomes ingrained in their behavior and can lead to anxiety-related disorders. For example, a dog who has had negative experiences with thunderstorms may exhibit signs of fear and anxiety whenever they hear loud noises, even if they are not related to thunderstorms. Over time, this generalized fear response can affect the dog's overall well-being and quality of life.

The Role of Fear in Canine Survival in the Wild

Heightened Awareness and Perception

When a dog experiences fear, their senses become hyper-alert, allowing them to detect subtle changes in their environment. Their hearing becomes more acute, enabling them to pick up on distant sounds that may indicate danger. They may also become more sensitive to smells, allowing them to detect potential threats or unfamiliar scents. Additionally, their vision becomes more focused, allowing them to observe minute details and movements in their surroundings. This heightened awareness and perception serve as a defense mechanism, helping dogs anticipate and respond to potential threats more effectively.

Fight or Flight Response

The fight or flight response is a physiological reaction triggered by fear. When faced with a perceived threat, a dog's body prepares for immediate action. The sympathetic nervous system activates, releasing adrenaline into the bloodstream. This surge of adrenaline provides a burst of energy, enabling the dog to either confront the threat head-on or flee from it. The fight response may manifest as aggressive behavior, while the flight response involves evasive actions such as running away or seeking cover. The choice between fight or flight is influenced by various factors, including the dog's temperament, previous experiences, and the perceived level of danger. If a dog just goes to fight or bite, they are subject to be put down.

Social Signaling and Hierarchy Establishment

Fear plays a crucial role in social interactions among canines, particularly in establishing hierarchical structures within a group. Dogs communicate their social status and intentions through fear-based signals. Submissive behaviors, such as lowered body posture, averted gaze, and tail tucking, indicate deference to more dominant individuals. These signals help maintain social order, reduce conflict, and prevent physical confrontations. Fear-based communication is an integral part of canine socialization and ensures cooperation and cohesion within a pack or group.

Learning from Negative Experiences

Fearful encounters contribute to a dog's learning and memory formation. When a dog experiences a negative event associated with fear, such as a painful or frightening experience, it creates a lasting impression in its memory. This memory helps the dog recognize and avoid similar situations in the future, allowing them to adapt and make better decisions to protect themselves. For example, if a dog receives a painful bite from another dog during an interaction, they may learn to be cautious or avoid similar encounters in the future. This learning mechanism enhances a dog's ability to survive and adapt to its environment, minimizing the risk of potential harm.

Coping with Fear in Domestic Settings

Creating a Safe Environment

Providing a secure and predictable environment can help alleviate fear in domestic dogs. Consistency in routines, familiar surroundings, and positive reinforcement can help build trust and reduce anxiety.

Gradual Desensitization

Gradual exposure to fear-inducing stimuli can help dogs overcome their fears. By starting with mild or controlled versions of the stimulus and gradually increasing intensity, dogs can learn to tolerate and cope with their fears.

Counterconditioning

Counterconditioning involves associating the fear-inducing stimulus with positive experiences. By pairing the stimulus with rewards or enjoyable activities, dogs can learn to form positive associations and reduce fear responses.

Professional Training and Behavior Modification

In severe cases of fear or anxiety, seeking professional help from a certified dog trainer or animal behaviorist is recommended. These experts can develop customized behavior modification plans to address specific fear-related issues and help dogs overcome their fears.

Ethical Considerations in Fear Management

Avoiding Punitive Measures

Punishment-based training methods can exacerbate fear and anxiety in dogs. It is important to avoid harsh corrections or punitive measures that may cause further distress and damage the bond between the dog and its owner.

Providing Emotional Support

Dogs experiencing fear or anxiety require emotional support and reassurance from their owners. Gentle and compassionate handling, soothing words, and physical contact can help comfort and calm fearful dogs.

Recognizing Individual Differences

Each dog has a unique temperament and response to fear. It is crucial to respect and understand the individual needs of dogs and tailor fear management strategies accordingly.

Conclusion

In conclusion, socialization plays a crucial role in a dog's life, facilitating positive relationships and overall well-being. By implementing controlled exposure, positive reinforcement, and individualized approaches, we can help dogs develop confidence and adaptability in social settings. Overcoming challenges like fear and aggression requires patience, gradual desensitization, and ethical methods that prioritize emotional support. Recognizing and respecting the unique needs of each dog allows us to create a safe and harmonious environment for their social development. In summary, responsible socialization contributes to the happiness and balanced behavior of our beloved canine companions.

Quiz

1. What is socialization?

Answer: Socialization refers to the process by which individuals learn and internalize the norms, values, customs, and behaviors of their society. It is a lifelong process that begins at birth and continues throughout our lives.

2. Why is socialization important?

Answer: Socialization is important for several reasons:

- It helps us develop a sense of self and identity.

- It teaches us social norms and acceptable behavior.

- It enables us to form relationships and maintain social connections.

- It prepares us to participate in society and fulfill social roles.

- It contributes to our emotional and psychological well-being.

3. What are the primary agents of socialization?

Answer: The primary agents of socialization are:

- Family: The family is usually the first and most influential agent of socialization, shaping our early beliefs, values, and behaviors.

- Education: Schools play a significant role in socializing children by teaching them academic knowledge and social skills.

- Peer groups: Friends and peers have a powerful influence on our socialization, especially during adolescence.

- Media: Mass media, including television, movies, and the internet, also shape our beliefs, attitudes, and behaviors.

4. What are the common challenges faced during socialization?

Answer: Common challenges faced during socialization include:

- Cultural differences: Navigating social interactions across cultures can be challenging due to varying norms, values, and customs.

- Peer pressure: The influence of peers can sometimes lead individuals to engage in risky behaviors or compromise their values.

- Social anxiety: Some individuals may experience anxiety or fear in social situations, making it difficult for them to form connections.

- Bullying: Bullying can hinder socialization by creating a hostile and intimidating environment.

- Social exclusion: Being excluded from social groups can lead to feelings of loneliness and isolation.

5. How does socialization contribute to the development of self-identity?

Answer: Socialization plays a vital role in the development of self-identity by providing individuals with a framework for understanding themselves within the context of society. Through interactions with others, we learn about our strengths, weaknesses, interests, and values, shaping our sense of self.

6. How can socialization affect our behavior?

Answer: Socialization influences our behavior by teaching us social norms, expectations, and acceptable ways of interacting with others. It helps us learn appropriate behavior in various contexts, such as school, work, and relationships.

7. What are the long-term effects of social isolation?

Answer: Prolonged social isolation can have adverse effects on individuals' mental and physical health. It may lead to feelings of loneliness, depression, anxiety, and reduced overall well-being. Social isolation can also impact cognitive functioning and increase the risk of various health conditions.

8. How does socialization vary across different cultures?

Answer: Socialization varies across different cultures due to variations in norms, values, customs, and social structures. Cultural factors such as religion, language, and traditions significantly shape the socialization process and influence how individuals interact with others.

9. What role does socialization play in gender identity development?

Answer: Socialization plays a significant role in the development of gender identity. Through socialization, individuals learn about societal expectations, roles, and behaviors associated with their assigned gender. These influences can shape how individuals perceive themselves and their gender roles.

10. How can11. How can socialization challenges be overcome?

Answer: Socialization challenges can be overcome through various strategies, including:

- Developing self-awareness: Understanding one's own values, beliefs, and boundaries can help navigate social situations more effectively.

- Seeking support: Connecting with trusted friends, family, or support groups can provide guidance and encouragement during challenging socialization experiences.

- Building social skills: Engaging in activities or classes that focus on improving communication, empathy, and assertiveness can enhance socialization skills.

- Practicing self-care: Taking care of one's physical and mental well-being can boost confidence and resilience in social interactions.

- Seeking professional help: In cases of severe socialization challenges, consulting a therapist or counselor can provide valuable guidance and support.

11. What is the role of socialization in the workplace?

Answer: Socialization in the workplace is crucial for fostering a positive work environment and effective collaboration. It helps new employees integrate into the organizational culture, learn job-specific skills, and establish relationships with colleagues. Additionally, socialization at work promotes teamwork, professionalism, and the sharing of knowledge and expertise.

12. How does technology impact socialization?

Answer: Technology has both positive and negative impacts on socialization. On the one hand, it facilitates communication and enables connections across distances. On the other hand, excessive reliance on technology can lead to decreased face-to-face interactions and a potential loss of essential social skills. It is important to strike a balance and use technology as a tool to enhance, rather than replace, real-life social interactions.

13. How does socialization contribute to a sense of belonging?

Answer: Socialization plays a significant role in fostering a sense of belonging by connecting individuals to social groups, communities, and cultures. Through shared experiences, values, and norms, socialization creates a sense of identity and acceptance, which in turn strengthens the feeling of belonging.

14. How does socialization impact mental health?

Answer: Socialization has a profound impact on mental health. Positive social interactions, support systems, and a sense of belonging contribute to improved mental well-being. Conversely, social isolation, loneliness, and difficulties in socialization can increase the risk of mental health issues such as depression, anxiety, and low self-esteem.

15. What are the effects of socialization on personal growth?

Answer: Socialization promotes personal growth by exposing individuals to new ideas, perspectives, and experiences. It encourages learning, adaptation, and the development of critical thinking skills. Through socialization, individuals can expand their knowledge, challenge their beliefs, and broaden their horizons.

16. How does socialization contribute to cultural transmission?

Answer: Socialization is the primary mechanism through which cultural transmission occurs. It enables the passing down of cultural values, traditions, beliefs, and practices from one generation to another. Through socialization, individuals learn about their cultural heritage and become active participants in preserving and perpetuating their culture.

17. How does socialization impact moral development?

Answer: Socialization plays a vital role in shaping moral development. Through interactions with others, individuals learn about ethical values, principles, and social norms that guide their behavior. Socialization helps internalize moral values and develop a moral compass that influences decision-making and actions.

18. What are the benefits of diverse socialization experiences?

Answer: Diverse socialization experiences provide numerous benefits, including:

- Increased cultural understanding and empathy.

- Expanded perspectives and openness to new ideas.

- Enhanced problem-solving and conflict-resolution skills.

- Improved communication and collaboration across diverse groups.

- Enriched personal growth and self-awareness.

19. How does socialization continue throughout adulthood?

Answer: Socialization continues throughout adulthood as individuals engage in new relationships, work environments, and social contexts. Life transitions, such as marriage, parenthood, career changes, and retirement, present opportunities for continued social

Unit 14:
Traveling with Your Canine Companion

Traveling with your furry companion can be an incredibly rewarding and unforgettable experience. Whether you're embarking on a short road trip or a long-distance adventure, careful planning and preparation are essential to ensure a safe and comfortable journey for both you and your dog. In this chapter, we will guide you through the essential steps to prepare for travel with your dog, enabling you to create lasting memories while exploring new places.

Think of other people when you travel

Research and Plan

Before setting off on your adventure, it's crucial to research your destination to ensure that it's pet-friendly. Look for accommodations, parks, and attractions that warmly welcome dogs. Additionally, familiarize yourself with any local regulations or restrictions concerning pets, such as leash laws or breed-specific regulations. Being well-informed will help you plan your itinerary and ensure a smooth experience.

Visit the Veterinarian

Schedule a visit to the veterinarian well in advance of your trip. Make sure your dog is up to date on vaccinations, and obtain a health certificate if it's required by your destination. Take this opportunity to discuss any specific concerns or necessary preventive measures for the area you'll be visiting, such as tick or mosquito protection. Your vet can provide valuable advice and recommendations tailored to your dog's health needs.

Pack Essential Supplies

Creating a checklist of essential items for your dog is a must. Some items to include are:

- Food and water bowls: Ensure you have portable bowls for on-the-go meals and hydration.

- Sufficient food for the duration of the trip: Pack enough of your dog's regular food to last the entire journey.

- Medications and any required prescriptions: Bring an ample supply of your dog's medications, along with copies of prescriptions.

- Collar with identification tags and a sturdy leash: Double-check that your dog's collar fits properly and that the tags are up to date with your contact information. Pack a reliable leash for walks and outings.

- Bed or blanket for comfort: Familiar items like your dog's bed or blanket can provide comfort and a sense of home while traveling.

- Favorite toys and chews for entertainment: Pack a selection of your dog's favorite toys and chews to keep them entertained during downtime.

- Waste bags for cleanup: Responsible waste disposal is crucial, so carry an adequate supply of waste bags.

- First aid kit for emergencies: Prepare a first aid kit specifically for your dog, including essentials like bandages, antiseptic wipes, and any necessary medications.

- Grooming supplies (brush, shampoo, etc.): Bring grooming tools to maintain your dog's hygiene throughout the trip.

- Travel crate or carrier if needed: If your dog requires a crate or carrier, ensure it's appropriately sized, comfortable, and secure for travel.

Prepare Your Dog for Travel

Help your dog become accustomed to traveling by taking short practice trips in the car. Start with brief outings and gradually increase the duration and distance to acclimate your dog to being in a moving vehicle. If your dog experiences anxiety or motion sickness, consult your veterinarian for possible solutions or medications to alleviate their discomfort.

Ensure Safety in the Car

When traveling by car, your dog's safety and security should be a top priority. Utilize a seat belt harness, crate, or travel carrier to restrain your dog during the journey. This prevents them from roaming inside the vehicle or getting injured in the event of sudden stops or accidents. Never allow your dog to ride in the front seat or stick their head out of the window, as it poses a significant risk.

Plan for Regular Breaks

During long car trips, plan regular breaks to allow your dog to stretch their legs, relieve themselves, and have a drink of water. Research rest areas or dog-friendly parks along your route where your dog can safely exercise and enjoy some fresh air. These breaks will help prevent your dog from becoming restless or uncomfortable during the journey.

Stay Hydrated and Fed

Hydration and nutrition are vital for your dog's well-being while traveling. Ensure your dog has access to fresh water throughout the trip by carrying a portable water dispenser or a spill-proof travel bowl. Stick to your dog's regular feeding schedule and pack their food in airtight containers to maintain freshness. Avoid feeding your dog a large meal right before traveling to minimize the chances of car sickness.

Comfort and Calming Techniques

Creating a comfortable and familiar space for your dog in the car can greatly contribute to their well-being during the journey. Utilize their bed or blankets to provide them with a cozy spot to rest. Additionally, consider using calming aids such as pheromone sprays, natural supplements, or anxiety wraps to help your dog relax and feel secure while on the road.

Air Travel and Shipping a Dog

Air travel and shipping dogs require careful consideration and preparation to ensure the well-being and safety of your furry friend. Whether you are planning a trip with your dog or need to transport them to a different location, understanding the process is essential. In this chapter, we will explore the various aspects of air travel and shipping dogs, including preparations, regulations, and tips to minimize stress and create a comfortable journey for your beloved pet.

Assessing Your Dog's Suitability for Air Travel

Before planning air travel, it is important to assess your dog's suitability for the journey. Consider their health, age, and temperament. Consult with your veterinarian to ensure your dog is fit to fly and discuss any necessary vaccinations or medications.

Choosing the Right Airline

Research different airlines' pet policies to find the one that suits your needs. Look for information on size and breed restrictions, fees, and options for in-cabin or cargo travel. Choose an airline that prioritizes the well-being of pets and provides appropriate facilities and services.

Preparing for the Trip

To prepare your dog for air travel, acquire an airline-approved pet carrier that meets size and safety requirements. Gradually introduce your dog to the carrier to familiarize them with it. Ensure your dog wears a secure collar with identification tags, and consider microchipping as an added precaution. Pack necessary items such as food, water, leash, toys, and any required documents, such as health certificates.

Regulations and Documentation

Research the specific regulations and requirements of your destination, including quarantine rules if applicable. Obtain a health certificate from your veterinarian within the specified time frame. Keep all necessary documents, including vaccination records, identification, and contact information, readily accessible.

Tips for a Stress-free Flight

To make the flight more comfortable for your dog, exercise them before the trip to help burn off excess energy. Avoid feeding a large meal before the flight to minimize the chances of an upset stomach. Provide comfort and reassurance during the journey using familiar scents or toys. Stay calm and composed, as dogs can sense your emotions and take cues from your behavior.

Shipping a Dog via Cargo

Understanding the Process

Evaluate if shipping your dog via cargo is necessary or if alternative options are available. Research reputable pet shipping services that prioritize the safety and well-being of animals.

Choosing a Pet Shipping Service

Verify the credentials and experience of the shipping company. Inquire about specific services, such as crate requirements, temperature-controlled environments, and tracking systems.

Preparing Your Dog for Shipping

Schedule a visit to your veterinarian to ensure your dog is in good health and meets the necessary requirements. Follow the instructions provided by the shipping service regarding crate training, feeding schedules, and required documentation.

Crate Preparation

Acquire a sturdy, well-ventilated crate that meets the shipping service's specifications. Familiarize your dog with the crate gradually and make it a comfortable space for them.

Ensuring Safety and Comfort

Provide familiar bedding and toys inside the crate to make it more comfortable and secure. Consider including an item with your scent to help your dog feel more at ease during the journey. Double-check that the crate is securely locked and labeled with your contact information.

Conclusion

Air travel and shipping a dog require careful planning, adherence to regulations, and consideration of your dog's well-being. By assessing your dog's suitability, choosing the right airline or shipping service, and adequately preparing for the journey, you can ensure a safe and comfortable experience. Following guidelines for crate preparation, safety, and comfort will further contribute to a positive travel experience for both you and your beloved pet.

Road Trips with Dogs - Safety and Comfort

Road trips can be an exciting adventure for both you and your furry friend. However, it's important to ensure the safety and well-being of your dog throughout the journey. In this chapter, we will discuss essential guidelines for taking dogs on road trips, including preventing dogs from being left in cars, avoiding closed windows while parked, and the importance of not letting dogs hang their heads out of windows. Additionally, we will emphasize the need to bring a pop-up kennel for your dog to ensure they have a comfortable space and avoid being on hotel beds.

Preventing Dogs from Being Left in Cars

Understanding the dangers

Leaving dogs in cars during road trips can pose serious risks, including heatstroke, dehydration, and suffocation. Understanding these dangers is crucial for ensuring your dog's safety.

Planning ahead

Instead of leaving your dog in the car, plan ahead and explore alternatives. Look for pet-friendly attractions, parks, or restaurants where your dog can accompany you.

Safe pit stops

Research and identify dog-friendly rest areas and establishments along your route. These stops will provide opportunities for your dog to stretch their legs, relieve themselves, and get some fresh air.

Avoiding Closed Windows while Parked

Proper ventilation

It is essential not to leave dogs in cars with closed windows, as this can lead to heat buildup and suffocation. Ensure proper ventilation by cracking the windows or using sunshades to allow air circulation.

Parking in shaded areas

When parking, choose shaded areas to minimize the impact of direct sunlight on your dog. This helps prevent overheating and discomfort during the journey.

Monitoring temperature

Consider using temperature monitoring devices to keep track of the temperature inside the car. This can alert you to any dangerous spikes in temperature and prompt you to take immediate action to protect your dog.

Discouraging Dogs from Hanging Their Heads out of Windows

Potential hazards

Allowing dogs to hang their heads out of moving vehicles can be risky. They may be at risk of injury from debris, insects, or sudden stops. Understanding these hazards is important for their safety.

Secure containment

Utilize appropriate restraints, such as harnesses or dog seat belts, to ensure your dog remains safely contained inside the vehicle. This prevents them from accidentally falling or jumping out of the window.

Providing alternative stimulation

To keep your dog engaged during the journey, provide them with toys, treats, or interactive puzzles. This helps redirect their attention and prevent them from seeking stimulation by hanging their heads out of windows.

The Importance of a Pop-Up Kennel for Accommodation

Establishing a safe space

A pop-up kennel provides a safe and comfortable space for your dog during rest stops and overnight stays. It gives them a familiar and secure area where they can relax and feel at ease.

Selecting the right size

When choosing a pop-up kennel, ensure it is spacious enough for your dog to stand, turn around, and lie down comfortably. Adequate space is essential for their comfort and well-being.

Hotel regulations

If you plan to stay at hotels, familiarize yourself with their pet policies and guidelines. Follow these regulations to prevent dogs from being on hotel beds, maintain cleanliness, and prevent any damage.

Conclusion

Taking your dog on a road trip can be an enriching experience for both of you. By adhering to the guidelines outlined in this chapter, you can ensure your dog's safety and comfort throughout the journey. Remember, preventing dogs from being left in cars, avoiding closed windows while parked, and discouraging dogs from hanging their heads out of windows are crucial aspects of responsible pet ownership. Additionally, bringing a pop-up kennel will provide your dog with a familiar and secure space, ensuring a relaxing stay at hotels and preventing them from being on the beds. With proper preparation and care, your road trip with your beloved canine companion is bound to be a memorable and enjoyable experience for all.

Responsible Dog Ownership in Public Spaces

In this section, we will explore the importance of responsible dog ownership in public spaces. We will discuss the significance of controlling your dog in public, including the necessity of leash training and proper behavior management. Additionally, we will emphasize the importance of picking up after your dog to maintain cleanliness and respect for others. By the end of this unit, dog owners will understand the responsibilities and etiquette associated with taking their dogs into public spaces.

Lesson 1: Controlling Your Dog in Public

The first lesson focuses on why control is essential in public spaces. Unleashed dogs can pose potential risks and hazards to themselves, others, and the environment. We will discuss these risks and highlight the importance of respecting the comfort and safety of other people. Additionally, we will teach you leash training techniques to improve control and communication with your dog, ensuring their safety and the safety of those around them. We will also address common behavior issues and provide tips for effective behavior management.

Activity: Leash Training Practice

To reinforce the lessons learned, we will engage in a hands-on activity. You will pair up with a volunteer who will act as a dog while you demonstrate leash training techniques. This interactive exercise will allow you to receive feedback and suggestions for improvement.

Lesson 2: Picking Up After Your Dog

Our second lesson centers around the importance of picking up after your dog. We will explain the health and environmental risks associated with leaving dog waste in public areas and discuss the impact of irresponsible waste disposal on the community and its perception of dog owners. Proper waste disposal methods will be taught, including using poop bags and taking advantage of waste disposal stations available in public spaces. We will also discuss the benefits of carrying extra poop bags and educating fellow dog owners on responsible waste management.

Activity: Waste Disposal Scenarios

You will participate in group discussions, where various waste disposal scenarios will be presented. Together, you will propose appropriate solutions or actions to address each situation effectively.

Lesson 3: Etiquette and Respect in Public Spaces

The third lesson focuses on proper etiquette and respectful behavior while taking your dog into public spaces. We will emphasize the importance of asking permission before allowing your dog to approach strangers or other dogs. You will learn appropriate ways to respond when someone expresses discomfort or fear of dogs. We will also discuss the need to be mindful of leash laws, designated dog-friendly areas, and areas where dogs should be kept away, such as food establishments.

Activity: Responsible Dog Owner Presentation

Each student will prepare a short presentation on responsible dog ownership, covering key points from the lessons and incorporating personal experiences or examples. This activity will enhance your understanding of responsible dog ownership and allow you to share your knowledge with the class.

Lesson 4: Safety Precautions in Public Spaces

Our fourth lesson revolves around implementing safety precautions while taking your dog into public spaces. We will discuss common hazards, such as busy roads, toxic substances, and aggressive animals. You will learn how to identify potential dangers and react to keep your dog safe.

Additionally, we will cover the use of safety equipment like identification tags, microchips, reflective gear, harnesses, and muzzles, if necessary. Basic first-aid techniques for dogs will also be taught, along with the importance of having emergency veterinary contact information readily available.

Activity: Safety Plan Creation

In small groups, you will create safety plans for different scenarios you may encounter while walking your dogs in public spaces. These plans will include hazard identification, preventive measures, and emergency response strategies.

Lesson 5: Continuous Training and Socialization

The fifth lesson emphasizes the importance of continuous training and socialization for dogs in public spaces. We will discuss the need for ongoing training to maintain good behavior and control. You will learn how to reinforce commands and behaviors learned during initial training sessions. Exposure to different environments and stimuli will also be discussed, along with the benefits of gradually introducing dogs to new environments to prevent fear or anxiety. Finally, we will encourage you to engage in obedience classes and group activities, such as agility training or visiting dog parks, to enhance structured training and socialization opportunities.

Activity: Obedience Training Demonstration

Each student will demonstrate basic obedience training commands with their dogs in a controlled environment, showcasing their dog's ability to respond to commands and display good behavior.

Lesson 6: Being a Responsible Community Member

The final lesson centers around being a responsible community member as a dog owner. We will discuss the importance of promoting positive interactions between dogs and community members. Respecting public spaces and regulations will be emphasized, highlighting the consequences of disregarding rules and their negative impact on other community members. Lastly, we will encourage you to be a role model by demonstrating responsible dog ownership in your daily life and fostering positive perceptions and attitudes towards dogs and their owners.

Activity: Community Awareness Campaign

You will design and implement a community awareness campaign to promote responsible dog ownership. This campaign can involve creating posters, organizing informational events, or distributing educational materials to engage and educate community members.

By actively practicing responsible dog ownership in public spaces, you can contribute to safer, cleaner, and more inclusive communities. Through effective control of your dogs, responsible waste disposal, respectful behavior, continuous training, and community involvement, you can foster a culture of responsible dog ownership that benefits everyone.

Remember, being a responsible dog owner is a commitment that extends beyond your home. Let's work together to create a positive and harmonious environment for dogs and humans alike.

Unit 15 Choosing a Breeder

Introduction

Bringing a new puppy into your life is a decision that requires careful consideration, and choosing a reputable breeder is paramount to ensure not only the well-being of the puppy but also your own satisfaction as a responsible dog owner. Reputable breeders play a significant role in a dog's life, starting from the moment of conception and continuing through the puppy's early development, socialization, and eventual transition into a loving home. In this section, we will explore in detail the importance of selecting a reputable breeder and the impact it can have on both the puppy and your experience as a pet owner. All too often, a person gets a dog from a bad source, and their household is not prepared for one.

Section 1: Criteria for Choosing a Breeder

Breeder's Reputation and Experience

The reputation of a breeder is an essential factor to consider during your search for the perfect puppy. Begin by conducting thorough research into the breeder's background and reputation. They will have paperwork and references. Utilize online platforms, such as websites, social media, and

304

forums, to find reviews and feedback from previous customers. Positive testimonials from satisfied pet owners are strong indicators of a breeder's commitment to producing healthy and well-adjusted puppies.

Membership in recognized breed clubs or associations is another positive sign. Reputable breeders often seek affiliation with these organizations, as it demonstrates their involvement in the dog community and their adherence to breed standards and ethical breeding practices.

Moreover, exploring the breeder's involvement and history with the breed can provide valuable insights. Understanding their passion for the breed and any achievements, awards, or recognitions they have received related to the breed can instill confidence in their ability to produce well-bred and healthy puppies. Reputable breeders do not design

Health Testing and Genetic Screening

Responsible breeders prioritize the health and well-being of their dogs by conducting thorough health tests and genetic screenings for their breeding stock. Before choosing a breeder, inquire about the specific health tests they perform on their dogs and request to see the results. Common health tests may include evaluations for hip and elbow dysplasia, eye conditions, and genetic tests for hereditary diseases prevalent in the breed.

A reputable breeder may offer health guarantees or warranties for their puppies. These guarantees provide buyers with assurance that the puppy is free from certain hereditary conditions. They may also provide options for recourse should any health issues arise.

Breeding Practices

Visiting the breeder's facility or home is an essential step in evaluating their breeding practices. Reputable breeders are usually open to welcoming potential buyers to see where their dogs and puppies are raised. During your visit, observe the living conditions of the dogs and puppies. Clean and well-maintained living spaces indicate a breeder's commitment to the health and welfare of their animals.

Socialization is a crucial aspect of a puppy's early development. Inquire about how the breeder socializes their puppies. Puppies should be exposed to various stimuli and experiences at an appropriate age to ensure they grow into well-adjusted and confident dogs.

Knowledge and Communication

A reputable breeder possesses in-depth knowledge about the breed, including its history, temperament, and specific care requirements. They should be eager to share their expertise with potential buyers, answering questions and providing guidance on choosing the right puppy for your lifestyle.

Openness and responsiveness in communication are essential traits of a reputable breeder. A breeder who is readily available to answer your queries and maintains open lines of communication during the puppy selection process is likely to be invested in the well-being of their puppies even after they leave their care.

Breeder's Support and Policies

The support offered by a breeder doesn't end when you take the puppy home. Reputable breeders often provide ongoing guidance and support as you acclimate to life with your new pet. This support may include advice on training, health care, and general well-being.

Understanding the breeder's policies regarding puppy returns is also crucial. Responsible breeders will have a plan in place to handle situations where a puppy needs to be returned or rehomed due to unforeseen circumstances.

Recommendations provided by the breeder, such as feeding guidelines, grooming tips, and training resources, can be invaluable to new pet owners, helping them ensure the best possible care for their puppy.

Section 2: Red Flags to Avoid in a Breeder

Reputable breeders adhere to strict breeding standards set forth by kennel clubs and breed organizations. These standards outline the desirable traits, physical characteristics, and temperament of the breed. A breeder who doesn't follow or disregard these standards may be breeding for profit rather than maintaining the breed's integrity. Such practices can lead to a loss of breed characteristics, including temperament and appearance, and may produce puppies that do not conform to the breed standard.

No Socialization or Interaction

Socialization is crucial for puppies' development, and responsible breeders understand the significance of early socialization. A red flag is a breeder who keeps the puppies isolated or lacks proper interaction with them during their early weeks. Puppies that aren't exposed to different environments, sounds, people, and other animals during their critical socialization period may grow up to be fearful, anxious, or aggressive. A reputable breeder should actively work to expose the puppies to various stimuli to promote their emotional well-being and ensure they become well-adjusted pets.

Lack of Screening for Potential Buyers

A reputable breeder cares about the well-being of

their puppies even after they leave their premises. A concerning sign is a breeder who shows little interest in screening potential buyers. Ethical breeders will often ask potential buyers questions to ensure the puppy is going to a suitable and loving home. They may inquire about the buyer's living situation, previous pet ownership experience, and how they plan to care for the puppy. This screening process helps ensure that the puppy will be placed in a responsible and caring environment.

No Return Policy or Health Guarantee

A reputable breeder stands behind the health and well-being of their puppies. A lack of a return policy or health guarantee is a significant red flag. A responsible breeder should be willing to take back a puppy if, for any reason, the new owner cannot keep it. Additionally, they should provide a health guarantee that covers any genetic health issues that may arise during the puppy's early life. This commitment demonstrates that the breeder is dedicated to producing healthy and happy puppies and is willing to support the new owners in case of unexpected health problems.

Unwillingness to Show the Breeding Facility or Provide References

An open and transparent breeder will have no issues inviting potential buyers to their breeding facility or providing references from previous buyers. If a breeder is hesitant or outright refuses to show their facilities or provide references, it could be a warning sign. A reputable breeder should be proud of their breeding practices and the care they provide to their dogs and puppies. Being able to visit the facility and speak with previous buyers can give you valuable insights into the breeder's reputation and the conditions in which their dogs are raised.

Lack of Transparency

Lack of transparency in a breeder can be a major red flag and may suggest that they have something to hide. Many reputable breeders will restrict visitors to help prevent illness or disease from being brought unknowingly. But in these cases, they provide lots of videos. Here are some additional details on what to be cautious of regarding transparency:

1. Vague or Inconsistent Information
   If a breeder provides unclear or inconsistent answers to your questions, it's a cause for concern. Reputable

breeders will be able to explain their breeding program, the health testing they conduct, and the lineage of their dogs in a straightforward manner. Inconsistencies in their responses may indicate a lack of knowledge or an attempt to mislead potential buyers.

2. Reluctance to Provide Documentation

   A responsible breeder should have no problem providing documentation to support their claims about health testing, pedigrees, and registrations. If a breeder is hesitant to share these documents or gives excuses for not having them readily available, it raises doubts about the legitimacy of their breeding practices.

3. Unwillingness to Allow Visits

   Transparency extends to allowing potential buyers to visit the breeder's facility or home to see the conditions in which the dogs and puppies are raised. A breeder who avoids on-site visits or makes excuses for why they cannot accommodate them might be hiding inadequate living conditions or other issues.

4. Lack of Online Presence or Referrals

   Reputable breeders often have an online presence, such as a website or social media page, where they share information about their breeding program, their dogs, and past litters. They may also have positive reviews or referrals from previous buyers. A breeder who lacks an online presence or refuses to provide references may be trying to avoid scrutiny.

5. Non-Disclosure of Health Issues

A transparent breeder will openly discuss any health issues that may be present in their breeding dogs or past litters. They should be forthcoming about the steps they are taking to breed healthy puppies and address any genetic concerns within the breed. Hiding or downplaying health issues is a major red flag.

6. Lack of Contract or Written Agreement

A reputable breeder will have a clear and comprehensive contract that outlines the terms of the sale, health guarantees, and responsibilities of both the breeder and the buyer. If a breeder avoids providing a written agreement or contract, it can leave you vulnerable to potential issues in the future.

Remember that responsible breeders take pride in their breeding program and are eager to share information with potential buyers. They prioritize the health and well-being of their dogs and puppies and strive to build trusting relationships with their customers. Choosing a transparent breeder ensures that you are supporting ethical practices and increases the likelihood of bringing home a healthy and happy puppy.

Pushy Sales Tactics

Pushy sales tactics from a breeder can be a significant red flag and indicate that their primary concern is profit rather than the well-being of their puppies. Here are some additional details on what to watch out for regarding pushy sales tactics:

1. High-Pressure Sales

   If a breeder tries to rush you into making a decision or insists that their puppies are in high demand and may not be available for long, it's a warning sign. Reputable breeders understand that bringing a puppy into your home is a significant commitment and will give you the time you need to make an informed choice.

2. Emotional Manipulation

Be cautious of breeders who try to use emotional manipulation to sway your decision. They might tell you heart-wrenching stories about their puppies to evoke sympathy or guilt. A responsible breeder will provide you with honest information about their dogs without resorting to emotional tactics.

3. Lack of Transparency

If a breeder avoids answering your questions directly, deflects concerns, or tries to divert your attention away from potential issues, it's a sign that they may be hiding something. An ethical breeder will be open and transparent about their breeding practices, the health of their dogs, and the living conditions of their puppies.

4. Discounted Offers

Some unethical breeders may offer significant discounts or promotions to entice you to buy a puppy quickly. They might claim that these discounts are time-sensitive or exclusive to you, which can create a sense of urgency. Reputable breeders will price their puppies fairly based on their quality and the care they have received without resorting to manipulative pricing tactics.

5. Lack of Concern for Your Lifestyle

A pushy breeder may disregard your lifestyle and living situation, trying to convince you that their breed is suitable for anyone, regardless of their circumstances. However, responsible breeders understand that different breeds have different needs and temperaments, and they will inquire about your lifestyle to ensure the puppy is a good fit for your home.

6. Guilt-Tripping

Avoid breeders who try to guilt-trip you into buying a puppy, such as claiming that not buying from them would be detrimental to the dogs or that you are not supporting responsible breeding. Ethical breeders focus on educating potential buyers and fostering a positive relationship rather than using guilt as a tactic.

Remember that choosing a puppy should be a well-considered decision based on compatibility, responsibility, and the desire to provide a loving and permanent home. A reputable breeder will support your decision-making process, provide you with all the necessary information, and

be there to assist you even after you bring your new puppy
home.

Conclusion

Choosing a reputable breeder is a decision that
should not be taken lightly, as it has a profound impact on
the well-being of the puppy and your experience as a pet
owner. Throughout this exploration, we have emphasized the
significance of careful breeder selection and the red flags to
avoid in order to find a responsible and caring source for
your new furry companion.

Thorough research is crucial when searching for a
breeder, and it involves investigating their reputation, health
testing practices, breeding conditions, knowledge, and
support. By doing so, you can ensure that the breeder you
choose is committed to producing healthy, well-adjusted,
and genetically sound puppies.

Prioritizing animal welfare is paramount when
engaging with a breeder. Responsible breeders have a
genuine passion for the breed and prioritize the health and
happiness of their dogs above all else. By supporting ethical
breeders, you contribute to the betterment of the breed and
discourage unethical breeding practices that may lead to
health issues and behavioral problems in dogs.

Additionally, the relationship between owners and breeders extends far beyond the moment the puppy leaves the breeder's care. A reputable breeder is invested in the well-being of their puppies throughout their lives, offering ongoing guidance and support to ensure they lead happy and fulfilling lives in their new homes.

In conclusion, selecting a reputable breeder is a decision that holds tremendous importance for both the puppy and you as an owner. Through thorough research, prioritization of animal welfare, and choosing responsible breeders, you can embark on a rewarding journey with your new puppy, knowing that you have made the best possible choice for your furry family member. The lifelong relationship between owners and breeders can be a source of continued support, guidance, and joy as you share your life with your beloved canine companion.

Unit 16 Dog Genetics

Introduction

In this chapter, we will delve into the fascinating world of dog genetics. Genetics is the study of heredity and how traits are passed down from one generation to the next. It plays a crucial role in understanding the unique characteristics and behaviors of different dog breeds. By examining the principles of genetics as they relate to dogs, we can gain valuable insights into the inheritance patterns of various traits, as well as the potential health concerns that may arise.

Definition of Genetics

Genetics is the branch of biology that focuses on the study of genes, heredity, and variation in living organisms. Genes are segments of DNA (deoxyribonucleic acid) that carry the instructions for the development, functioning, and appearance of an organism. They determine the traits that are passed from parents to their offspring, influencing factors such as coat color, body structure, temperament, and susceptibility to certain diseases.

Importance of Understanding Dog Genetics

Understanding dog genetics is of paramount importance for several reasons. Firstly, it allows breeders to make informed decisions when selecting mating pairs, aiming to produce offspring with desired traits while minimizing the risk of inheriting genetic disorders. By understanding the patterns of inheritance, breeders can work

319

towards maintaining breed standards and improving overall breed health.

Additionally, a comprehensive understanding of dog genetics helps veterinarians and researchers identify potential genetic diseases or health issues that may affect specific breeds. This knowledge aids in early detection, prevention, and treatment of these conditions, ultimately contributing to the overall well-being of dogs.

Furthermore, understanding dog genetics can also be beneficial for dog owners and enthusiasts. It allows them to make informed choices when selecting a new pet, considering factors such as breed-specific traits, potential health concerns, and compatibility with their lifestyle.

In conclusion, genetics provides a fundamental framework for comprehending the inheritance patterns and diversity within dog breeds. By studying dog genetics, breeders, veterinarians, and dog owners can make informed decisions that promote the health, welfare, and preservation of various dog breeds. In the following sections of this chapter, we will explore the principles of dog genetics in more detail, including modes of inheritance, genetic disorders, and the impact of selective breeding on the canine population.

Dog Genetics Fundamentals

DNA, or deoxyribonucleic acid, is a molecule found in the cells of living organisms, including dogs. It carries the genetic information that determines the characteristics and traits of an individual. DNA has a double-helix structure, resembling a twisted ladder or spiral staircase.

Each DNA molecule is made up of two strands that are connected by nucleotides. A nucleotide consists of a sugar molecule called deoxyribose, a phosphate group, and one of four nitrogenous bases: adenine (A), thymine (T), cytosine (C), or guanine (G). The two strands of DNA are held together by hydrogen bonds between complementary bases: A always pairs with T, and C always pairs with G.

The sequence of nucleotides along the DNA strands forms the genetic code. This code carries the instructions for building and maintaining an organism, including the development of physical characteristics, metabolism, and behavior.

Genes as units of inheritance

Genes are specific segments of DNA that contain the instructions for producing a particular protein or functional RNA molecule. Proteins are the building blocks of cells and play a crucial role in determining an organism's traits. Genes act as units of inheritance, passing on specific traits from one generation to the next.

In dogs, genes determine various characteristics such as coat color, eye color, size, and predisposition to certain diseases. Each gene has a specific location on a chromosome, which is a thread-like structure in the cell nucleus. Chromosomes come in pairs, with one inherited from each parent. Dogs typically have 39 pairs of chromosomes, except for some breeds with variations.

Different versions of a gene are called alleles. For example, there are multiple alleles for coat color genes, such as black, brown, or white. An individual dog inherits one allele from each parent for a given gene. The combination of alleles determines the specific trait or characteristic expressed in the dog.

Genes can be dominant or recessive. Dominant genes express their traits even if there is only one copy of the allele present, while recessive genes require two copies for the trait to be expressed. For example, the gene for black coat color in dogs is dominant over the gene for brown coat color. A dog with one black allele and one brown allele will have a black coat because the black allele is dominant.

Understanding genes and their inheritance patterns is essential for breeders who aim to produce specific traits or avoid genetic disorders in their breeding programs. By studying the genetic makeup of dogs and the inheritance patterns of various traits, researchers and breeders can make informed decisions to promote healthier and desired characteristics in future generations of dogs.

Chromosomes

Organization and Structure of Chromosomes

Chromosomes play a crucial role in the storage and transmission of genetic information within cells. These thread-like structures are found in the nucleus of eukaryotic cells and are composed of DNA molecules tightly wound around proteins. In this section, we will explore the organization and structure of chromosomes in greater detail.

1.　**Chromosome Composition**

Each chromosome consists of a single long DNA molecule that is associated with various proteins. The DNA molecule carries the genetic instructions necessary for the development, functioning, and reproduction of organisms. Proteins called histones help in the packaging and compaction of DNA, forming a complex known as chromatin.

2.　**Chromatin Structure**

Chromatin undergoes further coiling and folding to condense into a highly compact structure, visible during cell division. This condensed form of chromatin is essential for the orderly distribution of genetic material to daughter cells. When chromatin is highly compacted, it is visible under a microscope as distinct structures called chromosomes.

3. **Chromosome Number**

The number of chromosomes varies across different species. Humans, for example, typically have 46 chromosomes, organized as 23 pairs. Each pair consists of two homologous chromosomes, one inherited from each parent. The two chromosomes in a pair are similar in size and shape and carry genes for the same traits. However, there are exceptions, such as the sex chromosomes, which determine an individual's biological sex.

4. **Centromeres and Telomeres**

Chromosomes have specific regions called centromeres and telomeres. The centromere is a specialized region where sister chromatids, replicated copies of a chromosome, are held together until they separate during cell division. Telomeres, on the other hand, are found at the ends of chromosomes and protect them from degradation and fusion with other chromosomes.

325

Role in Inheritance

Chromosomes play a fundamental role in the inheritance of traits from one generation to the next. The organization and behavior of chromosomes during cell division are crucial for maintaining the stability and integrity of the genetic material. Let's delve into the role of chromosomes in inheritance.

Mendelian Inheritance

Gregor Mendel's experiments laid the foundation for understanding the principles of inheritance. His work showed that genes, the units of heredity, are located on chromosomes. Genes are specific segments of DNA that code for particular traits. Mendel's laws of segregation and independent assortment describe how genes are passed from parents to offspring via chromosomes during sexual reproduction.

Meiosis and Gamete Formation

Meiosis is a specialized form of cell division that occurs in reproductive cells, leading to the formation of gametes (sperm and eggs). During meiosis, homologous chromosomes pair up and exchange genetic material through a process called recombination or crossing over. This genetic recombination contributes to genetic diversity in offspring.

Chromosomal Aberrations

Chromosomal abnormalities, such as deletions, duplications, inversions, and translocations, can occur due to errors during chromosome replication or recombination. These aberrations can have significant effects on an individual's phenotype, potentially leading to genetic disorders or developmental abnormalities.

Sex Chromosomes and Sex Determination

In many species, including humans, sex chromosomes determine an individual's biological sex. The presence or absence of specific sex chromosomes (such as XX in females and XY in males in humans) determines the development of sexual characteristics. The inheritance patterns of sex-linked traits, which are located on the sex chromosomes, differ from those of autosomal traits.

Inheritance Patterns

Inheritance patterns and genetic traits play a crucial role in shaping the characteristics and health of dogs. Understanding these patterns is essential for responsible breeding practices, identifying potential health risks, and predicting the traits that offspring may inherit. Let's delve deeper into the discussed topics:

Mendelian Inheritance

Mendelian inheritance, based on the work of Gregor Mendel, describes the transmission of genetic traits from parents to offspring. This classic form of inheritance involves dominant and recessive alleles. Dominant traits are expressed when at least one copy of the dominant allele is present, while recessive traits are only expressed when two copies of the recessive allele are inherited. Breeders must consider these patterns to predict the potential traits of future generations and avoid certain undesirable traits.

Co-dominance and Incomplete Dominance

Co-dominance and incomplete dominance are variations of Mendelian inheritance. Co-dominance occurs when both alleles of a gene are expressed, resulting in a distinct phenotype that combines both traits. Incomplete dominance, on the other hand, leads to an intermediate phenotype when the heterozygous genotype shows a blending of the homozygous phenotypes. These patterns are relevant in understanding traits such as blood types in dogs or coat patterns like Merle's.

Polygenic Inheritance

Polygenic inheritance involves multiple genes contributing to a single trait, leading to a continuous range of variation in phenotypes. Traits like height, weight, and some behavioral characteristics are polygenic, making them more complex to predict and control through selective breeding. Breeders need to consider these interactions to maintain or modify certain traits in a breeding program effectively.

Genetic Terminology

Understanding genetic terminology, such as alleles, genotypes, and phenotypes, is fundamental to comprehending the underlying principles of inheritance. Alleles are different forms of a gene, and their combinations in the genotype determine the observed phenotype. Responsible breeders use this knowledge to make informed decisions to achieve desired traits while avoiding genetic diseases.

Genetic Diseases and Traits

Inherited disorders are a significant concern for dog breeders and owners. Genetic mutations passed down from parent dogs can result in various health conditions. Some inherited disorders are monogenic, caused by mutations in a single gene, while others are complex, involving interactions between multiple genes and environmental factors. Responsible breeding practices aim to reduce the incidence of these disorders through health testing and selective breeding.

Breed-Specific Traits

Dog breeds have been selectively bred over centuries for specific purposes, such as herding, hunting, or companionship. As a result, each breed has distinctive characteristics and traits associated with its purpose and appearance. Understanding breed-specific traits is vital for breeders, as it helps maintain the breed's standard and preserve its unique qualities.

Understanding Inherited Dog Diseases

Inherited diseases can significantly impact the health and well-being of our beloved canine companions. These conditions are passed down from one generation to another through genetic factors, making it crucial for dog owners and breeders to be knowledgeable about them. By understanding inherited dog diseases, we can take proactive measures to prevent or manage these conditions and ensure the overall health of our furry friends. In this chapter, we will explore the concept of inherited dog diseases, their causes, common examples, and strategies for prevention and management.

Understanding Inherited Diseases

Inherited diseases, also known as genetic diseases or hereditary conditions, are disorders that are passed down from parent dogs to their offspring through genetic material. These diseases result from variations or mutations in specific genes that control various aspects of the dog's biology. Inherited diseases can affect dogs of any breed or mix, although certain breeds are more prone to particular conditions due to their genetic makeup.

Causes of Inherited Dog Diseases

The causes of inherited dog diseases can be attributed to genetic mutations. Mutations are alterations in the DNA sequence, which can affect the normal functioning of genes. These mutations can be inherited from one or both parents and can result in a wide range of health conditions in dogs.

Types of Inherited Dog Diseases

Inherited dog diseases can be broadly classified into two categories: single-gene disorders and complex disorders.

1.   Single Gene Disorders

Single-gene disorders are caused by a mutation in a specific gene. They are relatively rare but can have a significant impact on a dog's health. Some examples of single-gene disorders in dogs include:

2.   Progressive Retinal Atrophy (PRA)

PRA is a group of inherited diseases that cause degeneration of the retina, leading to progressive vision loss and, in some cases, blindness.

3.   Von Willebrand's Disease (vWD) vWD is a bleeding disorder caused by a deficiency of von Willebrand factor, a protein involved in blood clotting.

4.   Canine Hip Dysplasia (CHD)

CHD is a common orthopedic condition where the hip joint develops abnormally, leading to joint instability, pain, and difficulty in movement.

5.   Complex Disorders

Complex disorders are influenced by multiple genes as well as environmental factors. They are more common than single-gene disorders and can be challenging to diagnose and manage. Examples of complex disorders in dogs include:

6.   Allergies

Dogs can inherit a predisposition to allergies, such as food allergies, environmental allergies (atopy), or flea allergies. These conditions can cause itching, skin irritations, and gastrointestinal problems.

7. Epilepsy

Canine epilepsy is a neurological disorder characterized by recurrent seizures. It can have a genetic basis, although the exact causes are not fully understood.

8. Cancer

Certain dog breeds are prone to specific types of cancer, indicating a genetic component to the disease. Examples include hemangiosarcoma in German Shepherds and osteosarcoma in large and giant breeds.

9. Prevention and Management

Preventing and managing inherited dog diseases requires a multi-faceted approach involving responsible breeding practices, genetic testing, and proactive healthcare measures.

10. Responsible Breeding

Breeders play a crucial role in preventing inherited diseases by carefully selecting mating pairs. They should prioritize breeding dogs with healthy genetic backgrounds, ideally free from known hereditary conditions. Genetic testing of parent dogs can help identify carriers of specific mutations and minimize the risk of passing on disease-causing genes to offspring.

11.   Genetic Testing

Genetic testing allows breeders and owners to identify specific mutations associated with inherited diseases. By testing breeding dogs, it becomes possible to make informed decisions about mating pairs and reduce the incidence of inherited diseases in subsequent generations. Advances in genetic research have made testing more accessible and affordable, providing breeders with valuable information to improve the overall health of their breeding lines.

Conclusion

Conclusively, it can be said that genetic testing has revolutionized the field of dog breeding and pet care, providing breeders and owners with powerful tools to enhance the health and well-being of canine populations. Through genetic testing, breeders can identify specific mutations associated with inherited diseases, enabling them to make informed decisions about mating pairs and reduce the incidence of genetic disorders in subsequent generations. The ability to pinpoint carriers of genetic mutations has led to more responsible breeding practices, as breeders can strategically select mates to avoid producing affected puppies.

Advancements in genetic research and technology have significantly expanded the scope and accuracy of available tests. New tests are continuously being developed, covering a wider range of inherited diseases and traits, providing breeders with comprehensive insights into their breeding lines. Moreover, the decreasing cost of genetic testing has made it more accessible to breeders and pet owners, democratizing the benefits of this invaluable tool.

Genetic testing not only benefits breeders but also empowers dog owners with essential health information about their pets. Testing can reveal potential health risks and predispositions, allowing veterinarians to develop personalized healthcare plans and early intervention strategies. By being proactive in managing potential health concerns, pet owners can extend their furry companions' lifespans and improve their overall quality of life.

However, while genetic testing is a powerful tool, it is essential to interpret the results accurately and within the context of the specific breed's health concerns. Not all genetic mutations are associated with disease, and some breeds may have naturally occurring variants that do not pose health risks. Therefore, collaboration between breeders, veterinarians, and geneticists is critical in ensuring that genetic testing is used responsibly and ethically.

Incorporating genetic testing into breeding programs has had a profound impact on the betterment of various dog breeds. By selectively breeding for healthier traits and reducing the incidence of inherited diseases, breeders play a significant role in safeguarding the genetic diversity and long-term health of their chosen breeds. As a result, future generations of dogs are more likely to lead healthier, happier lives.

Quiz

1. Q: What is genetics?

   A: Genetics is the study of genes and heredity, including how traits are passed from parents to offspring.

2. Q: What are genes?

A: Genes are segments of DNA that contain instructions for building and maintaining an organism. They determine the traits and characteristics of an individual.

3. Q: How many chromosomes do dogs have?

    A: Dogs typically have 39 pairs of chromosomes, for a total of 78 chromosomes.

4. Q: What is a dominant trait?

    A: A dominant trait is a characteristic that is expressed when an individual has one or two copies of the corresponding gene. It masks the presence of a recessive trait.

5. Q: What is a recessive trait?

    A: A recessive trait is a characteristic that is only expressed when an individual has two copies of the corresponding gene. It is masked by the presence of a dominant trait.

6. Q: Can you give an example of a dominant trait in dogs?

    A: Sure! An example of a dominant trait in dogs is the black coat color. If a dog has one or two copies of the gene for black coat color (Bb or BB), it will have a black coat.

7. Q: Can you give an example of a recessive trait in dogs?

A: Certainly! An example of a recessive trait in dogs is the white coat color. If a dog has two copies of the gene for white coat color (bb), it will have a white coat.

8. Q: What is a genotype?

A: A genotype refers to the genetic makeup of an individual, specifically the combination of alleles (alternative forms of a gene) it possesses for a particular trait.

9. Q: What is a phenotype?

A: A phenotype is the observable physical or biochemical characteristics of an organism, which are determined by its genotype and influenced by environmental factors.

10. Q: Can a dog with a dominant phenotype have a recessive genotype?

A: Yes, it is possible. If a dog has a dominant phenotype, it means that the dominant trait is expressed, but its genotype can still carry a recessive allele that may be passed on to its offspring.

11. Q: What is the purpose of selective breeding in dogs?

A: Selective breeding in dogs is performed to enhance or eliminate specific traits, such as coat color, size, temperament, or working ability. It aims to produce offspring with desired characteristics.

12. Q: What is genetic diversity, and why is it important in dog populations?

A: Genetic diversity refers to the variety of different genes within a population. It is important in dog populations to maintain overall health and reduce the risk of inherited diseases or disorders.

13. Q: Can two dogs with the same phenotype have different genotypes?

A: Yes, it is possible. Dogs with the same phenotype can have different genotypes if they carry different combinations of alleles for the trait in question.

14. Q: What is a mutation, and how can it affect dog genetics?

A: A mutation is a change in the DNA sequence of a gene. It can occur spontaneously or be caused by external factors. Mutations can introduce new traits or alter existing ones, impacting dog genetics.

15. Q: How can understanding dog genetics help in responsible breeding practices?

A: Understanding dog genetics allows breeders to make informed decisions about which dogs to breed, taking into account traits, health considerations, and genetic diversity. This helps promote healthier and more predictable offspring.

16. Q: What is a hereditary disease in dogs?

A: A hereditary disease in dogs is a genetic disorder or condition that is passed down from parents to offspring through their genes. These diseases are caused by mutations or abnormalities in specific genes.

17. Q: Can two dogs with the same genotype have different phenotypes?

A: Yes, it is possible. The expression of certain traits can be influenced by other genes or environmental factors, leading to variations in the phenotype even when the genotype is the same.

18. Q: What is a carrier in dog genetics?

A: A carrier is an individual who possesses one copy of a recessive gene for a particular trait but does not show any signs or symptoms of that trait. Carriers can pass on the gene to their offspring.

19. Q: How can genetic testing be beneficial for dog breeders?

A: Genetic testing can provide valuable information about a dog's genotype, including the presence of disease-causing genes, carrier status for certain traits, and genetic diversity. Breeders can use this information to make informed breeding decisions and reduce the risk of inherited diseases.

20. Q: Can genetic traits be influenced by environmental factors?

A: Yes, environmental factors can influence the expression of certain genetic traits. For example, the coat color of a dog can be affected by exposure to sunlight or temperature changes, leading to variations in the phenotype.

21. Q: What is hybrid vigor or "the outbreeding effect"?

A: Hybrid vigor, also known as heterosis or the outbreeding effect, refers to the improved performance or characteristics observed in offspring

341

resulting from the mating of genetically diverse parents. It often leads to increased vitality, health, and performance compared to inbred individuals.

22. Q: Can you explain polygenic inheritance in dogs?

A: Polygenic inheritance refers to the inheritance of traits that are controlled by multiple genes, each with a small additive effect. Examples of polygenic traits in dogs include height, weight, and certain behavioral traits. The expression of these traits is influenced by the cumulative effect of multiple genes.

23. Q: What is the role of DNA sequencing in dog genetics?

A: DNA sequencing allows for the analysis of an individual dog's entire genome, providing detailed information about its genetic makeup. It helps identify specific genes, mutations, or variations associated with traits, diseases, or inherited conditions, aiding in the understanding of dog genetics.

24. Q: How can breed standards affect dog genetics?

A: Breed standards outline the ideal physical and behavioral characteristics of a particular dog breed.

The selective breeding practices based on these standards can shape the genetics of the breed over time, emphasizing specific traits and potentially leading to genetic predispositions or health issues.

25. Q: What is epigenetics, and how does it relate to dog traits?

A: Epigenetics is the study of heritable changes in gene expression or cellular phenotype that do not involve alterations to the DNA sequence itself. Environmental factors and experiences can affect gene expression, potentially influencing the development and expression of certain traits in dogs.

Unit 17 Understanding Dog Aging and Health Issues

Introduction

As beloved companions and faithful friends, dogs bring immeasurable joy to our lives through their unwavering loyalty and boundless affection. Watching them embark on the journey of growing and aging alongside us is a remarkable experience that every dedicated dog owner cherishes.

343

As our furry friends transition into their senior years, they require special attention and care to ensure their continued comfort and quality of life. Understanding the intricacies of the aging process becomes crucial at this stage. It's a time when silver muzzles and graceful movements replace the exuberance of youth, yet the love they radiate remains as strong as ever.

Providing appropriate care for senior dogs involves a holistic approach that encompasses not only their physical health but also their emotional well-being. Tailoring their diet, exercise routine, and living environment to their changing needs becomes paramount. Creating a serene and nurturing space allows them to age gracefully, surrounded by the love they've always known.

Furthermore, recognizing common health issues that tend to arise as dogs age is a vital skill for responsible pet owners. Aches, pains, and the potential for chronic conditions demand vigilant observation and proactive management. This unit goes beyond the surface, delving into these potential challenges, offering insights on how to identify early signs of discomfort, and guiding dog owners in seeking appropriate veterinary care.

By delving into these essential topics, this unit aims to equip dog owners with the knowledge and tools they need to navigate the golden years of their beloved companions. As each dog's journey through life is unique, so too is the path they take into their senior years. Armed with a deeper understanding of aging, health, and care, dog owners can ensure that their loyal friends continue to experience a life filled with love, comfort, and happiness.

Understanding the Aging Process in Dogs

Just as in humans, the aging process in dogs is a tapestry woven with intricate threads of physical changes and behavioral shifts. These changes unfold in a personalized manner, influenced by factors such as breed, size, genetics, and overall health. It's a dynamic process that evolves over time, marking the passage of years in a way that's both fascinating and poignant. Here's a closer look at the stages that compose this remarkable journey:

Puppyhood and Adolescence

The opening act of a dog's life is a whirlwind of growth and discovery. Much like the first few chapters of a novel, puppies undergo rapid transformations as they develop both physically and emotionally. Teething becomes a rite of passage, with tiny teeth giving way to a strong set that will serve them throughout their lives. House training and socialization fill their days, imprinting the foundations of behavior and interactions that will carry them into adulthood. Every bark and playful tumble is a brushstroke, painting the vibrant hues of youthful exuberance.

Adulthood

As the curtain rises on adulthood, dogs find themselves in a stage of stability and vitality. Physically and mentally mature, they embody a unique blend of personality traits that define them as individuals. This is the era of peak activity, where hikes, runs, and spirited play sessions are commonplace. Their energy seems boundless, matched only by the enthusiasm they bring to every adventure. It's during this phase that the true depth of the human-canine bond becomes evident as they accompany us through life's joys and challenges.

Middle Age

Around the age of 7, the script takes a subtle twist as dogs transition into middle age. This is a phase characterized by a blending of youth's vigor with a burgeoning sense of maturity. While the playfulness and zest for life remain, they may become interspersed with moments of reflection and repose. Joints might creak a bit more, signaling a natural wear and tear that accompanies the passage of time. The dog who once bounded effortlessly might now approach activities with a measured approach as if savoring each experience a bit more deeply.

Senior Years

With the years advancing, the final acts of the aging process take center stage. Around 9 to 10 years old, many dogs embark on their senior years—a phase that leaves an indelible mark. The vibrant coat of yesteryears might now glisten with touches of silver, a visual representation of the wisdom that comes with age. Internally, joints may be more prone to stiffness, and muscles may require more tender care. Every wag of the tail and soulful gaze carries with it the weight of shared memories and the wisdom that only a life well-lived can bestow.

Each of these stages weaves together a narrative of companionship and resilience, a testament to the profound connection that humans and dogs share. By understanding the intricacies of this journey, we are better equipped to provide the care and attention necessary to ensure that our canine friends age with grace and dignity, continuing to enrich our lives with their unwavering love and presence.

Caring for Older Dogs: Nurturing Their Golden Years

As our loyal companions age, their needs evolve, necessitating adjustments to their daily routines and overall care. The art of caring for older dogs involves a delicate blend of attentive consideration and specialized adjustments to ensure their continued well-being and comfort.

Nutrition

The culinary canvas of a senior dog's life requires a thoughtful palette. While their appetite might not wane, their metabolism and energy expenditure tend to change. Crafting a diet that provides essential nutrients while being mindful of calorie intake is crucial. Foods rich in joint-supporting nutrients like glucosamine and chondroitin can aid in maintaining mobility. Collaborating with a veterinarian can yield a tailored dietary plan, addressing individual needs and preventing obesity while sustaining optimal health.

Exercise

A symphony of movement remains essential in the lives of aging dogs, but the composition changes. Brisk walks and low-impact activities replace the high-energy romps of youth. The goal is to strike a balance between keeping joints limber and muscles engaged without overexertion. These gentler exercises not only maintain physical health but also foster a profound emotional bond between the dog and its caregiver.

Regular Vet Check-ups

The veterinary clinic becomes a haven of health in a senior dog's life. Regular visits are akin to preventive medicine, allowing the early detection of potential issues.

Blood work, joint assessments, and other diagnostics are the instruments for intercepting potential ailments, enabling interventions that can significantly improve their quality of life. The vet's skilled touch guides the journey, ensuring that each chapter is one of comfort and well-being.

Dental Care

Time may have woven silver threads into their fur, but it can also unveil dental concerns. Oral health becomes a priority as the risk of dental issues increases with age. Regular cleaning and check-ups prevent dental discomfort and potential complications that might ripple through their overall health. The rewards of maintaining strong teeth extend far beyond aesthetics, ensuring the joy of eating and the prevention of systemic issues.

Comfort and Environment

With age comes the potential for aches and pains, often stemming from joint issues and arthritis. The physical environment must become a sanctuary of solace. Plush

351

bedding cushions weary bones, and ramps transform stairs from obstacles to manageable inclines. A warm and cozy setting not only eases physical discomfort but also nurtures their spirit, fostering a sense of security and well-being.

Mental Stimulation

The landscape of aging encompasses not only the body but also the mind. Cognitive function requires exercise just as muscles do. Puzzle toys challenge their intellect, interactive games engage their curiosity, and training sessions provide mental agility. The richness of their experiences keeps cognitive decline at bay, preserving their vibrant personality and zest for life.

In the symphony of caring for older dogs, each note is a gesture of love and respect. It's a journey where understanding their evolving needs forms the foundation of a harmonious relationship. By making adjustments that cater to their physical, emotional, and mental well-being, we ensure that their twilight years are a melody of contentment, cherished moments, and enduring companionship.

Navigating Common Health Issues in Senior Dogs: A Compass for Compassionate Care

As our faithful companions venture deeper into their golden years, their bodies become chapters that tell tales of resilience and challenges. Just as we grow with them, it's essential to understand the health issues that may arise, allowing us to shepherd them through this final act of their journey with grace and comfort.

Arthritis and Joint Pain

The echoes of a lifetime spent in motion might manifest as arthritis, a common companion of senior dogs. Their once-joyful leaps might transform into measured steps, and a hint of stiffness may grace their movements. Observant eyes will catch these subtle changes—limping, hesitation while rising, or a reluctance to engage in boisterous play. To ease their discomfort, joint supplements rich in glucosamine and chondroitin can be incorporated into their diet. Medications under the watchful eye of a veterinarian may also join the ensemble, orchestrating a symphony of relief.

Dental Problems

Time's embrace can sometimes manifest as dental issues. Gum disease, tooth decay, and unwelcome halitosis can march forward with age. The overture to preventive care starts with a daily ritual of dental hygiene. Brushing becomes a gesture of love, accompanied by regular professional cleanings—a choreography that prevents pain and maintains the joy of chewing. Through this routine, we ensure that their smiles remain as radiant as their spirits.

Vision and Hearing Loss

Just as the sun sets gracefully, so too might a senior dog's senses of vision and hearing. The world that once was vibrant and clear may soften into a canvas of muted tones. Patience becomes a virtuous practice as we guide them with gentle signals, serving as their eyes and ears when they falter. Through our unwavering presence, they continue to navigate life's landscapes, relying on the bond that transcends words.

Cognitive Dysfunction Syndrome (CDS)

In the symphony of aging, a poignant melody emerges—Cognitive Dysfunction Syndrome. Like a shadow of the mind, it can cast confusion and disorientation upon our cherished friends. Altered sleep patterns may dance in harmony with changes in behavior, tugging at our heartstrings. Amid these moments, we stand as anchors, providing reassurance and engaging in activities that keep their minds agile. Each puzzle toy and playful interaction becomes a thread woven into the fabric of their cognitive well-being.

Cancer

With time, the specter of cancer might cast its shadow. Yet, vigilant eyes can intercept its advance. Regular check-ups are the sentinel guards, equipped to identify any suspicious lumps or bumps that dare to encroach. With a swift and skilled evaluation, the curtain might rise on early intervention, turning the tide in favor of their continued well-being.

Heart and Kidney Issues

Heart and kidney issues are common health concerns that often afflict senior dogs, necessitating careful attention and proactive care from their owners. As our canine companions age, their bodies undergo a natural process of gradual change, making them more susceptible to certain ailments. Among the most prevalent concerns are heart disease and kidney problems, both of which demand vigilant monitoring and early detection to ensure a high quality of life for these loyal companions.

As we stand at the intersection of time and companionship, we become their advocates in health and comfort. By knowing the challenges that aging may unveil, we become stewards of their twilight years, ensuring that each chapter is defined by love, support, and a commitment to granting them the dignity they so richly deserve.

When is it Time? Navigating the Difficult Decision

Among the myriad chapters written in the book of pet ownership, one stands as the most heart-wrenching—the chapter titled "When is it Time?" This question, heavy with emotion, is a crossroads that every dog owner inevitably faces. A poignant blend of love, compassion, and a profound understanding of their well-being guides this pivotal decision.

Guided by Quality of Life

In the silent symphony of aging, the dog's quality of life becomes the poignant melody that echoes in our hearts. This compass guides us through the labyrinth of uncertainty. The decision hinges on their comfort, happiness, and ability to partake in the joys of life. It's an intricate tapestry woven with threads of pain, appetite, mobility, and enthusiasm. When pain usurps the pleasures, when meals become a

burden, and when once-beloved activities lose their luster,
the heart is stirred to ponder what is best for our cherished
companions.

The Heartache of Goodbye

The bittersweet truth is that this decision arises from
the depths of love. It's an acknowledgment that our devotion
to their well-being extends to the heart-rending act of letting
go. When their eyes, once bright with joy, reflect a quiet
sadness, we stand on the precipice of a painful yet
compassionate choice. It's a decision born of empathy,
driven by the understanding that their comfort and dignity
take precedence.

Consulting the Compassionate Guide

In this chapter, the wisdom of veterinary expertise
becomes a beacon of light. Consulting with a veterinarian
during this emotional crossroads provides a lifeline of
insights. They bring clinical acumen, a compassionate heart,
and a depth of understanding that can navigate the
complexities of the decision. Their counsel offers a balanced

perspective that complements our love, paving the way for an informed choice.

Conclusion

As the final paragraphs of our canine companions' lives unfold, they remain steadfast sources of joy, loyalty, and love. Understanding their aging journey, embracing the unique challenges it presents, and ensuring their well-being becomes a testament to the depth of our bond. With attentive care, thoughtful decisions, and unwavering love, we provide a closing chapter that mirrors the vitality and grace that marked their lives. The legacy they leave is one of cherished moments, shared experiences, and the profound connection that transcends time.

Unit 18 Therapy Dogs and Their Role

Therapy dogs have garnered remarkable recognition due to their invaluable contributions to enriching human well-being across a wide array of settings. These highly trained canines play a pivotal role in delivering emotional support, solace, and unwavering companionship to individuals experiencing various forms of distress. Their presence offers a distinct and exceptional form of therapy, effectively fostering enhancements in mental, emotional, and even physical health.

Within this comprehensive unit, we will delve deeply into the myriad advantages presented by therapy dogs. From alleviating anxiety to promoting a sense of calm, these four-legged companions have demonstrated their ability to make a meaningful impact on the lives of those they interact with. We will explore the diverse range of therapy dog programs available, each tailored to address specific needs across healthcare facilities, educational institutions, and rehabilitation centers.

Furthermore, this unit will intricately outline the rigorous training process that transforms these dogs into the empathetic and perceptive beings they become. Their ability to read human emotions, provide non-judgmental support, and offer unconditional affection requires a carefully structured training regimen that highlights their innate traits while refining their responses to various situations.

Champion Master Hunter Cooper

Cooper The Profound Benefits of Therapy Dogs

The impact of therapy dogs on individuals' physical, emotional, and psychological well-being is both profound and multifaceted. The presence of these four-legged healers has been extensively studied, revealing a tapestry of positive effects that span various aspects of human health. Delving into the intricate details, we uncover a wealth of benefits that therapy dogs bring to those in need:

1. **Stress Reduction and Anxiety Alleviation**: The
   therapeutic power of therapy dogs lies in their ability
   to provide immediate stress relief and anxiety
   reduction. The act of interacting with these gentle
   creatures triggers a cascade of physiological
   responses that promote relaxation. Research has
   shown that the simple act of petting a dog releases
   oxytocin, often referred to as the "cuddle hormone."
   Oxytocin not only reduces stress hormones but also
   fosters a sense of emotional connection and bonding.
   This hormonal release translates into a palpable
   sense of tranquility, making therapy dog interactions
   a veritable oasis in the midst of life's demands.

2. **Elevating Mood and Alleviating Loneliness**: The
   emotional impact of spending time with therapy dogs
   is nothing short of remarkable. These nonjudgmental
   beings exude unconditional love and companionship
   that can effortlessly brighten even the darkest of
   moods. For individuals grappling with feelings of
   loneliness or depression, a therapy dog's presence
   can be a beacon of hope. The sheer joy of connecting
   with a furry friend who holds no expectations or

judgments can ignite a renewed sense of purpose and happiness.

3. **Holistic Physical Health Improvement**: The benefits of therapy dogs extend beyond the emotional realm into the realm of physiological well-being. Engaging with these animals can lead to tangible improvements in physical health. The gentle act of petting a therapy dog has been linked to reductions in blood pressure and heart rate, providing a natural and enjoyable means of managing cardiovascular health. Moreover, this interaction triggers the release of endorphins, the body's natural pain relievers, leading to a heightened sense of well-being and comfort.

4. **Cultivating Social Interaction**: One of the most remarkable facets of therapy dogs is their ability to break down barriers and facilitate social interaction. For individuals who struggle with social engagement due to conditions like autism or social anxiety, therapy dogs act as extraordinary catalysts for connection. These furry companions create a shared point of interest and conversation, allowing individuals to engage in meaningful interactions that

might have otherwise seemed daunting. The simple act of petting a therapy dog opens doors to conversations, fostering friendships and connections that enrich lives.

5. **Nurturing Cognitive Stimulation**: The profound impact of therapy dogs on cognitive processes is a testament to their versatility. Engaging in activities with therapy dogs, such as teaching them tricks or participating in interactive games, demands cognitive focus and memory recall. This engagement not only stimulates mental faculties but also provides a platform for individuals with cognitive impairments to exercise their cognitive abilities. The therapeutic potential of these interactions cannot be overstated, as they offer avenues for cognitive growth and mental agility.

So, therapy dogs are not merely companions; they are conduits of healing that touch every facet of human existence. From alleviating stress and anxiety to bolstering emotional resilience, from fostering social bonds to stimulating cognitive functions, these remarkable beings enrich lives in immeasurable ways. The profound benefits they offer are a testament to the unique and enduring connection between humans and animals, demonstrating the incredible capacity of dogs to serve as healers, mentors, and friends.

Diverse and Specialized Landscape of Therapy Dog Programs

The world of therapy dog programs unfolds as a meticulously designed mosaic, each piece crafted to address distinct needs in a myriad of environments. As we delve into the intricacies of these programs, we uncover a vast spectrum of interventions that not only embrace the therapeutic potential of dogs but also extend a healing touch to various corners of society.

1. **Animal-Assisted Therapy (AAT):** The intricate synergy between certified therapists and therapy dogs forms the foundation of Animal-Assisted Therapy (AAT). In this immersive therapeutic approach, a licensed therapist collaborates with a trained therapy dog to achieve specific, measurable treatment objectives. Within the clinical confines of hospitals, rehabilitation centers, and mental health facilities, AAT transcends conventional methods. The empathetic presence of the therapy dog facilitates emotional breakthroughs, empowers communication, and promotes the rebuilding of cognitive and motor skills. The tactile connection between the therapy dog and the patient serves as a conduit for emotional expression, creating a bridge toward healing.

2. **Animal-Assisted Activities (AAA):** The canvas of Animal-Assisted Activities (AAA) is painted with

strokes of comfort, companionship, and joy. These gentle interventions transcend the confines of traditional therapy spaces, weaving their magic in schools, nursing homes, community events, and beyond. The essence of AAA lies in its ability to uplift spirits and provide emotional support without the burden of defined therapeutic goals. Whether engaging with children in educational settings or offering solace to the elderly in nursing homes, therapy dogs become beacons of warmth, allowing individuals to bask in the genuine companionship and unconditional acceptance they provide.

3. **Reading Assistance Programs:** In the realm of education, therapy dogs assume the role of literacy catalysts, ushering children into the enchanting world of books. Reading Assistance Programs capitalize on the unique bond between children and dogs to enhance reading skills. Children who might hesitate to read aloud to peers or adults find solace and encouragement in reading to a non-judgmental and attuned audience. As the child navigates the pages of a book, the dog listens attentively, nurturing confidence, fluency, and a love for learning.

4. **Crisis Response Teams:** Amid the chaos of crisis and turmoil, therapy dog teams emerge as beacons of comfort and compassion. These specially trained teams possess the remarkable ability to provide immediate emotional support to individuals affected by catastrophic events. Whether in the aftermath of natural disasters, mass shootings, or other traumatic incidents, the presence of therapy dogs serves as a soothing balm to frayed nerves and shattered emotions. Their unwavering companionship and intuitive empathy bridge the gap between anguish and healing, offering a tangible lifeline amidst the storm.

In essence, the panorama of therapy dog programs is a testament to the versatility and adaptability of our canine companions. From clinical settings to the wider fabric of society, these programs intricately weave the threads of comfort, connection, and healing. As we explore these diverse initiatives, we uncover the profound impact that therapy dogs have on human lives, transcending boundaries and enriching the tapestry of our collective well-being.

Training a Therapy Dog

Training a therapy dog is an intricate and meticulous process that demands unwavering dedication, patience, and a comprehensive strategy to cultivate a canine companion that exudes impeccable behavior and compassion in a wide array of circumstances. The journey towards creating a therapy dog that becomes a beacon of comfort and emotional support is multifaceted, encompassing a series of meticulously designed steps.

1. **Basic Obedience:** The foundation of a proficient therapy dog starts with ingraining fundamental obedience commands into their repertoire. These commands—such as "sit," "stay," "come," and "leave it"—are not merely mundane exercises but the cornerstones of control that allow the dog to respond promptly and predictably regardless of the environment they find themselves in. By mastering these commands, the dog's handler gains the ability to guide and manage their behavior seamlessly, laying the groundwork for the more complex tasks ahead.

2. **Socialization:** Crafting a therapy dog that exudes unshakeable confidence and poise in the face of

368

novel situations hinges on thorough socialization. This process involves systematically exposing the dog to a diverse array of people, places, sounds, and scenarios. From bustling city streets to tranquil parks and from the gentle hum of everyday life to the cacophony of bustling crowds, the dog must become acquainted with the full spectrum of human experiences. This not only diminishes anxiety but cultivates a calm resilience that is pivotal in the therapeutic role they are destined to undertake.

3. **Good Manners:** At the heart of therapy dog training lies the cultivation of impeccable manners that harmonize with their role as a source of solace and tranquility. A therapy dog must embrace gentle gestures and be at ease with the touch, petting, and embraces of individuals from all walks of life. Straying away from the rambunctiousness of jumping or the discordant notes of excessive barking, the dog must embrace a demeanor that resonates with the serenity they bring to their interactions.

4. **Desensitization:** Navigating the intricacies of therapeutic environments requires a therapy dog to be unfazed by the presence of medical paraphernalia,

wheelchairs, crutches, and other equipment typically encountered in healthcare settings. Through the process of desensitization, the dog learns to view these objects not as potential sources of concern but rather as innocuous elements in their surroundings. This precludes any undue agitation or anxiety, enabling the dog to perform its role with equanimity and poise.

5. **Therapy-Specific Training:** The culmination of the training process involves honing skills that are tailored to the specific therapeutic context the dog is destined to engage. Whether it's the gentle approach they adopt while interacting with individuals, the serene act of lying beside patients to provide comfort, or their capacity to remain unperturbed in the face of unforeseen noises, these specialized skills exemplify the refined finesse of a well-trained therapy dog. This phase of training aligns the dog's capabilities with the nuanced demands of their role, ensuring they can navigate the delicate nuances of their interactions with the utmost grace and efficacy.

In conclusion, the journey of training a therapy dog is an intricate tapestry woven from meticulous attention to detail, unwavering patience, and an unwavering commitment to fostering an animal companion that stands as a beacon of solace and emotional support. Each step of this process is a testament to the symbiotic bond between humans and dogs, encapsulating the transformative power of patient guidance and unconditional love.

Service Dogs vs. Therapy Dogs

In the intricate tapestry of canine companionship, the distinction between service dogs and therapy dogs emerges as a testament to the multifaceted roles these remarkable creatures play in enhancing the lives of individuals they touch. This comparison delves into the intricacies of their roles, legal considerations, and the profound impact they have on the fabric of human experience.

Service Dogs

Service dogs are the embodiment of unwavering dedication, meticulously trained to perform a myriad of tasks that redefine independence for individuals with disabilities. These canine champions are not just pets; they are lifelines, providing an unparalleled level of support that enables their handlers to navigate the world with newfound autonomy. From guiding the visually impaired through the labyrinth of life's obstacles to offering crucial assistance to individuals with mobility limitations, service dogs are both a physical extension and an emotional anchor.

Legal Rights and Protections

A pivotal differentiator lies in the legal rights bestowed upon service dogs. These exceptional animals are more than mere companions; they are recognized as essential tools for mitigating the challenges of disabilities. As such, service dogs are granted the legal privilege to accompany their handlers in public spaces, transcending societal barriers that would otherwise impede full participation. The legal protections they command serve as a beacon of inclusivity, a testament to the power of partnership between humans and canines.

Therapy Dogs

While service dogs are celebrated for their utilitarian contributions, therapy dogs embody a different facet of canine influence—one that traverses emotional landscapes and nurtures the human spirit. Their primary role is not to perform specific tasks but to be the bearers of solace and companionship. From the gentle touch of a paw to the warmth of their presence, therapy dogs carve out a space in the hearts of individuals they encounter.

Setting the Stage

Therapy dogs thrive in environments carefully curated to elicit emotional responses and facilitate healing. Hospitals, schools, nursing homes, and disaster relief settings become the canvas upon which these dogs paint strokes of comfort and connection. Their impact is profound, extending far beyond the realm of medicine. In the hushed corridors of a hospital, therapy dogs offer a moment of respite; in the echoing halls of a school, they become beacons of calm during exam stress.

The Legal Spectrum

However, it's important to recognize that the legal landscape differs for therapy dogs. They do not hold the same elevated status as service dogs, and their access to public spaces is contingent upon individual establishments' policies. While therapy dogs often receive permission to enter certain spaces to fulfill their therapeutic role, their reach is not as expansive as that of their service counterparts.

Impact on Well-being

In the symphony of well-being, therapy dogs play a harmonious tune. Their presence has been scientifically proven to reduce stress, elevate moods, and even contribute to physical health improvements. The gentle caress of a therapy dog's fur can act as a salve for wounds that aren't visible, soothing the soul and soothing frayed nerves.

Conclusion

As the chapters of this comparison draw to a close, the indelible mark of service dogs and therapy dogs on the human narrative is undeniable. Service dogs redefine possibilities, rewriting the stories of those they serve with courage and tenacity. Therapy dogs, on the other hand, hold space for vulnerability, encouraging emotional connections and facilitating the healing journey.

In a world that sometimes seems fraught with challenges, these four-legged companions emerge as beacons of hope and agents of transformation. Whether it's through the sturdy partnership of service dogs or the gentle touch of therapy dogs, the tale of canine contributions to human lives is one that unfolds with every wag of a tail, every nuzzle, and every unspoken understanding.

Unit 19 Working Dogs: Legacy and Training

Introduction

Working dogs, widely acknowledged as the often uncelebrated yet indispensable pillars of human society, have played a pivotal role in shaping the course of our existence over the span of centuries. These exceptional canine confidants embody a tapestry of innate proficiencies meticulously refined through the intricate interplay of selective genetic heritage and rigorous pedagogical endeavors. In the units that follow, this exploration embarks on an illuminative journey into the intricate tapestry of the world inhabited by working dogs. With a discerning gaze, we shall navigate through the diverse pantheon of these canines, unraveling their varied typologies, tracing the footprints of their historical eminence, and engaging in a contemplative dissection of the elaborate science and artistry that orchestrates the unveiling of their latent potentials.

Overview of Different Types of Working Dogs: Herding Dogs

Among the diverse array of roles that working dogs occupy, herding dogs emerge as a vivid exemplar of the symbiotic tapestry woven between humans and animals within the framework of agricultural societies. Channeling an instinct deeply ingrained within their genetic makeup, these remarkable canines epitomize the harmonious collaboration between two species. Their exceptional ability to not merely gather and corral livestock but to do so with an almost choreographic precision renders them indispensable companions to farmers and herders alike. In this dynamic relationship, breeds such as the Border Collie, Australian Shepherd, and Shetland Sheepdog take center stage, showcasing an extraordinary aptitude for herding that transcends mere utility. Employing a fusion of calculated eye contact, fluid movement, and measured barks, they orchestrate a symphony of control that guides livestock across expanses of pastureland.

Service Dogs

The realm of service dogs stands as an embodiment of the transformative influence that canines can wield in the lives of individuals confronted with diverse disabilities. These exceptional dogs serve as living testaments to the potency of the human-canine bond, orchestrating a dance of companionship and assistance that transcends mere task execution. Their training, often spanning months and even years, endows them with the uncanny ability to become sensory extensions, emotional support pillars, and even lifelines for those in need. In this arena, the roles they assume are as diverse as the challenges they alleviate. From guiding those with visual or auditory impairments with steadfast dedication to providing critical aid to individuals navigating the intricate labyrinth of psychiatric conditions like PTSD, their contributions encompass a spectrum that spans physical, emotional, and psychological realms. Retrieving dropped items becomes a gesture of independence, alerting the deaf to auditory cues becomes an act of empowerment, and offering stability to those with mobility limitations transforms into an embodiment of unwavering support.

Search and Rescue Dogs

Within the narrative of valor and selflessness, search and rescue dogs emerge as the embodiment of unwavering dedication, proving themselves as true sentinels of hope in times of crisis. Armed with an olfactory prowess that defies human comprehension, these dogs unravel the intricate scent trails left by those in distress, traversing treacherous terrains with a resolute spirit. Their agility and courage transform disaster-stricken landscapes into canvases of potential rescue as they work tirelessly alongside human counterparts to locate the missing and the imperiled. This partnership between humans and canines, forged in the crucible of adversity, offers a glimmer of hope amid chaos. Their contributions extend beyond the realm of duty; they are a living testament to the extraordinary capabilities that emerge when nature's instincts meet the training nurtured by human hands. In the face of natural calamities, accidents, and other emergencies, search and rescue dogs stand as silent yet thunderous heralds of hope, saving lives with each paw step and every determined sniff of the air.

Police and Military Dogs

In the intricate tapestry of law enforcement and military operations, police and military dogs stand as stalwart exemplars of dedication, vigilance, and symbiotic partnership between humans and canines. Beyond their role as mere companions, these remarkable dogs inhabit a realm where their finely honed senses, unswerving loyalty, and undaunted valor coalesce into indispensable assets. Trained

to an exacting standard, these dogs become veritable
extensions of their human handlers, embodying a unity of
purpose that transcends species boundaries. Their roles
encompass a diverse spectrum, ranging from tracking elusive
suspects through urban labyrinths to deploying their
extraordinary olfactory prowess in detecting explosives and
narcotics concealed from human senses. With a keen eye and
an unwavering spirit, they apprehend criminals who might
otherwise elude justice, providing a tangible link between
canine instinct and the human pursuit of order. In the
intricate theater of security operations, their presence
resonates as a testament to the profound depths of the
human-canine partnership, where mutual respect and
reliance forge a bond that serves to protect and uphold
society's values.

Therapy Dogs

Within the realm of healing and emotional well-
being, therapy dogs manifest as emissaries of solace and
empathy, their furry presence echoing the power of the
human-animal connection. These four-legged healers
personify the embodiment of comfort, providing a haven of
compassion for individuals navigating the challenging
landscapes of hospitals, nursing homes, and rehabilitation

centers. In these settings, the touch of a gentle paw and the unconditional affection of a wagging tail create a sanctuary of emotional respite. The scientific underpinnings of their impact are remarkable: interactions with therapy dogs have been scientifically linked to the reduction of stress hormones, mitigation of anxiety, and even alleviation of pain perception in patients. Through this silent language of empathy, therapy dogs orchestrate a symphony of healing that transcends the boundaries of spoken words, offering solace to those whose hearts and bodies bear the weight of affliction.

Guard Dogs

Guard dogs, bearing the legacy of generations of purposeful breeding, assume a mantle of protective guardianship that traces its roots back to ancient bonds between humans and wolves. This lineage of vigilance is embodied by breeds such as the stalwart German Shepherd, the watchful Doberman Pinscher, and the steadfast Rottweiler. Their innate territorial behavior and unshakable loyalty to their human families define their role as sentinels of security. These canines, often endowed with imposing physical stature, represent an embodiment of deterrence, their presence alone often serving as a formidable deterrent to potential threats. With a fusion of watchfulness, caution, and readiness, guard dogs become the living embodiment of an unspoken agreement: they protect and serve, standing as resolute sentries against the backdrop of modern challenges. In safeguarding property and individuals, they channel an ancestral legacy, breathing life into a tradition where the howl of a dog and the warmth of its protective presence convey an unwavering promise of safety.

The History of Working Dogs

Ancient Beginnings

The intricate interplay between humans and dogs finds its roots in the annals of ancient history, a saga woven with threads of companionship, utility, and shared survival.

Tracing back to the enigmatic caves adorned with vibrant paintings, evidence suggests that early humans recognized the invaluable partnership that could be forged with these four-legged allies. Dogs, the first domesticated species, embarked on their journey alongside humanity, offering their acute senses and loyalty in exchange for sustenance and camaraderie. In the dawn of civilization, their roles encompassed hunting assistance, protection against predators, and a steadfast presence at the fireside.

Middle Ages and Renaissance

The Middle Ages witnessed the blossoming of dogs' roles into a rich tapestry of responsibilities that spanned far beyond their original functions. As human societies burgeoned and diversified, so did the repertoire of dogs' contributions. They transformed into multifaceted companions, guardians of flocks, and even formidable assets in warfare. As feudal societies took root, the rise of nobility paved the way for a newfound fascination with selective breeding. The development of specialized breeds tailored for hunting pursuits and elevated companionship began to take shape. The Renaissance era ushered in a renaissance of a different sort for dogs—a cultural renaissance. These loyal companions, once relegated to the background, emerged as subjects of admiration, immortalized in art as symbols of fidelity, loyalty, and the enduring bond between humans and canines.

Industrial Revolution and Modern Times

The thunderous echoes of the Industrial Revolution reverberated not just through factories and machinery but through the trajectory of working dogs' roles. Amid the clatter of progress, dogs stepped onto new stages of responsibility, tethering their destinies to the wheels of change. Cart-pulling and sled-dragging canines became unsung engines of transportation, while their uncanny ability to navigate dark tunnels and narrow shafts turned them into irreplaceable companions in mining operations. As the urban landscape unfolded, the canine narrative shifted once more, embracing the demands of evolving societies. The roles of service, therapy, and search and rescue dogs emerged in response to the dynamic needs of humanity. In these contemporary chapters, dogs transitioned from mere tools of labor to steadfast allies, enriching lives and saving them with every bark, wag, and attentive gaze.

Contemporary Roles

In the age of pixels and algorithms, the roles of working dogs continue to metamorphose, taking on novel forms to suit novel challenges. These extraordinary animals now stand at the forefront of cutting-edge innovation, wielding their innate talents with an adaptability that mirrors the era they inhabit. With an olfactory acumen that defies the confines of technology, dogs are now capable of detecting diseases like cancer with astonishing accuracy through scent alone. Their presence in schools and disaster-stricken regions has evolved into an embrace of emotional support, nurturing the well-being of those who traverse the complex terrain of human experience. From modern medical marvels to solace amid the ruins, working dogs are the steadfast guardians of our shared journey into the unknown, their history an unbroken thread of loyalty that stitches the tapestry of human existence.

How to Train a Working Dog?

Early Socialization and Basic Obedience

The foundational steps in crafting a capable working dog commence with early socialization, a process that shapes the core temperament and adaptability of these extraordinary canines. During their tender puppyhood, working dog candidates are introduced to a mosaic of stimuli, a symphony of sights, sounds, and sensations that transcend the familiar confines of their birthplace. This exposure forms the cornerstone of their resilience, ensuring that they navigate diverse environments with poise. As this symphony unfolds, the notes of basic obedience commands begin to resonate. These initial chords—commands like "sit," "stay," and "come"—compose the rudimentary vocabulary that underpins more advanced training. Through this foundation, the seeds of discipline and responsiveness are sown, which will later blossom into intricate symphonies of skill and precision.

Task-Specific Training

Just as a painter selects the precise brushstroke to create their masterpiece, working dog trainers tailor their approach to the intricate palette of tasks a dog will undertake. This specialized training blueprint aligns a dog's natural proclivities with the demands of its designated role. Whether it's the delicate dance of scent detection for search and rescue dogs or the choreography of assistance tasks for service dogs, each protocol is calibrated to harness the unique abilities of these canines. This precision ensures that the symphony of skills woven into their beings is conducted in harmony with the needs of their human counterparts.

Positive Presentation and Bond Building

The symphony of training takes on a harmonious cadence when conducted through the prism of positive presentation. This method, akin to bestowing the sweetest notes upon a musician, utilizes treats, toys, and lavish praise to encourage desired behaviors. As these canine virtuosos execute commands with precision, they are met with rewards that reaffirm their brilliance. Beyond the superficial rewards, the deeper melody lies in the bonds forged between handler and dog. With each treat shared and every moment of playfulness, a profound connection deepens, sowing the seeds of trust and companionship that amplify their shared prowess.

Complex Simulations and Real-Life Scenarios

The rehearsal hall for working dogs is a domain of intricately choreographed simulations where real-life scenarios are distilled into controlled environments. In these dynamic arenas, the echoes of real emergencies and challenges reverberate. Search and rescue dogs navigate intricate mazes to unearth hidden scents, while service dogs enact the symphony of tasks tailored to their handlers' needs. Through these staged dramas, these canines develop the ability to perform seamlessly, even under the spotlight of high-pressure situations. These rehearsals shape their instincts into finely tuned instruments, ready to orchestrate harmony amid chaos.

Handler Skills and Communication

The handler, a conductor of the working dog symphony, holds the baton of guidance and connection. This role isn't merely one of command-giving; it's a nuanced dance of understanding canine cues, deciphering body language and forging a connection that transcends words. Handlers undergo rigorous training of their own, delving into the lexicon of canine behavior and psychology. The art of communication is an intricate one, where the slightest cues and the gentlest touches lead to harmonious performances.

Continuous Learning and Adaptation

The composition of a dog's journey isn't finalized upon its debut; it's an evolving symphony that must resonate with the ever-changing rhythms of the world. Continuous learning becomes the refrain that keeps their skills sharp and their adaptability finely tuned. Just as a musician practices their scales, dogs engage in ongoing training to remain at the zenith of their abilities. The complexities of modern society introduce new notes into their repertoire—new challenges that demand innovative solutions. With each passing day, these remarkable canines stand ready to adapt, harmonize, and lead us into the future with the boundless melody of their skills.

Conclusion

Dogs, with their rich history, diverse roles, and remarkable abilities, epitomize the deep connection between humans and animals. Their contributions to agriculture, security, healthcare, and disaster response are immeasurable. As society continues to evolve, dogs will undoubtedly play an integral role in shaping our future, adapting their talents to meet the ever-changing needs of humanity. Through meticulous training and dedicated handlers, these extraordinary dogs continue to inspire and enrich our lives in countless ways.

Unit 20 Managing Multi-Pet Households

Introduction

The dynamics of multi-pet households offer a blend of rewarding and challenging experiences. The decision to share your living space with an array of animals, ranging from dogs and cats to smaller companions like rabbits or birds, promises the enrichment of companionship and the joys that come with it.

Yet, the coexistence of diverse creatures necessitates a profound comprehension of the complexities involved in integrating pets, addressing the inevitable obstacles that arise, and sustaining an equilibrium that is pivotal for the success of a multi-pet household. In the ensuing chapter, we embark on an exploration of the intricate art of orchestrating and managing multi-pet households.

Our journey will traverse through the strategic introduction of pets, the adept handling of common challenges that arise, and the nurturing of an environment that harmoniously accommodates the diverse needs of cohabiting animals. As we navigate through these nuances, it becomes evident that the tapestry of a successful multi-pet household is woven from a tapestry of patience, insight, and astute management. Yet we as humans must understand just because we want them to get along doesn't mean they will. Some pets are prey to the other, and some should be run off.

Introducing Dogs to Other Pets

Assessing Compatibility

Introducing a new pet into a multi-pet household requires a thoughtful assessment of compatibility, taking into account the distinct characteristics of each species and the individual temperaments of the pets involved. It's imperative to recognize that certain dog breeds possess inherent traits such as prey drive or territorial instincts, which can significantly influence their interactions with other pets. For instance, a breed known for its strong prey drive might not be the best match for a household with smaller mammals or birds. In contrast, breeds with a more sociable disposition might be better suited for harmonious coexistence.

Gradual Introduction

The process of introducing a new dog to existing pets demands a patient and methodical approach. Gradual and controlled introductions are paramount to prevent undue stress or conflicts. To begin, allow the pets to become familiar with each other's scents through closed doors, thereby laying the foundation for recognition without direct contact. Subsequently, progress to supervised meetings in neutral territory. This neutral setting reduces territorial tension and allows the animals to become acquainted without feeling threatened in their established spaces.

Supervised Interaction

During the initial interactions between the new dog and the existing pets, it's crucial to maintain a vigilant presence and ensure that both pets are on leashes. This measure serves to minimize the risk of aggressive behaviors or fear-based reactions. Close supervision facilitates immediate intervention if tensions arise and helps in gauging the comfort levels of all parties involved. Observing the body language and vocalizations of the animals can provide insights into their emotional states and aid in gauging the progress of their interactions.

392

Direction Reinforcement – With Positive Presentation

The foundation of successful introductions lies in reinforcing positive behaviors and interactions. Offering treats, praise, and affection when pets engage in calm and friendly behaviors fosters a positive association with one another's presence. This conditioning underscores the idea that being around other pets results in pleasant experiences, encouraging repeated harmonious interactions over time. It's important to note that the timing of reinforcement is crucial, as it should immediately follow the desired behavior to effectively establish the connection.

Separate Spaces

To cultivate a harmonious multi-pet environment, it's essential to ensure that each pet has access to its own designated space. These spaces serve as retreats where pets can seek solace if interactions become overwhelming or tense. Having separate areas equipped with comfortable bedding, toys, and resources prevents conflicts arising from resource guarding and offers a sanctuary for pets to recharge.

Providing each pet with its own space enhances their sense of security and minimizes the potential for territorial disputes.

Common Challenges with Multi-Pet Households

Resource Guarding

Resource guarding, a natural instinct in animals, can become a significant challenge when managing a multi-pet household. It's imperative to recognize the signs of resource guarding, which can manifest as growling, snapping, or even aggression when a pet feels threatened over possessions such as food, toys, or resting spots. Early detection and intervention are vital to prevent conflicts from escalating. Strategies to address resource guarding include teaching pets to associate the presence of others with positive outcomes, practicing controlled feeding times, and employing desensitization techniques to reduce possessive behavior.

Territory Issues

Territorial behavior is particularly pronounced in dogs, and it can lead to disputes over space within the household. To mitigate this challenge, ensuring that each pet has its designated areas is paramount. Establishing personal territories not only reduces potential confrontations but also provides pets with a sense of security. Additionally, gradual introductions to shared spaces can help pets acclimate to each other's presence, diminishing territorial tensions over time.

Communication Breakdown

Pets communicate through a complex array of body language and cues, which may not always be understood by other species. Misinterpretations of signals can result in conflicts. Enhancing your understanding of these nonverbal cues is essential for identifying potential confrontations before they escalate. For instance, recognizing signs of anxiety, stress, or discomfort, such as lowered ears, tucked tails, or raised fur, allows for timely intervention to diffuse tensions and promote peaceful cohabitation.

Jealousy and Attention

Changes in attention distribution, such as when a new pet enters the household, can trigger feelings of jealousy and result in behavioral changes. To address this challenge, it's crucial to allocate quality time and individual attention to each pet. Maintaining established routines and engaging in activities that foster bonding can help alleviate any perceived sense of neglect. Moreover, involving pets in positive group experiences, like playtime or training sessions, can strengthen their associations with one another and mitigate feelings of rivalry.

Health Considerations

When introducing a new pet, it's imperative to consider the health conditions and vulnerabilities of existing pets. Certain medical issues, such as chronic illnesses or heightened stress levels, can impact an animal's ability to adapt to changes in the household. Consulting with a veterinarian before introducing a new pet ensures that the transition is orchestrated in a manner that minimizes stress and prioritizes the well-being of all pets involved. Tailoring the introduction process to accommodate the specific needs of each pet can greatly contribute to a smoother adjustment period.

Successfully managing a multi-pet household necessitates a comprehensive understanding of these common challenges and the implementation of proactive strategies to address them. By fostering an environment of open communication, respect for individual boundaries, and equitable attention distribution, pet owners can create a harmonious living space where the rewards of companionship far outweigh the inherent challenges.

Tips for Maintaining Harmony among Pets

Routine and Predictability

Consistency in routine serves as the cornerstone of effective multi-pet household management. Establishing and maintaining a predictable schedule for feeding, playtime, and rest significantly contributes to the well-being of all pets involved. Animals, much like humans, find comfort in routines. Predictable daily activities create a sense of security, helping pets anticipate their needs being met. This anticipation, in turn, minimizes stress and anxiety as pets learn to rely on the dependable rhythm of their environment.

Individual Attention

Recognizing and celebrating the individuality of each pet is essential for nurturing a harmonious atmosphere.

397

Dedicated one-on-one time with each pet deepens the bond you share and reaffirms their unique place within the household. Through grooming sessions, interactive play, and heartfelt interactions, you reinforce the special connection between you and each pet. Regular individual attention mitigates feelings of competition for your affection and attention, fostering a sense of emotional security.

Environmental Enrichment

Enrichment activities are a cornerstone of preventing boredom and curbing potential behavioral challenges in multi-pet households. These activities encompass a wide spectrum, from puzzle toys that stimulate cognitive abilities to scratching posts that satisfy natural instincts. Introducing novel experiences through toys, puzzles, and interactive games engages pets mentally and physically, channeling their energy constructively. This engagement not only prevents destructive behaviors but also enriches their lives by catering to their innate exploratory nature.

Training and Socialization

Obedience training and socialization are vital components in nurturing well-adjusted pets within a multipet setting. Dogs, in particular, thrive on clear communication and well-defined boundaries. Through direction reinforcement training, pets learn to respond to commands, promoting orderly interactions and minimizing potential conflicts. Socialization efforts expose pets to diverse experiences, animals, and people, fostering adaptability and reducing the likelihood of fear-based reactions. The synergy of training and socialization creates a cohesive and understanding multi-pet environment.

Professional Guidance

The introduction of a new pet or the emergence of persistent conflicts can sometimes necessitate expert guidance. Professional animal behaviorists (Big D's Dog Training) possess specialized knowledge to address nuanced challenges within multi-pet households. Their assessments consider factors ranging from pet personalities and communication styles to environmental dynamics. The solutions they provide are tailored to the specific needs of your pets and the intricacies of their interactions. Seeking professional advice underscores your commitment to the well-being of your pets and ensures that the necessary interventions are informed by expert insight.

Incorporating these nuanced strategies into your approach to managing a multi-pet household elevates your capacity to navigate challenges successfully. By embracing routine, celebrating individual connections, embracing environmental enrichment, prioritizing training and socialization, and valuing professional guidance when required, you create a dynamic and flourishing environment. This environment not only accommodates the diverse needs of your pets but also embodies the essence of companionship and cooperation that exemplify the beauty of a harmonious multi-pet household.

Conclusion

In summary, successfully managing a household with multiple pets necessitates a blend of patience, empathy, and dedication to ensuring optimal living conditions for each individual animal. The intricate process of introducing different pets, coupled with the proactive resolution of common issues and the strategic deployment of harmonization techniques, lays the groundwork for harmonious coexistence. This endeavor culminates in the establishment of a nurturing and engaging home environment where animals of diverse species can not only cohabit but also flourish in contentment. By adeptly overseeing these dynamics and upholding the principles of responsible pet ownership, the cohabitation of a variety of pets in a single household can indeed prosper. This journey promises to deliver a gratifying and cheerful encounter for both the animals and their human caretakers, reinforcing the notion that a well-orchestrated multi-pet household can be a source of profound mutual enrichment.

Unit 21: Exploring Canine Sports

In the world of dogs, there is much more than meets the eye. Beyond being faithful companions and loving family members, dogs have an incredible capacity for physical and mental athleticism. Canine sports have gained immense popularity over the years, offering an outlet for dogs and their owners to engage in exciting activities that go far beyond a simple game of fetch in the backyard. In this chapter, we will embark on a journey through the multifaceted world of canine sports, exploring their diversity, the training required to excel in them, and how you can get involved to create lasting memories with your four-legged friend.

Section 1: An Overview of Different Types of Canine Sports

Dogs, with their boundless energy and diverse breeds, are natural athletes. This innate athleticism forms the foundation for various canine sports that cater to different skills and interests. Let's delve into some of the most popular canine sports:

Agility

Agility is a thrilling sport that tests a dog's speed, agility, and obedience. It involves navigating a timed obstacle course consisting of jumps, tunnels, weave poles, and other challenges. The dog and handler work as a team to complete the course as quickly and accurately as possible. Breeds like Border Collies and Shetland Sheepdogs often excel in agility due to their intelligence and agility.

Flyball

Flyball is a high-octane relay race where teams of four dogs race against each other. Each dog must jump over hurdles, trigger a spring-loaded box to release a tennis ball, and then race back with the ball to their handler. The next dog in line repeats the process, and the first team to have all four dogs complete the course wins. It's a sport that combines speed, agility, and teamwork, making it perfect for energetic breeds like the Whippet and Border Collie.

Disc Dog

Disc dog, also known as canine disc, is all about precision and aerial acrobatics. Dogs and their handlers team up to perform jaw-dropping tricks, throws, and catches using flying discs. This sport requires not only physical fitness but also a deep connection between the handler and their furry partner. Breeds like the Australian Shepherd and Border Collie excel in this dynamic sport.

Obedience

Obedience trials test a dog's ability to follow commands and exhibit good behavior in various scenarios. Dogs are judged on their ability to perform tasks like heeling, staying, and coming when called. Obedience competitions can range from basic to advanced, and they are an excellent way to develop a strong bond with your dog while reinforcing essential training skills. Breeds like the German Shepherd and Labrador Retriever often excel in obedience trials.

Canine Freestyle

Imagine combining the grace of dancing with the enthusiasm of your dog - that's canine freestyle. In this sport, handlers choreograph routines set to music, showcasing the dog's agility and obedience. It's an artistic expression of the bond between handler and dog, where creativity knows no bounds. Any breed with the right temperament and training can participate in canine freestyle.

Herding Trials

Herding trials tap into a dog's instinctual herding abilities. Dogs are tasked with moving livestock through a designated course while responding to the handler's commands. Breeds such as the Border Collie and Australian Shepherd, known for their herding heritage, excel in this sport. Herding trials are a way to honor a dog's historical role as a working companion.

CH Krisma's Cabaret Queen

Canine Scent Work

Dogs have an exceptional sense of smell, and canine scent work harnesses this ability. In this sport, dogs use their noses to locate specific scents hidden in various environments. It's an excellent way to engage a dog's mental faculties while providing them with a satisfying challenge.

Breeds like the Bloodhound and German Shepherd are known for their scenting abilities.

Canicross and Skijoring

For those who enjoy running or skiing, canicross and skijoring offer a unique experience of being towed by your dog. Canicross involves running with your dog while skijoring is done on skis in the snowy terrain. Both activities require specialized equipment and training but can be immensely rewarding for active individuals and their dogs. Breeds with high endurance, like the Siberian Husky and Alaskan Malamute, excel in these sports.

Dock Diving

Dock diving, also known as dock jumping, is a sport where dogs leap off a dock into a pool of water to fetch a toy or ball. It's a test of a dog's strength, speed, and jumping ability. Breeds like the Labrador Retriever and Belgian Malinois are often top contenders in this thrilling aquatic sport.

Section 2: Training for Canine Sports

Participating in canine sports is not just about having a well-trained dog; it's also about honing your own skills as a handler. Successful training is the key to excelling in these

sports and ensuring the safety and enjoyment of both you and
your dog.

Basic Obedience Training

Before diving into any specific canine sport, it's
essential to establish a solid foundation in basic obedience.
Commands like sit, stay, come, and heel are fundamental and
serve as building blocks for more advanced training. Basic
obedience training ensures that your dog understands and
responds to your commands reliably.

Sport-Specific Training

Once your dog is well-versed in basic obedience, you
can begin sport-specific training. Each canine sport has its
own set of skills and commands. For agility, you'll need to
work on obstacle navigation and sequencing. For a disc dog,
you'll focus on catching and retrieving discs. Tailor your

training to the chosen sport, and consider seeking guidance from experienced trainers who specialize in that area.

Direction Reinforcement

Direction reinforcement Positive presentation is the cornerstone of effective training. Reward your dog with treats, praise, and play when they perform well during training sessions. This not only motivates your dog but also strengthens your bond. Understand punitive methods, as they can reduce your dog's trust and enthusiasm.

Consistency and Patience

Consistency is vital in training. Use the same commands and cues consistently, and practice regularly to reinforce learning. Be patient with your dog, as progress may be gradual. Celebrate small victories along the way to keep both you and your dog motivated.

Handler Fitness: A Crucial Component of Canine Sports Success

When embarking on the exciting journey of participating in canine sports, it's imperative to remember that it's not just your furry companion who needs to be in peak condition. Yes, your dog's athleticism is undoubtedly important, but let's not underestimate the significance of your own fitness. In sports such as agility and canine cross, where the bond between you and your canine partner is put to the test, your physical prowess plays a vital role in the equation.

The Human Side of Canine Sports

Canine sports are a thrilling blend of teamwork, skill,

and agility, but they can also be physically demanding. Handlers, that's you, must be prepared to match the energy, enthusiasm, and stamina of your four-legged athlete. Imagine navigating an intricate agility course or running alongside your dog in a canicross race; it's no walk in the park. To keep up with the intensity and excitement of these sports, it's essential that you invest in your own fitness.

The Benefits of Regular Exercise

Regular exercise and conditioning for handlers offer a multitude of advantages. First and foremost, it boosts your stamina, allowing you to actively participate in the sport without tiring quickly. Improved endurance not only benefits your performance but also enhances the overall experience for both you and your dog. Furthermore, staying physically fit reduces the risk of injuries, ensuring that you can enjoy a long and rewarding journey in canine sports.

Finding a Trainer for Guidance

For those new to the world of canine sports or seeking specialized training, enrolling in classes with a qualified trainer is a wise choice. The trainer you select can significantly impact your success and the well-being of your dog. When seeking a trainer, prioritize those with experience in the specific sport you're interested in. Look for

410

professionals who have a track record of employing positive, reward-based training methods that create a harmonious partnership between you and your dog. Great consulting source: Big D's Dog Training – Professor Cooper

Safety Above All Else

In the thrill of competition and training, it's crucial to keep safety as your utmost priority. Safety encompasses multiple aspects, including equipment, physical preparedness, and adherence to regulations.

Equipment Check: Always ensure that your equipment is in excellent condition. Faulty gear can lead to accidents and injuries for both you and your dog. Regularly inspect and maintain your equipment to prevent any mishaps during training or competition.

Physical Preparation: Before diving into rigorous training or competitions, both you and your dog should be physically prepared. Gradually increase the intensity of your workouts and adhere to a well-structured conditioning program. This gradual approach minimizes the risk of strains, sprains, and other injuries. You have to think of your safety as well. Because it's not as if a dog will hurt you; it's when!

Rule Adherence: Canine sports often have governing bodies and established rules to maintain fairness and safety. Familiarize yourself with these regulations and ensure strict compliance. Following the rules not only keeps everyone safe but also upholds the integrity of the sport.

Section 3: How to Get Involved in Canine Sports

Now that you're familiar with the exciting world of canine sports and the training required, it's time to explore how you can get involved and start your journey with your furry friend.

Research the Sport

Begin by researching the specific canine sport that piques your interest. Learn about its rules, equipment, and any local clubs or organizations that host events. The more you know, the better prepared you'll be to embark on this adventure.

Find Local Clubs and Organizations

Joining a local canine sports club or organization can be a great way to connect with like-minded individuals and gain access to training facilities and resources. These groups often host competitions and events, providing opportunities for you and your dog to participate and socialize.

Attend Competitions and Events

Even if you're not ready to compete, attending canine sports competitions and events as a spectator can be informative and inspiring. You'll get a firsthand look at the sport, observe different breeds in action, and connect with experienced handlers and trainers.

Start Training

Begin training with your dog, starting with basic obedience and gradually progressing to sport-specific skills. Enroll in classes if necessary, and practice regularly to build your dog's confidence and competence in the chosen sport.

Set Realistic Goals

Setting realistic goals is essential to stay motivated and track your progress. Whether your goal is to complete an agility course, earn a title in obedience, or simply have fun, having a clear objective will keep you focused on your canine sports journey.

Enjoy the Journey

Remember that canine sports are not solely about winning competitions. They are an opportunity to bond with your dog, stay active, and create lasting memories together. Embrace the journey, cherish the moments, and celebrate the milestones, no matter how big or small.

Embrace the Community

One of the most rewarding aspects of canine sports is the community of passionate dog lovers you'll meet along the way. Attend club meetings, connect on social media, and engage with fellow enthusiasts. The camaraderie and shared experiences will enhance your enjoyment of the sport.

Stay Informed

Stay informed about developments and updates in your chosen canine sport. Rules and regulations may change, and new training techniques or equipment may emerge. Continuous learning and adaptation are key to staying competitive and enjoying the sport to the fullest.

Conclusion

Canine sports offer a world of adventure, bonding, and excitement for both dogs and their human companions.

From agility and obedience to dock diving and herding trials, there's a canine sport to suit every dog's talents and every owner's interests. With the right training, dedication, and a supportive community, you can embark on a fulfilling journey in the world of canine sports, creating lasting memories and unforgettable experiences with your four-legged friend. So, lace up your shoes, grab your dog's leash, and get ready to explore the incredible world of canine sports together.

Unit 22 GSPs: The Hunting Maestros

Introduction

In the world of hunting dogs, the German Shorthaired Pointer (GSP) stands out as a breed known for its versatility, intelligence, and unwavering loyalty. In this chapter, we will delve into the characteristics and training of one exceptional GSP named Dan, who played a pivotal role in the adventures of his owner, Cooper.

Breed Overview

History

The captivating tale of Dan, the extraordinary German Shorthaired Pointer, stands as a testament to a breed that boasts a storied history dating back to the late 19th century in Germany. Originally conceived for the noble purpose of hunting, GSPs (German Shorthaired Pointers) were meticulously bred to be all-encompassing hunting companions, capable of a trifecta of skills: tracking, pointing, and retrieving game.

Appearance

GSPs, much like the illustrious Dan, command attention with their striking appearance. Adult males typically reach a majestic height, standing tall at 23 to 25 inches at the shoulder and exhibiting a robust weight ranging between 55 to 70 pounds, while their female counterparts sport a slightly more delicate stature. Their coat is a masterpiece in itself, short, dense, and designed to repel water, rendering them not only aesthetically pleasing but also eminently suited for outdoor adventures. The spectrum of their coat colors, including liver, black, or a captivating combination of liver and white, ensures they are a vision to behold in any setting.

Temperament

The temperament of the German Shorthaired Pointer (GSP), exemplified by the unforgettable Dan, is a captivating blend of intelligence, boundless energy, affection, and unwavering loyalty. It is this unique amalgamation of qualities that sets this breed apart in the world of dogs.

Intelligence

GSPs are often regarded as one of the most intelligent dog breeds in existence. They exhibit an exceptional ability to solve problems, making them stand out as paragons of cognitive prowess among their canine counterparts. This remarkable intelligence equips them with a keen understanding of their surroundings, enabling them to swiftly adapt to various situations. It is this innate intelligence that makes GSPs such quick learners, making them a preferred choice for activities that require mental acumens, such as hunting and obedience training. Whether deciphering complex hunting cues or mastering intricate obedience commands, GSPs like Dan effortlessly rise to the occasion, showcasing their intellectual dexterity.

Energetic

GSPs are often likened to dynamic powerhouses, brimming with an uncontainable wellspring of energy. This boundless enthusiasm for life and activity is a defining characteristic of the breed. Dan, with his seemingly endless vitality, was a living testament to the GSP's athletic prowess. This energy is not just a trait but a lifestyle requirement. GSPs thrive when engaged in regular physical activity and mental stimulation. Whether it's running through open fields, participating in agility courses, or simply playing fetch, they need outlets to channel their exuberance. Their high energy levels also make them excellent companions for those who lead active lives and seek four-legged partners to keep up with their adventures.

Affectionate

Despite their high-octane exterior, GSPs possess hearts brimming with affection. These dogs are deeply social and thrive on human interaction. They are known for forging deep and meaningful bonds with their families. Dan, for instance, was not just a pet to Cooper but a cherished family member. The affectionate nature of GSPs is what endears them to their owners and makes them exceptional companions. They crave companionship and thrive when they can be close to their human loved ones. This affection extends beyond their immediate families, as GSPs are often known for their friendly and approachable demeanor, making them great additions to households with children and other pets.

Loyalty

Among the myriad remarkable traits of GSPs, their unwavering loyalty to their human companions is perhaps the most profound. As exemplified by the unwavering devotion of Dan in our narrative, this loyalty surpasses mere companionship. It manifests as a profound and enduring commitment, often marked by selfless actions that reflect their profound attachment to their human counterparts. Dan's loyalty was a living testament to the profound bond that can be forged between a GSP and its owner, a bond that transcends time and circumstance.

Training a GSP

Hunting Skills

Dan's remarkable journey as an exceptional retriever specialized in waterfowl exemplifies the inherent hunting prowess deeply ingrained within the GSP (German Shorthaired Pointer) breed. This breed's extraordinary hunting abilities can be broken down into several key facets, each of which contributes to their reputation as top-tier hunting companions.

Pointing

GSPs possess an instinctual ability to point at game birds, a behavior that serves as a crucial asset during hunting escapades. This innate talent allows them to silently signal the location of the game to the hunter, granting the opportunity for an approach without startling their quarry. With an uncanny ability to lock onto the scent of birds, GSPs freeze in a distinctive pointing stance, their tails rigidly pointing toward the hidden prey. This natural inclination to "point" is a testament to their genetic predisposition to assist hunters in locating elusive game birds.

Retrieving

Within the realm of retrieving, GSPs shine both on land and in the water, a quality made evident by Dan's exceptional feats in our narrative. These dogs are versatile retrievers, equally at home in marshy wetlands as they are in rugged terrains. Their robust swimming skills, combined with unwavering determination, render them invaluable when it comes to retrieving downed waterfowl. GSPs are known to fearlessly plunge into icy waters or navigate through dense vegetation, ensuring that no game is left uncollected. Their acute sense of smell aids them in pinpointing the exact location of fallen birds, and their gentle mouths ensure that the retrieved game remains intact for the hunter's use.

Tracking

Another formidable hunting skill in their repertoire is tracking. GSPs exhibit an impressive aptitude for tracing the path of the wounded game, an ability that proves indispensable in the recovery of downed birds or injured prey. This talent stems from their acute sense of smell, which is finely tuned to detect even the faintest traces of blood or scent markers left by wounded game. Their relentless determination comes to the fore as they meticulously follow the scent trail, navigating challenging terrain and obstacles with remarkable agility. Whether in dense forests, rocky hillsides, or open fields, GSPs are reliable trackers, ensuring that no wounded game goes unrecovered.

Obedience Training

Owing to their remarkable intelligence, GSPs are highly receptive to obedience training. Fundamental commands like 'sit,' 'stay,' and 'come' are not only essential for their safety but also pivotal for effective hunting endeavors. Cooper's triumphant partnership with Dan was firmly anchored in a rigorous regimen of obedience training. This ensured that Dan would respond promptly to commands in the field, facilitating seamless coordination between the hunter and his loyal companion.

Socialization

The significance of proper socialization from an early age cannot be overstated when it comes to GSPs. This critical process guarantees that they grow into well-mannered and adoptable dogs, comfortable in a variety of settings. Dan, with his inherently sociable nature, was a sheer delight to be around, whether he was out in the field, mingling with fellow hunting dogs or enjoying the coziness of his home environment. His ease in diverse social situations underscored the importance of early and comprehensive socialization in shaping a GSP into an affable and well-behaved companion.

Dan's Extraordinary Traits

Exceptional Retrieval Skills

Dan, a proud representative of the German Shorthaired Pointer breed, possessed exceptional retrieval skills that showcased both his innate abilities and extensive training. He was a shining example of the breed's potential when it came to waterfowl retrieval.

When the sharp report of a shotgun pierced the air, signaling the goose's fall from the sky into the serene marsh waters, Dan's instincts kicked in. His remarkable endurance and unwavering determination in retrieving games came to the fore, marking him as an extraordinary retriever.

Dan moved through the cool waters with grace and precision, exhibiting a swimming prowess that left observers in awe. Every stroke was deliberate, every movement purposeful as he homed in on the fallen goose, which had created rippling disturbances across the tranquil marsh.

As minutes stretched into what felt like hours, Cooper, Dan's human companion, anxiously watched. His initial confidence in Dan's abilities began to waver, and he contemplated the possibility of something going wrong in the depths of the marsh. The tension hung thick in the air, and Cooper considered diving into the water himself to assist Dan.

Just as Cooper teetered on the brink of making that decision, a triumphant sight finally emerged on the horizon. It was Dan, emerging from the water with the goose securely held in his mouth, marking his triumphant return and reinforcing his reputation as an exceptional retriever.

Sense of Fairness and Loyalty

As Dan approached with the goose, his pace slow and dignified, a palpable tension filled the air. His proud demeanor was evident, and Cooper's initial worry was quickly replaced by sheer admiration for Dan's remarkable endurance and perseverance. However, what happened next left both Cooper and the stranger who had shot the goose in profound amazement.

In a surprising turn of events, instead of heading straight for Cooper, Dan bypassed his owner and made a direct route toward the stranger who had fired the shot. The man, still astonished by Dan's grand entrance, looked at Cooper, awaiting an explanation.

Cooper, torn between embarrassment and admiration for his loyal companion, couldn't help but offer an apologetic explanation with a sheepish grin. "Sorry about that," he chuckled. "Dan must have thought it was only right to return the goose to the one who shot it. He's quite the character."

The stranger, his initial surprise giving way to amusement and respect, warmly patted Dan's wet fur, expressing his gratitude. "You've got one incredible dog there, my friend. Not only a fantastic retriever but a true gentleman as well."

Cooper nodded, sharing the sentiment. He understood that Dan's actions that day transcended mere training; they were a testament to the deep bonds that German Shorthaired Pointers often form with their owners and their innate sense of fairness and loyalty.

Conclusion

The German Shorthaired Pointer, represented by Dan in our story, is a breed that seamlessly combines intelligence, athleticism, and loyalty in a remarkable manner. Whether as a steadfast hunting companion or a cherished family pet, GSPs like Dan hold a special place in the hearts of those fortunate enough to share their lives with them.

Cooper and Dan's adventures, marked by moments of extraordinary skill and unwavering loyalty, quickly became legendary tales in their local community. The story of Dan's exceptional retrieve, where he returned the fallen goose to the man who had shot it, was a staple at gatherings and campfires. Yet, their story extended far beyond hunting prowess; it was a narrative of friendship, trust, and the profound bond between a man and his dog.

As Cooper and Dan continued to embark on their adventures, their bond deepened with each passing day. Their journeys became cherished memories, and they learned that no matter the challenges they encountered, they could always rely on each other. Their unbreakable friendship guided them through every twist and turn, serving as an enduring testament to the extraordinary potential and remarkable qualities of the German Shorthaired Pointer breed.

PAWSITIVELY PAWESOME: THE ULTIMATE DOG LOVER'S HANDBOOK

Unit 23:
My Story

In the beautiful state of Minnesota, there lived Cooper. From a very young age, Cooper had a deep passion for animals, especially dogs. Growing up in the city, surrounded by homes, he developed an unnatural affinity for understanding and working dogs.

Cooper's journey with dogs began when his cousin had a stray dog come to the farm they named Scraps. Scraps was an energetic and playful pup, but he needed some training to become a well-behaved companion. Cooper, eager to play with a dog, just started working Scrap on the farm. I'm receiving his own dog that was a gift from his sister Phyllis (Special Thanks). The Fox Terrier Munica started it all!

Inspired by his love for dogs and his desire to help others, Cooper started a pet food delivery and training service as a kid (K9 Hotline). He would ride his bicycle around the neighborhood, delivering high-quality pet food to his customers while offering training tips and tricks to help them better communicate with their furry friends.

As Cooper grew older, he pursued his passion for working with animals by attending the University of Wisconsin-River

Falls (UWRF). He studied animal science and dog behavior and training, soaking up knowledge from experienced professionals and experts in the field (Lora I Delany, Richard Walters, Po Pervis, and Bob Gates) for a short list. Cooper's dedication and hard work paid off when he became the first Distinguished Honor Grad of his class with the US Air Force.

After graduating, Cooper sought to enhance his skills even further. He embarked on an apprenticeship under renowned trainers such as Bob Gate, Richard Walter, and Mary Foster. Under their guidance, he honed his training techniques and deepened his understanding of dog behavior.

But Cooper's journey didn't stop there. Driven by his desire to serve others, he while in the United States Air Force and specialized in search and rescue and bomb detection operations. Cooper became a national search and rescue evaluator, working with hundreds of police departments across the country to train and evaluate search and rescue dogs.

Through his experiences, Cooper realized that the key to successful dog training was a positive and compassionate approach to giving the dog directions. He firmly believed in the power of diction reinforcement and

431

developed innovative training methods that focused on building a strong bond between humans and dogs. Cooper's expertise and dedication led him to write this book called "Pawpositive," which aimed to empower dog owners with effective training knowledge and promote a harmonious relationship with their pets. Being the first Text book of its kind.

Cooper hopes the book, "Pawpositive," will become a bestseller, reaching dog lovers worldwide and helping countless people develop a deeper understanding of their furry companions. His work at the Brooklyn Pet Hospital in Minnesota, combined with his vast experience, canine influence, and knowledge, made him a trusted authority in the field of dog training.

Today, Cooper continues to inspire and educate dog
owners through his training programs, workshops, canine
consulting courses, podcasts, and speaking engagements.
His passion for dogs and his commitment to their well-being
have made him a true advocate for direction reinforcement
training and a beloved figure in the world of dog lovers
everywhere. As Cooper's reputation as a skilled dog trainer
grew, he started receiving invitations to conduct training
seminars and workshops in different parts of the country. He
traveled worldwide, sharing his knowledge and expertise
with eager audiences.

During his travels, Cooper had the opportunity to

work with various police departments and their K-9 units. He collaborated with these dedicated teams, providing advanced training techniques and guidance to enhance their search and rescue efforts. Cooper's collaboration with law enforcement agencies earned him a stellar reputation in the field of canine search and rescue.

One of Cooper's most memorable experiences involved working with a police department in a small town. The community had been devastated by a recent natural disaster, and their search and rescue capabilities were stretched thin. Cooper arrived with his expertise and a team of highly trained search dogs, Jim Couch with his dog. Together, they scoured the debris and wreckage, bringing hope and solace to the affected families by reuniting them with their missing loved ones.

Cooper's dedication to his craft and his unwavering commitment to helping both dogs and humans alike earned him numerous accolades and recognition. He was awarded the National Canine Hero Award for his exceptional contributions to the field of search and rescue and Life Time Achievement Award Marquette Who Who. Cooper's passion for dogs and his tireless efforts to make a positive impact on their lives truly made a difference.

Throughout his journey, Cooper remained humble and grounded, always emphasizing the importance of compassion, patience, and understanding when working with dogs. He believed that every dog had the potential to be a loving and well-behaved companion with the right guidance and training.

"Pawpositive," his book, became a go-to resource for dog owners, trainers, and enthusiasts around the world. It offered practical tips, step-by-step training methods, and heartwarming stories that inspired readers to forge a deeper bond with their furry friends.

Cooper's legacy continues to thrive as he mentors aspiring dog trainers and dog owners, works with rescue organizations, and advocates for the humane treatment of animals. His dedication to promoting successful training methods and nurturing the human-animal bond has left an indelible mark on the world of dog training and behavior.

With each success story and every transformed dog-human relationship, Cooper's impact grows, reminding us all of the power of love, patience, and the pawpositive approach to training our four-legged companions. As Cooper's influence continued to expand, he embarked on a new endeavor that aimed to revolutionize the field of dog training. He founded the Pawpositive Academy, a state-of-the-art Education program that offered comprehensive certifications for those who want to start their dig business, and Big D's Dog Training of all breeds, and all ages for their dog training needs.

The Big D's Dog Training Academy became renowned for its innovative training techniques, which emphasized direction reinforcement and customized approaches tailored to each individual dog's needs. Cooper

assembled a team of expert trainers who shared his
philosophy and passion for nurturing the potential in every
dog.

Big D's Dog Training's success has attracted dog
owners from far and wide, seeking solutions for various
behavioral challenges. Cooper and his team worked closely
with each client, providing personalized training plans and
ongoing support to ensure long-lasting results. The academy
became a hub for education and collaboration, hosting
seminars, workshops, and guest speakers from around the
world.

Recognizing the importance of community
involvement, Cooper initiated partnerships with local animal
shelters and rescue organizations. He implemented training
programs to help prepare shelter dogs for adoption,
increasing their chances of finding loving homes. Cooper
firmly believed in the power of second chances and
dedicated himself to rehabilitating and rehoming as many
dogs as possible.

As Cooper's expertise grew, he also delved into the
world of canine sports and competitions. He trained and
coached numerous dogs to success in agility, obedience, and
scent work, earning them prestigious titles and recognition.

Cooper's ability to unlock a dog's full potential through positive training methods garnered admiration from fellow trainers and competitors alike.

In addition to his work at the Big D's Dog Training, Cooper remained involved in the academic community. He regularly guest lectured at events, sharing his knowledge and experiences with aspiring veterinarians, animal behaviorists, and dog trainers. Cooper's commitment to education and mentorship ensured that his positive training philosophy would continue to thrive in future generations.

Cooper's impact extended beyond the boundaries of his training facility and the local community. He started Big D's Dog Training, dedicated to promoting animal welfare

and supporting initiatives that improved the lives of dogs in
need.

As the years went by, Cooper's dedication to dogs
and their well-being remained unwavering. His compassion,
expertise, and passion for positive training methods
transformed countless lives, both human and canine.
Through his book and academy, he left an enduring legacy
that continues to shape the way we understand and interact
with our four-legged companions.

Cooper's story serves as an inspiration to all who
aspire to make a difference in the lives of animals. His
journey from a young boy in the city to a farm to a renowned
dog trainer and advocate demonstrates the profound impact
one person can have when they follow their passion and
work tirelessly to create a more compassionate world for our
beloved pets. Certainly! Let's dive deeper into Cooper's story
and explore some additional aspects of his journey.

As Cooper's reputation grew, he caught the attention
of media outlets and was invited to share his expertise on
television shows and in interviews. His warm personality and
wealth of knowledge made him a sought-after guest,
allowing him to reach an even wider audience and spread his
message of positive training methods.

439

One of the most memorable moments in Cooper's career was when he was invited to be a keynote speaker at a prestigious international dog training conference. Sharing the stage with renowned experts, Cooper captivated the audience with his engaging storytelling and insightful teachings. His ability to connect with people on an emotional level and convey the profound impact that positive training had on the lives of both dogs and their owners left a lasting impression.

Cooper's dedication to the field of dog training led him to develop groundbreaking techniques that focused on strengthening the human-canine bond. He introduced innovative concepts such as mindfulness training, where both the dog and the owner learned to be fully present and attuned to each other's needs. This approach not only improved obedience but also nurtured a deeper sense of trust and understanding between dogs and their owners.

Recognizing the importance of continuing education, Cooper regularly attended conferences, workshops, and seminars to stay updated on the latest advancements in dog training and behavior. He collaborated with other industry leaders, exchanging ideas and pushing the boundaries of what was possible in the field. Cooper's commitment to lifelong learning and professional growth earned him the respect of his peers and solidified his position as a leading authority in the industry.

Throughout his career, Cooper remained dedicated to giving back to his community. He organized fundraising events, donating the proceeds to local organizations. He also volunteered his time to train therapy dogs that brought comfort and joy to hospital patients, nursing home residents, and children with special needs. Cooper believed in the transformative power of dogs and their ability to positively impact people's lives.

As the years went by, Cooper's work and contributions were recognized with numerous accolades and awards. He was invited to join prestigious professional organizations and served on advisory boards, where he played a crucial role in shaping industry standards and promoting ethical training practices.

Cooper's story not only inspired dog owners and trainers but also motivated countless individuals to follow their passions and make a difference in the lives of animals. His journey from a young boy on a farm to a respected expert and advocate demonstrated the profound impact that one person can have when they combine their passion with knowledge and compassion.

Today, Cooper's legacy lives on through the countless dogs and owners who have benefited from his teachings, the graduates of his academy who continue to spread his positive training methods, and the ongoing efforts of the Big D's Dog Training to improve the lives of dogs in need.

Cooper's remarkable journey serves as a reminder

that with dedication, empathy, and a deep love for animals, we have the power to create a world where every dog receives the care, training, and respect they deserve.

Cooper's journey began with the Bracco, a beautiful hunting dog known for its keen sense of smell and strong hunting instincts. Cooper had the opportunity to work with several Braccos and successfully trained them for hunting trials. Through his dedication and expertise, he helped many Braccos achieve champion titles in various competitions. Cooper's skill in handling these dogs quickly gained recognition in the Italian dog community.

Next, Cooper delved into working with the Spinone, a gentle and versatile hunting breed. Though less well-known internationally, the Spinone had a devoted following in Italy. Cooper focused on training Spinones for both field trials and dog shows, highlighting their natural abilities and elegant appearance. The Spinones, under Cooper's guidance, won numerous accolades and contributed to the breed's growing recognition outside Italy.

Cooper's international journey continued with the Neapolitan Mastiffs, a majestic and powerful breed known for its protective nature. Despite their imposing size, these dogs possess a gentle and affectionate temperament. Cooper worked closely with Neapolitan Mastiffs, emphasizing their obedience and temperament training. With his guidance, many Neapolitan Mastiffs excelled in obedience trials and gained recognition for their well-rounded abilities. Also to include (Dane, Papion, Doberman, Corgi, Dachshund, Collie, Labrador, Newfoundland, and Weimaraner).

In addition to the breeds mentioned above, Cooper also had the opportunity to handle Boxers, a well-known breed with a strong following worldwide. While Boxers were not as rare as the other breeds, Cooper's expertise and dedication helped him train Boxers to their full potential. He worked with them in both conformation shows and various dog sports, showcasing their agility, intelligence, and natural athleticism.

One remarkable aspect of Cooper's journey in Italy
was how working with dogs helped him overcome language
barriers. Cooper's Italian language skills were limited
initially, but the universal language of dogs bridged the
communication gap. He found that his passion for dogs and
the shared understanding of training techniques brought him
closer to fellow dog enthusiasts and breeders in Italy.
Cooper's dedication and commitment to the dogs he handled
allowed him to forge strong connections and gain respect
within the Italian dog community.

Cooper's experience in handling rare dog breeds in
Italy, including the Bracco, Spin one, Neapolitan Mastiffs,
and Redbone Coonhound, showcased his talent as a trainer
and his ability to bring out the best in each breed. His
successes in the show ring and various competitions

445

highlighted his expertise and passion for working with dogs. Ultimately, Cooper's journey in Italy not only enriched his own life but also contributed to the recognition and appreciation of these unique breeds within the international dog community.

Most every fall, we hosted a field training clinic. One attendee was a proud owner of a lively Britney Spaniel, "Charlie." Charlie, his owner, was eagerly always exploring the outdoors and embarking on new adventures.

One sunny day, Charlie went to a field training clinic. It was a popular spot for hunting enthusiasts, particularly those training for rigorous hunting activities and trials. This field was renowned for its tough exercises that required both mental and physical agility.

Eager to teach his dog hunting skills and to bond with his four-legged friend, John eagerly enrolled himself and Charlie in the field's renowned training program. The program was led by a group of experienced instructors of Big D's Dog Training who specialized in pushing individuals and their dogs to their maximum potential. John hoped to enhance Charlie's obedience and hunting skills while improving his own endurance.

With great enthusiasm, John and Charlie threw themselves into the intense training sessions. Together, they navigated through high grass. I was impressed by the duo's determination and the close bond they shared.

During one particularly demanding session, disaster struck. John caught up in the heat of the moment, lost his phone in the field. Distraught, we searched frantically but couldn't find it. In his distress, he had to leave the training field without his phone.

Two weeks went by, and John couldn't help but feel a sense of emptiness without his device. It wasn't just the phone itself but the countless memories and important information stored within. Despite our efforts to retrace his steps, the phone remained elusive.

Desperate for a solution to a problem with the whoa command, John returned to Big D's training field with Charlie for another training session. As we worked the field, Charlie went south on the field as we went north. Charlie began sniffing around the area. Something caught his attention, and he wouldn't leave it. Charles was pointing. It was at this point that I said trust your dog. Which I've said hundreds of times, thinking Charlie was on a bird

Intrigued, Charlie followed his nose, leading John through the field they had once covered. The other participants and instructors watched in awe as the determined Britney Spaniel quartered the field.

Finally, after a captivating display of canine acrobatics, Charlie triumphantly stood over some thicket of bushes, his tail wagging vigorously. Pointing to the long-lost phone, slightly scratched but still functional.

The incredible bond between John and Charlie had not only led to the recovery of the lost phone but had also sparked a brilliant idea. I saw the potential for a new sport that combined physical training with the extraordinary abilities of our four-legged friends—the sport of Action Dog.

Action Dog gained popularity in 2020 as people realized the practicality and usefulness of training their dogs to find misplaced items. Dogs of various breeds and sizes were now being trained to locate cell phones, keys, remote controls, glasses, wallets, and more. Action Dog competitions sprang up around the world, attracting participants eager to showcase the incredible skills of their beloved companions.

The birth of Action Dog not only brought joy and entertainment but also highlighted the remarkable intelligence and capabilities of our faithful canine companions.

And so, thanks to the extraordinary journey of John and Charlie, the world gained a new sport that celebrated the unique partnership between humans and dogs, forever changing the way we perceive our furry friends and the incredible feats they can achieve.

The sun shone brightly on a beautiful day in Florida as y Echo and I, the client's spirited dog, arrived at the prestigious National Rally Obedience Event. Excitement bubbled within me, knowing that this event would showcase the skills and bond between Echo and me. Little did I know that this day would be filled with unexpected twists and turns.

As I walked through the gates of the event, Echo immediately caught the attention of fellow participants and spectators. Her energy was palpable, her tail wagging furiously as she pranced by my side. However, as I neared the starting line, Echo abruptly sat down, seemingly uninterested in what lay ahead. I was taken aback, unsure of what had suddenly caught her attention.

In that split second, Echo's ears perked up, and in a burst of energy, she bolted off, sprinting through the course with unparalleled speed and enthusiasm. Gasps and laughter filled the air as onlookers marveled at Echo's spontaneous display of agility as if to were reading the course signs.

As Echo neared the end of the course, I held my breath, uncertain of what would happen next. Miraculously, as if guided by some invisible force, Echo suddenly slowed down, and with incredible precision, she flawlessly executed the remaining commands. With a final triumphant leap, she returned to my side, perfectly poised and ready to proceed.

451

The judge, who had been observing the whirlwind performance, approached me with a bemused smile. "Are you ready?" she asked, unable to hide her amusement. I hesitated, convinced that Echo's spontaneous adventure had surely caused us to fail. Nevertheless, I decided to press on, determined to make the most of the situation and just have some fun.

We almost flawlessly maneuvered through the course; Echo followed my lead with a newfound focus and determination. The connection and trust with each other were evident in every command and response. Cheers and applause echoed through the arena as spectators recognized the remarkable synergy between Echo and myself.

Finally, I crossed the finish line, my heart racing with a mix of disbelief and exhilaration. Despite the unexpected detour, we successfully completed the course. But would it be enough to secure a respectable placement? The anticipation built as the judge calculated our score.

Moments later, the judge stepped forward, holding the score sheet, and announced the placements. and "In second place, with a score of 195, we have our dynamic duo!" I couldn't believe my ears. A wave of joy washed over me as the crowd erupted in applause and cheers, recognizing the unique bond you and Echo shared.

As you stepped forward to receive your well-deserved recognition, Echo looked up at me with bright, proud eyes. It was a moment of pure bliss and accomplishment, a testament to the incredible journey we had embarked on together. This Rally Obedience Event had not only showcased Echo's vibrant personality but also the indomitable spirit of teamwork and resilience.

The rest of the day was filled with celebrations and shared stories of Echo's spontaneous adventure that had turned into a victorious triumph. People approached us,

453

eager to congratulate us on our impressive performance. I couldn't help but bask in the joy and revel in the memories of this unforgettable day.

From that day forward, Echo's tale became legendary in the Rally Obedience community. People would recall the spirited dog who, against all odds, brought joy and excitement to the event. My bond with Echo grew even stronger, and together, we continued to conquer new challenges of an AKC Champion Title, leaving a lasting impression wherever we went.

And so, as the sun set on that beautiful Florida evening, Echo and I embarked on new adventures, ready to face the world with a newfound confidence and a heart full of unforgettable memories.

In my world of dogs, there are many enthusiasts, None more than I, Big D, who dedicated their my to training dogs and teaching people how to handle them in shows and event rings. Big D's I understood that training was not just about winning competitions or collecting ribbons but about creating a deep and meaningful bond between humans and their canine companions via communication.

As Big D's, training went beyond the technicalities

of commands and obedience. It was about bridging the gap between dogs and humans, facilitating effective communication, and fostering a harmonious relationship based on trust, respect, and love. I believed that dogs were not merely pets; they were cherished members of the family.

With boundless energy and enthusiasm, I embarked on a mission to provide families with the skills to nurture this special bond. Training sessions were not only focused on teaching dogs to sit, stay, or heel but also on understanding the needs, desires, and unique personalities of dogs and their owners. As Big D's, I recognized that each dog had its own learning style, and tailoring the training approach accordingly was key to unlocking their full potential.

In the show and event rings, Big D's taught aspiring handlers how to present their dogs with confidence and grace. Every movement, every gesture, and every interaction with the dog was carefully choreographed to showcase their beauty, elegance, and charisma. It was not simply about winning titles but about celebrating the remarkable partnership between humans and canines.

Big D's firmly believed that training was a lifelong journey. It was a continuous process of growth, adaptation, and learning for both dogs and their human counterparts.

Beyond the show ring, the lessons learned in training spilled over into everyday life, enriching the bond between families and their furry friends. Dogs became not only obedient companions but also sources of joy, comfort, and unwavering loyalty.

As the years passed, Big D's reputation grew, and their impact extended far beyond the show world. Families from all walks of life sought Big D's guidance, knowing that they would be equipped with the skills and knowledge to create a happy and fulfilling life with their dogs. Big D's training methods were celebrated for their effectiveness, compassion, and ability to transform the lives of both dogs and humans.

In the end, what training was all about for Big D was more than just a profession; it was a calling, a labor of love. It was about teaching people to handle dogs with care, empathy, and understanding. It was about nurturing the bond between dogs and humans, providing families with a source of lifelong joy, companionship, and unwavering love. And with every wagging tail and every happy family, Big D's legacy continued to shine, reminding the world that the true essence of training lies in the celebration of the incredible

connection between humans and their beloved four-legged
companions.

Chapter 23 My story is what has made up this book.
I was raised in South Minneapolis, Minnesota, as a young
boy named Daryl. From a very young age, I have always
been fascinated by dogs and their unique behaviors. In fact,
my love for dogs began in the third grade when I started a
K9 hotline project for a science fair. Blessed with my sister
Phyllis buying me a dog while she was in school abroad
(Mexico).

My project was a huge success, and I even won
several science fairs with my innovative ideas and
techniques for dog training. My passion for working with

457

dogs only grew stronger as I got older. Before I turned nine, he landed a helper job at the Brooklyn Pet Hospital, where I worked for fifteen years, learning everything I could about Veterinarian Medicine and the different breeds and their behavior.

The surprise gift from Phyllis would change my life forever. Phyllis presented me with a lively and mischievous Fox Terrier named Muncia. Muncia quickly became my best friend and partner in crime. But my rule for keeping the dog was I had to train her!

As the years passed, my passion for dogs continued to flourish. In the fourth grade, I started a dog food delivery service to provide high-quality and nutritious meals for his canine companions in the neighborhood. It was a hit, and I soon found myself with a growing list of satisfied customers.

In the fifth grade, my love for dogs took an adventurous turn. Along with my father and our neighbor, Mr. Brown, started a Coonhound hunting & competition. It was an exhilarating experience as we trained the dogs to track and chase raccoons through the woods. We formed a strong bond and spent countless nights and weekends exploring the wilderness with their loyal four-legged companions.

PAWSITIVELY PAWESOME: THE ULTIMATE DOG LOVER'S HANDBOOK

My father's friend Mr. McMillan exposed me to hunting over a German Shorthaired Pointer. After working with his dog under the excuse of exercising him, I was learning training skills and sales.

My journey didn't stop there. In the seventh grade, I saved up enough money to buy his very own German Shorthaired Pointer, whom I named Dan. This energetic and intelligent dog quickly became my most prized possession. Together, we embarked on countless adventures, honing our hunting skills and participating in various field trials.

As the years went by, my reputation as a skilled dog trainer grew far and wide. I decided to turn my lifelong passion into a full-fledged profession and opened "Big D's Dog Training." With my extensive knowledge, experience, and genuine love for dogs, I became the go-to person in town for anyone seeking help in training their furry companions.

From basic obedience to advanced tricks and specialized hunting training, Big D's Dog Training offers a wide range of services. My dedication and expertise helped transform countless dogs into well-behaved and happy pets, earning me the respect and admiration of the entire community.

But more than just training dogs, My ultimate goal was to foster a deep understanding and bond between humans and their four-legged friends. I believe that a well-trained dog is not only a joy to be around but also a reflection of responsible pet ownership.

Throughout my journey, I never forgot my basic beginnings. I have often shared the dog stories of my early endeavors and encouraged young children to explore their passions and follow their dreams, just as I have.

And so, the tale of Big D's Dog Training became legendary in the town of River Falls, Wisconsin. As college friend named the business after my dog Dan "Big D". My unwavering love for dogs is a lifelong dedication to their well-being, and my remarkable ability to communicate with them left an indelible mark on the hearts of all who knew. My passion for dogs had truly become a life's calling, and I continued to touch the lives of dogs and their owners for many years to come.

Learn additional animal care working on a dairy farm in Waverly, Minnesota, reinforcing my fascination about dogs and their incredible abilities. Watching the dogs work the dairy Cattle. I believed that with the right training, dogs could accomplish amazing feats.

One day, I got the brilliant idea to teach Dan to
deliver newspapers to each customer's door on my paper
route. I believed that this would not only be a helpful service
but also a great way to showcase Dan's intelligence and
trainability. I set out on a mission to turn my idea into a
reality.

I started by patiently training Dan to recognize the
newspaper and carry it in his mouth without tearing it apart.
I used direction reinforcement techniques and praise every
time Dan successfully completed a step. With consistent
training sessions, Dan quickly grasped the concept, but not
without retrieving all the papers back from the house the first
few times.

To everyone's amazement, the idea seemed to be
working perfectly. Dan would run from house to house,
dropping the newspapers at each doorstep with great
precision.

Determined to unravel the mystery behind Dan's
unusual behavior, I decided to delve deeper into animal
education. While driving to and from a farm in Waverly, I
started studying animal behavior and training techniques. I
immersed myself in learning about dogs, their instincts, and
the psychology behind their actions.

461

My passion continued in high school, where I excelled in football, basketball, and track. After completing high school. I decided to pursue a degree in Animal Science. I initially attended Hamline University and then transferred to River Falls, Wisconsin, where he obtained a Bachelor of Science in Animal Science.

My thirst for knowledge and love for dogs didn't stop there. I decided to join the US Air Force, being the first Disquieted Honor Grad, where I could further my education while serving his country. Stationed in Avaino, Italy, I participated in extension programs that allowed me to explore dog behavior and reproduction in depth. With dedication and hard work, I achieved one of my goals of obtaining a Ph.D. in Animal Behavior and Reproduction.

During my time in the Air Force, stationed in Italy, I continued to expand my knowledge and expertise in the field as an SP Dog Handler. My experiences abroad enriched his understanding of different animal behaviors and training methodologies. In the private sector, I handle Boxer, Brocho, Spinone, Neapolitan Mastiffs, and numerous others.

After completing my service and returning stateside, I decided to put his vast knowledge and skills to use, where I partnered with John Quimby and established "Big D's Dog Training," a renowned dog training & pet food delivery located in Lino Lakes, MN. As Big D's, we did stage shows on the shores of Game Fair from the late 1980s to the present day.

Throughout my training career, I've not only taught dogs basic obedience but also specialized in addressing behavioral issues and training dogs for specific purposes while consulting the people as well. I've become widely known for my ability to transform even the most challenging cases into well-behaved and obedient companions.

My journey, from teaching my dog, Dan, to delivering newspapers to founding a successful dog training center and education academy, was truly inspiring. My unwavering passion for animals, combined with my extensive knowledge and experience, allowed me to make a lasting impact on countless dogs and their owners.

And so, my story is a remarkable journey that serves as a reminder of the extraordinary things that can be achieved through dedication, perseverance, and a deep understanding of the animal kingdom. My path was not without challenges, but he overcame them through my unwavering determination and love for dogs.

Throughout my years running "Big D's Dog Training," I continued to innovate and refine his techniques. I implemented reward-based training methods that focused on direct reinforcement and building a strong bond between dogs and their owners. My approach emphasized understanding the unique needs and behaviors of each individual dog, ensuring tailored training programs that yielded remarkable results.

My expertise and the success stories that emerged from Big D's Dog Training. People from near and far sought my guidance, whether they had a new puppy in need of basic obedience training or a troubled dog with deep-seated behavioral issues. I'm dedicated to helping both dogs and their owners establish harmonious relationships become my trademark.

Beyond my work at "Big D's Dog Training," I have been an advocate for animal welfare and responsible pet ownership. I regularly volunteered at local events, offering my expertise to help rehabilitate and train rescue dogs, increasing their chances of finding forever homes.

My impact has extended beyond my local community. I have been invited to speak at national and international conferences on animal behavior and training.

Over the years, I have continued to expand my knowledge by collaborating with renowned experts in the animal behavior and training industry. I remained at the forefront of advancements, incorporating cutting-edge techniques into his programs to provide the best possible outcomes for dogs and their owners.

I have worked with students from all walks of life who sought to learn from my expertise. I have become a mentor and instructor, passing on my knowledge and passion to aspiring dog trainers who share my vision of creating happier, healthier, and well-behaved canine companions.

My dedication to animal education and his contributions to the field of animal behavior and training have earned me accolades and recognition. I have received numerous awards and honors, solidifying my place as a respected authority in the industry.

But beyond the accolades and accomplishments, my greatest reward was seeing the transformations in the dogs I've worked with and the joy I've brought to their owners' lives as service dogs. The stories of dogs once deemed untrainable or aggressive, who went on to become loving and obedient companions, fueled my passion and inspired me to continue the work.

Over the years in dog training, dogs have not changed, but people's thinking has. "Big D's Dog Training" has become a symbol of excellence and a testament to the power of compassionate and effective training methods. My expertise and love for animals have left an indelible mark on the world of dog training and forever changed the lives of countless dogs and their owners.

So, this book showcases the remarkable journey of a man who turned a simple idea of teaching his dog to deliver newspapers into a lifelong pursuit of animal education and an unwavering commitment to improving the lives of dogs everywhere.

Rich's dog goes to make a retrieve with no one watching him. I found myself captivated by the beauty of a peaceful lake shore. The sun's golden rays gently kissed the water's surface, creating a shimmering dance of light. As I stood there, appreciating nature's canvas, a young and spirited yellow Labrador Retriever caught my eye.

This energetic lab had been watching the dock intently, eagerly awaiting a chance to retrieve a floating bumper that had been cast into the water. With an irrepressible burst of excitement, the dog leaped off the dock, soaring through the air like a graceful dolphin, driven by its insatiable love for the game of fetch.

However, amidst the thrill of the moment, an unexpected challenge emerged. The bumper had been cleverly secured as a tie-off bowie, which meant the dog was inadvertently tethered to it. Panic ensued as the young lab realized it was rapidly descending into the depths of the lake, caught in the clutches of its own enthusiasm on Long Lake, Wisconsin. Without a moment's hesitation, a surge of adrenaline propelled me into action. Leaving my place at the lakeside restaurant, I sprinted towards the water's edge, driven by an instinctive desire to save the lab from harm. It was an urgent race against time, my heart pounding in my chest as the distance between me and the dog seemed to stretch infinitely.

As fortune would have it, a small John boat, powered by a modest 9.9 horsepower outboard engine, was conveniently tied to the dock. With a couple of pulls on the motor, I swiftly commandeered the vessel, knowing it was the only way to reach the imperiled lab in time. The gentle hum of the motor filled the air as the boat glided across the tranquil surface of the lake, propelled by a fervent sense of purpose.

Drawing closer, I could see the dog's struggle against the constraining rope, its eyes filled with both fear and trust. The pup would not let go. With one final burst of strength, I reached out, grasping the dog's collar, and pulled it towards the safety of the boat. The young lab, relieved and exhausted, nestled against my side as we began our journey back to shore.

The lakeside restaurant had become a hub of concerned onlookers, their faces reflecting a mix of worry and relief as they witnessed our successful rescue. Cheers and applause echoed through the air as we approached, acknowledging the shared sense of joy that comes from witnessing a small victory against the perils of fate.

From that day forward, the bond between the yellow lab paper "Rich" and I grew, rooted in the memory of our lakeside adventure. The dog, grateful for its second chance at play and exploration, continued to bring boundless love and endless joy to Rich. As we watched the sun sink below the horizon, casting a warm glow across the lake, we knew that the lake shore would forever hold a special place in our hearts, a testament to the enduring power of courage, compassion, and the unbreakable spirit of man's best friend.

Once upon a time, I had dedicated my life to the world of education, constantly seeking opportunities to inspire and guide young minds. My passion for dog training was not confined to traditional classrooms; He had a special connection with 4-H students from around the world.

My journey in canine education began early in my schooling. I found immense joy in helping their classmates understand complex concepts and uncover their true dogs' potential. Recognizing his gift for teaching. When I decided to pursue a career in dog training, driven by a desire to make a positive impact on as many young lives as possible.

My involvement with 4-H extended far beyond the confines of their local community. They actively sought opportunities to connect Big D's Dog Training with 4-H students from different corners of the globe, fostering cross-cultural exchange and learning. Through various channels like online forums, conferences, and workshops, Cooper built a vast network of 4-H enthusiasts, including students, teachers, and mentors, all sharing a common goal of empowering youth.

As a judge and evaluator for 4-H competitions and events, I played a crucial role in recognizing and celebrating the achievements of young participants. Their extensive knowledge and experience in education helped them provide valuable feedback, encouraging students to refine their skills and strive for excellence. My empathetic nature allowed me to nurture the students' confidence, making them believe in their abilities and inspiring them to aim higher.

Beyond the competitive aspect, as a dedicated mentor to countless 4-H students. They recognized the importance of guiding and supporting these young individuals as they

471

pursued their passions and navigated their personal journeys. Big D's Dog Training mentoring sessions were filled with wisdom, encouragement, and practical advice, helping students overcome challenges, set goals, and develop essential life skills.

Cooper's impact on 4-H students was immeasurable. They witnessed students transform from shy and uncertain individuals to confident and accomplished young leaders. Many of these students went on to achieve remarkable feats in their chosen fields, and they often credited Cooper's guidance as a catalyst for their success.

As the years passed, my influence on the 4-H community remained strong. Their commitment to nurturing the next generation of leaders persisted, and their legacy became a guiding light for educators and mentors worldwide.

And so, my story serves as a reminder that each of us has the power to make a difference in the lives of others. Through teaching, judging, evaluating, and mentoring, they exemplified the profound impact one individual can have on the world. I hope my journey will forever inspire others to empower the youth, unlock their potential, and shape a brighter future for generations to come.

Quiz

Question quiz about dogs in history, featuring both well-known and lesser-known facts.

- Which breed of dog was the loyal companion of President Franklin D. Roosevelt? o Answer: Scottish Terrier (Fala)

- What ancient civilization considered dogs sacred and often depicted them in their artwork?

  o Answer: Ancient Egyptians

- Which dog breed is famous for its role in the rescue operation during the 9/11 attacks?

  o Answer: Labrador Retriever

- What is the name of the dog that accompanied Lewis and Clark on their expedition? o Answer: Seaman

- Which dog breed was revered by the Native American tribe called the Chukchi? o

  Answer: Siberian Husky

- Which dog breed is often associated with the Swiss Alps and is known for its ability to rescue people in the snow?

473

- Answer: Saint Bernard

- What was the name of the dog who played the iconic role of Lassie in the television series?

  - Answer: Pal

- Which breed of dog was famously owned by the composer Ludwig van Beethoven?

  - Answer: Saint Bernard

- Which dog breed was the symbol of the Roman god of the Underworld, Pluto?

  - Answer: Cerberus (a mythical three-headed dog)

- Which dog breed was bred in Germany as a hunting dog and later became a popular police and military working dog? o Answer: German Shepherd

- Which dog breed is known for having a black tongue and originated in China?

  - Answer: Chow Chow

- What is the name of the dog who became the first animal to orbit the Earth in space?

  - Answer: Laika

- Which small dog breed was a favorite among European nobility during the Renaissance period? o Answer: Maltese

- What was the name of the dog who became the mascot for the Yale University football team in the early 20th century?

  o Answer: Handsome Dan

- Which dog breed is associated with the iconic movie "101 Dalmatians"? o Answer: Dalmatian

- What was the name of the dog who helped discover the remains of the ancient city of Pompeii? o Answer: Sophie

- Which dog breed was developed by monks in the Swiss Alps as a herding dog? o Answer: Bernese Mountain Dog

- Which dog breed is known for its distinctive curly coat and is often referred to as the "hypoallergenic" breed?

  o Answer: Poodle

- What is the name of the dog who accompanied Ernest Shackleton on his Antarctic expedition? o Answer: Samson

- Which small dog breed originated in Mexico and is known for its alert and spirited nature?

  o Answer: Chihuahua

Unit 24 Mac Story

Setting on the corner, there lived a man named Mac. Mac was known for his carefree and easygoing nature, always seeking adventure and fun. He enjoyed the freedom of life without any responsibilities tying him down. Being retired. That is until the day he stumbled upon a stray dog wandering alone on the road.

The dog, a small and timid creature with soulful eyes, seemed lost and scared. Mac's heart melted, and he couldn't bear to see the poor dog suffering. Without hesitation, he decided to take the dog home and give it the love, food, and care it needed.

Little did Mac know that this small act of kindness would completely transform his life. The responsibilities of dog ownership soon took hold. He had to ensure the dog's basic needs were met: food, water, and shelter. He learned about the importance of regular exercise, training, and socialization for his new furry companion. Mac realized that this little creature relied on him for everything.

As the days turned into weeks, Mac's carefree spirit began to evolve. He started waking up earlier to take the dog for walks, even in rain or snow. He researched the best food options and diligently scheduled veterinary appointments.

The once aimless retired man found himself organizing his life around the needs of his four-legged friend.

With each passing day, Mac grew more responsible and selfless and found meaning in life. He learned the power of unconditional love and the joy of caring for another being. The dog became his constant companion, providing comfort during life's ups and downs. The little pup gave him a sense of purpose and taught him the value of commitment and loyalty.

A dog to remember!

Mac's transformation did not go unnoticed. Friends and family marveled at his Cattle dog drive and dedication.

They saw how his life had been enriched by this furry bundle of joy. And while there were challenges and sacrifices along the way, Mac wouldn't trade his hound responsibilities for anything.

In the end, it wasn't just the dog that was saved that day. Mac's heart and soul were also rescued, and he discovered a depth of character he never knew he had. The dog had extended him, teaching him that true happiness comes not from freedom alone but from embracing the responsibility of caring for another life.

As time went on, Mac's bond with his dog deepened. He named him Buddy, a fitting name for his loyal companion. With Buddy by his side, Mac explored new horizons and discovered a world of possibilities he had never considered before.

The responsibility of caring for Buddy extended beyond the basics of food and shelter. Mac realized the importance of mental stimulation and enrichment for his furry friend. He spent hours researching and implementing training techniques, engaging Buddy in interactive play, and even taught him a few tricks. As he witnessed Buddy's growth and progress, Mac felt an immense sense of pride and accomplishment.

But it wasn't just the physical and mental aspects of caring for Buddy that extended Mac. The emotional connection they shared was truly transformative. Buddy became a constant source of love and support, always there to listen and provide comfort during both good times and bad. Mac found solace in Buddy's presence, knowing that no matter what challenges he faced, there was someone who believed in him unconditionally.

Mac's catalog responsibility didn't stop at just taking care of Buddy. He became more aware of the welfare of other animals in need. He started volunteering at the local animal shelter, helping to find homes for abandoned pets. He became an advocate for animal rights and joined community initiatives to raise awareness about responsible pet ownership.

The bond of dogs brings people Together.

Through his experiences with Buddy, Mac learned the value of selflessness and empathy. He understood that true happiness comes from giving and caring for others. The responsibility of dog ownership had opened his eyes to a world beyond his own desires and needs.

As the years passed, Mac and Buddy aged together, their bond growing stronger with each passing day. Mac often reflected on how his life had been forever changed by the little stray dog he found in the park. Buddy had extended him in ways he could have never imagined, shaping him into a compassionate, responsible, and loving individual.

And so, their story became an inspiration to others. Mac shared his journey, encouraging people to consider the transformative power of dog ownership. He emphasized that the responsibility of caring for a dog goes beyond mere obligation; it extends a person's heart, mind, and soul, bringing forth qualities they never knew they possessed.

The presence of Buddy had forever enriched Mac's life, and he was grateful for every moment they had together. In their journey, they both found purpose and a love that would endure for a lifetime.

As Mac continued on his journey of dog ownership, he discovered that the responsibilities extended beyond the confines of his home. Buddy became a catalyst for Mac's engagement with the community and the world around him.

Mac began attending local dog events, such as adoption drives and fundraising walks. He met other dog owners who shared his passion for animal welfare and formed lasting friendships. Together, they organized awareness campaigns and initiatives to promote responsible pet ownership.

Inspired by his experiences, Mac decided to take his involvement a step further. He enrolled Buddy in therapy dog training, recognizing the potential for their bond to bring comfort and joy to others. They visited hospitals, nursing homes, and schools, spreading happiness wherever they went. Mac witnessed firsthand the positive impact Buddy had on people's lives, and it fueled his determination to make a difference.

Word of Mac and Buddy's uplifting visits spread, and soon, they were invited to participate in various community events. They attended children's reading programs at libraries, where Buddy patiently listened as children read to him, instilling confidence and a love for books. They visited veterans' support groups, offering a listening ear and a wagging tail to those who had served their country.

Mac's involvement with Buddy expanded beyond their local community. He joined volunteer organizations that traveled to areas affected by natural disasters, providing support and aid to both humans and animals in need. Together, Mac and Buddy assisted in search and rescue efforts, offering comfort to those who had lost everything.

Mac discovered the immense power of responsibility and compassion through his journey with Buddy. He realized that dog ownership was not just about caring for one individual but had the potential to create a ripple effect of kindness and change in the world.

As the years passed, Mac and Buddy's impact continued to grow. Their story became an inspiration to others, motivating people to take action and make a difference in their own communities. Mac's transformation was evident in his character and the countless lives he and Buddy touched.

The responsibility of dog ownership had extended even far beyond his initial expectations. It awakened a deep sense of purpose within him and propelled him to be an agent of positive change. He knew that his journey with Buddy would forever shape his path and the lives of those they encountered.

In the end, it was clear that dog ownership was not merely about taking care of a pet. It was about embracing a greater responsibility—the responsibility to love, nurture, and make a difference in the world. Mac's story was a testament to the profound impact that can be achieved when one opens their heart and extends oneself for the wellbeing of another.

As Mac delved deeper into the world of dog ownership, he realized that the responsibilities he had assumed had expanded his horizons in unexpected ways. His connection with Buddy had not only transformed him personally but also opened doors to new opportunities and experiences.

One such opportunity presented itself when Mac stumbled upon a local dog training club. Intrigued, he decided to join, eager to enhance his understanding of dog behavior and training techniques. The club became a gathering place for like-minded individuals who shared a passion for dogs. Mac formed friendships with experienced trainers who mentored him, guiding him on his journey to becoming a skilled dog handler.

Through his involvement in the dog community,

Mac discovered a hidden talent for public speaking. He was often asked to share his experiences as a dog owner and advocate for responsible pet ownership. He realized that his journey with Buddy had not only transformed him but also held the power to inspire and educate others.

Mac seized the opportunity to spread awareness about the joys and challenges of dog ownership. He became a regular speaker at local schools, community events, and even pet expos. His talks emphasized the importance of responsible dog care, addressing topics such as proper nutrition, exercise, and the significance of positive reinforcement in training. Through his words, he sought to empower others to become responsible and compassionate dog owners.

Word of Mac's engaging presentations reached the ears of an animal welfare organization. They invited him to become a spokesperson, enabling him to reach an even wider audience. He began collaborating with the organization on campaigns promoting adoption, spaying and neutering, and responsible breeding practices. Mac's dedication and genuine love for animals resonated with people, prompting them to consider the impact they could make in the lives of their own pets.

485

As Mac reflected on his journey, he marveled at how dog ownership had extended him beyond his wildest imagination. What started as a simple act of kindness towards a stray dog had transformed into a lifelong commitment and a platform for positive change. Through the responsibilities he embraced, Mac discovered talents, passions, and a purpose he had never envisioned.

The story of Mac and Buddy became an inspiration to many, a testament to the transformative power of dog ownership. Their journey illustrated that taking on the responsibility of caring for a dog is not just about fulfilling basic needs but also about personal growth, community engagement, and making a lasting impact.

Mac's life had been forever enriched by the presence of Buddy, and he was grateful for the countless lessons they had learned together. They had embarked on a shared adventure, a journey that extended their hearts, minds, and spirits. And as they continued to make a difference in the lives of others, their story would forever be a reminder of the profound connection between responsibility, personal growth, and the incredible bond between a human and their canine companion.

As Mac's journey with Buddy continued, the
responsibility of dog ownership extended to him in ways he
never anticipated. It wasn't just about the day-to-day care and
training; it was about the lessons he learned and the personal
growth he experienced along the way.

One aspect that profoundly affected Mac was his
newfound sense of discipline. Taking care of Buddy required
consistency and structure. Mac had to establish a routine for
feeding, exercise, and training. He learned to prioritize and
manage his time effectively, ensuring that Buddy's needs
were met while still attending to his own responsibilities.
This discipline spilled over into other areas of Mac's life. He
became more organized, focused, and committed to pursuing
his own goals and ambitions.

Additionally, the responsibility of dog ownership
taught Mac about resilience and adaptability. There were
times when Buddy faced health challenges or behavioral
issues that required extra attention and care. Ethan had to
research, seek advice, and make difficult decisions for
Buddy's well-being. Through these experiences, he
developed a resilience that allowed him to navigate obstacles
and find solutions in other areas of his life. He became better

487

equipped to handle setbacks and embrace change with a positive mindset.

Mac also discovered a newfound sense of empathy and compassion. Being responsible for Buddy's happiness and well-being made him more attuned to the needs of others. He started noticing stray animals in his community and took it upon himself to help them find shelter and care. He reached out to neighbors in need, offering assistance and support. The unconditional love and loyalty Buddy showed him opened Mac's heart, making him more compassionate towards both animals and humans alike.

Moreover, the responsibility of dog ownership extended Mac's social circle. As he took Buddy on walks and to dog parks, he found himself striking up conversations with fellow dog owners. These chance encounters blossomed into meaningful friendships, creating a sense of community and belonging. The shared love for dogs served as a common bond, connecting Mac with people from different backgrounds and walks of life. Through these connections, he gained new perspectives, expanded his horizons, and built a support network that enriched his life.

In the end, Mac realized that the responsibilities of dog ownership had transformed him into a more well-rounded individual. The care and commitment he had invested in Buddy had extended his character, instilling discipline, resilience, empathy, and a sense of community.

The journey with Buddy had not only brought joy and companionship but had also shaped Mac's values and priorities.

As Mac and Buddy continued their adventures together, they embraced each day with gratitude and love. The responsibility of dog ownership had brought them closer, deepening their bond and enriching their lives in countless ways. As they navigated life's challenges and joys side by side, they both knew that their connection would endure, a testament to the power of responsibility and the remarkable impact that a dog can have on a person's life.

Unit 25:
The History and Interactive Relationship between Humans and Dogs

Introduction

Throughout history, humans and dogs have shared a remarkable bond that transcends time and culture. Dogs, often referred to as "man's best friend," have been loyal companions, protectors, and even working partners to humans for thousands of years. This interactive relationship has evolved and adapted, leaving an indelible mark on both species. This paper explores the fascinating history of the human-dog connection, highlighting five famous figures and their public relationships with their canine sidekicks. By examining these examples, we gain insight into the profound impact dogs have had on human lives.

Ron Schara and Raven

Ron Schara, the TV host of Minnesota Bound and a writer for the Star Tribune, is a well-known figure in the outdoor industry. Throughout his career, he has been accompanied by his faithful sidekick, Raven, a Labrador Retriever. Ron and Raven's partnership symbolizes the classic bond between a hunter and his hunting dog. Raven's presence on Ron's television show and in his writing not only showcases their mutual trust but also demonstrates the integral role dogs play in various outdoor activities.

Franklin D. Roosevelt and Fala

One of the most famous human-dog relationships in history is that of President Franklin D. Roosevelt and his Scottish Terrier, Fala. Fala was a constant companion to Roosevelt during his presidency and accompanied him on numerous public appearances. Fala's endearing presence helped humanize Roosevelt's image, making him relatable to the American people. Their relationship was so cherished that a statue of Fala was erected next to Roosevelt's monument in Washington, D.C., commemorating their bond.

John Steinbeck and Charley

Renowned American author John Steinbeck embarked on a cross-country journey in 1960, which he later chronicled in his book, "Travels with Charley." Steinbeck's loyal companion during this adventure was his Standard Poodle, Charley. The book serves as a testament to the deep connection between Steinbeck and Charley, portraying their shared experiences and the emotional support that Charley provided during their journey. "Travels with Charley" captures the essence of the human-dog relationship, emphasizing the comfort and companionship that dogs can offer in times of solitude.

Queen Elizabeth II and her Corgis

Queen Elizabeth II, the longest-reigning monarch in British history, has had a profound affection for Corgis throughout her life. Over the years, she has owned several Corgis, including Dookie, Jane, and Willow. The Queen's bond with her Corgis has been widely documented, with these loyal companions often accompanying her during public engagements and private moments. The presence of her beloved Corgis has become synonymous with her reign, showcasing the role of dogs as trusted and cherished companions, even for royalty.

Barack Obama and Bo

Former President Barack Obama and his family welcomed Bo, a Portuguese Water Dog, into their lives during their

time in the White House. Bo became a prominent figure in
the Obama family, capturing the hearts of many
Americans. Bo's popularity extended beyond the family,
with his charismatic personality and playful demeanor
making him a symbol of the Obama administration. This
public association between the President and his loyal dog
emphasized the power of dogs in fostering positive public
relations and promoting a relatable image.

Conclusion

The history and interactive relationship between
humans and dogs are profound and multifaceted. Through
the examples of Ron Schara and Raven, Franklin D.
Roosevelt and Fala, John Steinbeck and Charley, Queen
Elizabeth II and her Corgis, and Barack Obama and Bo, we
see the significant impact that dogs have had on the lives of
notable figures. These relationships exemplify the
unwavering loyalty, companionship, and emotional support
that dogs offer humans in various contexts, be it hunting,
politics, literature, or public appearances. As we continue to
evolve alongside dogs, this enduring bond reminds us of the
profound connection we share with our four-legged
companions.

Famous Dogs

The 50 most recognized dogs in history are legendary for their exceptional qualities and remarkable contributions. These dogs have left an indelible mark on our collective consciousness. Among them, Lassie stands out for her intelligence and loyalty, while Rin Tin Tin is celebrated for his acting prowess. Hachiko's unwavering devotion touched the hearts of millions, and Balto's heroic sled dog exploits saved countless lives. The iconic Snoopy from the beloved Peanuts comic strip and Lady and the Tramp, the lovable Disney duo, have charmed generations with their endearing personalities. Other notable dogs include Toto from The Wizard of Oz, Beethoven from the eponymous movie series, and Benji, the resourceful canine hero. Moving on to lesser-known dogs, we have Towser, a prolific mouser who reportedly caught over 30,000 mice in her lifetime. Then there's Hovawart, an ancient German breed known for its versatility and guarding abilities. The Cirneco dell'Etna, a sleek Italian hunting dog, is often overshadowed by its more famous counterparts. The Chinook, America's only native sled dog breed, is rarely recognized despite its vital role in polar exploration. These dogs and many others may not enjoy widespread fame, but they deserve recognition for their unique qualities and contributions to their respective fields.

Certainly! Here are 25 more lesser-known dogs:

Spanish Water Dog: A versatile working breed from Spain, known for its curly, waterproof coat and its proficiency in herding and retrieving.

Cirneco dell'Etna: A small, agile hound from Sicily, Italy, bred for hunting small game in rocky terrain.

Pumi: A Hungarian herding breed with a distinctive curly coat and a lively, intelligent disposition.

Sloughi: Also known as the Arabian Greyhound, this sighthound from North Africa is renowned for its speed and grace.

Stabyhoun: A versatile Dutch breed used for hunting, pointing, and retrieving, known for its friendly and gentle nature.

Peruvian Inca Orchid: A hairless breed from Peru, highly valued for its elegant appearance and its ability to adapt to various climates.

Polish Lowland Sheepdog: A shaggy herding breed from Poland recognized for its intelligence, agility, and strong herding instincts.

Belgian Laekenois: One of the four Belgian Shepherd breeds, the Laekenois is a versatile working dog with a protective nature and a rough, tousled coat.

Japanese Chin: A small, charming toy breed originally from China but associated with Japanese nobility, known for its expressive eyes and silky coat.

Puli: This Hungarian herding breed is instantly recognizable for its distinctive corded coat, which forms tight, dense cords.

Estrela Mountain Dog: A Portuguese breed used for guarding livestock, known for its loyalty, intelligence, and protective instincts.

Finnish Hound: A medium-sized hunting breed from Finland, prized for its excellent scenting ability and endurance.

Toy Fox Terrier: A small terrier breed from the United States, characterized by its intelligence, agility, and alert nature.

Shiba Inu: A small and spirited Japanese breed with a fox-like appearance, known for its independent nature and keen hunting instincts.

Grand Basset Griffon Vendéen: A French scent
hound with a long, droopy face and a keen sense of smell,
used for hunting small game.

Pachón Navarro: A Spanish hunting breed known for
its distinctive long ears, strong scenting abilities, and
friendly disposition.

Polish Tatra Sheepdog: A large and imposing Polish
breed with a dense white coat, bred for guarding livestock in
mountainous regions.

Alaskan Klee Kai: A small, spitz-type dog from
Alaska, resembling a miniature version of the Siberian
Husky, known for its striking appearance and playful nature.

Sealyham Terrier: A Welsh terrier breeds with a wiry,
weather-resistant coat and a courageous, spirited
temperament.

Czechoslovakian Wolfdog: Bred from a mix of
German Shepherd and Carpathian wolf, this striking breed
combines the loyalty and trainability of a German Shepherd
with the wild beauty of a wolf.

Glen of Imaal Terrier: A small Irish breed with a
distinctive body structure and a determined, spirited
personality.

Shikoku: A Japanese breed from the mountainous regions of Shikoku Island, known for its loyalty, strength, and hunting abilities.

Volpino Italiano: A small, foxy-looking Italian breed with a thick, double coat and a lively, playful nature.

American Eskimo Dog: Despite its name, this breed actually originated in Germany. It is known for its fluffy white coat and its intelligence.

Silken Windhound: A graceful and elegant breed developed in the United States, resembling a smaller version of the Borzoi, with a long, silky coat and a friendly temperament.

These lesser-known dogs each have their own unique traits, histories, and contributions, showcasing the diverse world of canine companions.

Dan, Preacher, and Lt. Dan: The Unstoppable Sidekicks

Introduction

Dan, Preacher, and Lt. Dan - a trio of extraordinary canines whose talents and entertaining performances have captured the hearts of audiences nationwide. These remarkable dogs have not only delighted crowds with their captivating acts, but their unwavering love for hunting and their steadfast companionship have cemented their status as the ultimate sidekicks. Together, they have formed an unbeatable team, bringing joy and excitement wherever they go.

Dan, the Charismatic Leader

At the helm of this dynamic trio is Dan, a charismatic and fearless dog with a heart full of determination. With a commanding presence and an unparalleled ability to engage the crowd, Dan steals the spotlight whenever he steps onto the stage. His energy is infectious, and his natural charisma has endeared him to audiences across the country. But Dan's true passion lies in the hunt, as his unwavering focus and impressive hunting skills have made him an invaluable asset to the team.

The preacher, the second member of the trio, is a natural-born entertainer. With his playful antics and mischievous charm, he effortlessly brings laughter and joy to every performance. Preacher's agility and precision in executing tricks and stunts make him a crowd favorite. Beyond his entertainment value, Preacher's keen instincts and exceptional tracking abilities have proved essential in their hunting expeditions, cementing his status as an indispensable part of the team.

Completing this exceptional trio is Lt. Dan, a loyal
and devoted companion to his fellow sidekicks. His
unwavering loyalty and courage have earned him the
admiration of both his teammates and the audience. Lt..
Dan's unwavering dedication to the hunt has elevated their
success, ensuring they remain a force to be reckoned with.
With his strong bond with Dan and Preacher, Lt. Dan stands
as the glue that holds this extraordinary team together.

The Perfect Balance

What truly sets these remarkable sidekicks apart is
the harmonious balance between their entertaining
performances and their shared love for hunting. While they
have captivated crowds nationwide with their charisma and
talent, their unity and shared passion for the hunt have made
them an unrivaled force. Their ability to seamlessly
transition from thrilling audiences with their acts to

embarking on hunting adventures showcases their versatility and unwavering commitment to their craft.

Conclusion

Dan, Preacher, and Lt. Dan have proven themselves to be the ultimate sidekicks, entertaining crowds with their captivating performances and astounding audiences with their hunting skills. The perfect blend of charisma, entertainment, and companionship, this remarkable trio continues to leave a lasting impression wherever they go. Together, they have cemented their status as number one sidekicks, winning the hearts of people across the country and leaving an indelible mark on the world of entertainment and hunting.

Meraki shows yes a Bulldog can do nosework

Final Exam

Dog Training, Dog Sports, and Responsibilities of Dog Ownership

Instructions: Read each question carefully and choose the correct answer from the options provided. Only one answer is correct for each question. Mark your answers on the provided answer sheet. Good luck!

1. Which training method relies on positive reinforcement and rewards to teach dogs desired behaviors?

   a. Punishment-based training

   b. Clicker training

   c. Dominance-based training

   d. Alpha dog training

   Answer: b) Clicker training

2. Which command is commonly used to teach a dog to sit?

   a. "Stay"

   b. "Down"

   c. "Come"

   d. "Sit"

   Answer: d) "Sit"

3. Which of the following is an example of a dog sport?

   a. Flyball

   b. Lure coursing

   c. Agility

   d. All of the above

   Answer: d) All of the above

4. In which dog sport does the dog navigate through a timed obstacle course?

    a. Rally Obedience

    b. Nose work

    c. Flyball

    d. Agility

    Answer: d) Agility

5. What is the purpose of crate training a dog?

    i.   To punish the dog for misbehavior

    ii. To provide the dog with a safe and comfortable space

    iii. To prevent the dog from escaping

    iv. To restrict the dog's movement

Answer: b) To provide the dog with a safe and comfortable space

6. Which of the following is an important responsibility of dog ownership?

    a. Regular exercise

    b. Providing proper nutrition

    c. Veterinary care

    d. All of the above

    Answer: d) All of the above

7. What is the recommended age to start socializing a puppy?

    a. 6 months

    b. 1 year

    c. 8 weeks

    d. 2 years

    Answer: c) 8 weeks

8. Which of the following should be part of a dog's daily routine?

    a. Training sessions

    b. Playtime and exercise

    c. Feeding and watering

    d. All of the above

    Answer: d) All of the above

9. Which dog sport involves dogs pulling a cart or sled?

    a. Disc dog

    b. Schutzhund

    c. Weight Pulling

    d. Canicross

    Answer: c) Weight pulling

10. Which of the following is a common challenge in dog ownership?

a. Shedding

b. Barking

c. Chewing

d. All of the above

Answer: d) All of the above

11. What is the first step in house training a puppy?

a. Using puppy pads indoors

b. Restricting access to certain areas

c. Establishing a consistent schedule

d. Punishing accidents

Answer: c) Establishing a consistent schedule

12. Which dog sport involves throwing a disc for a dog to catch and retrieve?

a. Flyball

b. Dock diving

c. Disc dog

d. Schutzhund

Answer: c) Disc dog

13. Which type of collar is designed to provide gentle control over a dog's pulling behavior?

a. Choke collar

b. Prong collar

c. Martingale collar

d. Shock collar

Answer: c) Martingale collar

14. What is the purpose of a dog's microchip?

a. To track the dog's location via GPS

b. To store the dog's medical records

c. To identify the dog if it gets lost

d. To monitor the dog's activity level

Answer: c) To identify the dog if it gets lost

15. Which dog sport focuses on training dogs for scent detection?

a) Canicross

b) Nose work

c) Rally Obedience

d) Herding

Answer: b) Nose work

16. What is the ideal temperature for walking a dog during hot weather?

a) 60°F (15°C)

b) 75°F (24°C)

c) 90°F (32°C)

d) 100°F (38°C)

Answer: a) 60°F (15°C)

17. What is the correct way to introduce two unfamiliar dogs to each other?

a) Hold the dogs tightly on a leash

b) Let them approach each other face-to-face

c) Allow them to sniff each other's rear ends

d) Keep them at a distance and observe their body language

Answer: d) Keep them at a distance and observe their body language

18. Which of the following is an example of an inappropriate punishment for a dog?

a) Time-out in a designated area

b) Verbal reprimand in a calm tone

c) Physical hitting or kicking

d) Ignoring the dog for a short period

Answer: c) Physical hitting or kicking

19. Which dog sport involves training dogs for protection work?

a) Flyball

b) Tracking

509

c) Schutzhund

d) Lure coursing

Answer: c) Schutzhund

20. What is the average lifespan of a dog?

a) 5-8 years

b) 10-12 years

c) 15-18 years

d) 20-25 years

Answer: b) 10-12 years

21. Which command is commonly used to teach a dog to lie down?

a) "Stay"

b) "Sit"

c) "Come"

d) "Down"

Answer: d) "Down"

22. Which of the following is an important aspect of responsible dog ownership?

a) Regular grooming

b) Providing proper identification

c) Cleaning up after the dog in public areas

d) All of the above

Answer: d) All of the above

23. Which dog sport involves dogs jumping into the water to retrieve objects?

a) Disc dog
b) Dock diving
c) Lure coursing
d) Weight Pulling

Answer: b) Dock diving

24. What is the best way to address a dog's separation anxiety?

a) Punish the dog when it displays anxious behaviors
b) Ignore the dog's anxious behaviors
c) Gradually desensitize the dog to being alone
d) Get another dog as a companion

Answer: c) Gradually desensitize the dog to being alone

25. Which type of dog training uses aversive methods to suppress unwanted behaviors?

a) Positive reinforcement training
b) Alpha dog training

511

c) Dominance-based training

d) Clicker training

Answer: c) Dominance-based training

26. What is the primary purpose of a dog's leash?

a) To restrict the dog's movement

b) To provide control and ensure safety

c) To display the dog's identification tags

d) To exercise the dog

Answer: b) To provide control and ensure safety 27.

Which dog sport involves dogs herding livestock?

a) Flyball

b) Dock

a. Certainly! Here are the remaining questions:

28. What is the purpose of socializing a dog?

a) To teach them basic obedience commands

b) To expose them to different environments, people, and animals

c) To make them more aggressive towards strangers

d) To discourage play behavior

Answer: b) To expose them to different environments, people, and animals

29. Which of the following is an important aspect of responsible dog ownership regarding public spaces?

a) Allowing the dog off-leash at all times

b) Failing to pick up the dog's waste

c) Training the dog to ignore commands from others

d) Keeping the dog leashed and cleaning up after them

Answer: d) Keeping the dog leashed and cleaning up after them

30. Which dog sport involves dogs running alongside their owners while attached to a waist belt?

a) Agility

b) Flyball

c) Canicross

d) Rally Obedience

Answer: c) Canicross

31. What is the proper way to introduce a dog to a new environment?

a) Allow the dog to explore freely without supervision

b) Immediately introduce the dog to other dogs in the area

c) Gradually introduce the dog while providing reassurance and positive experiences

513

d) Keep the dog confined to prevent any potential accidents

Answer: c) Gradually introduce the dog while providing reassurance and positive experiences

32. Which of the following is an important factor to consider when choosing a dog breed?

   a) Size and weight
   b) Exercise needs
   c) Grooming requirements
   d) All of the above

Answer: d) All of the above

33. Which dog sport involves dogs jumping over hurdles and through tunnels?

b)

c)

Nose work

Lure coursing

Disc dog

d) Agility

Answer: d) Agility

34. What is the purpose of a dog's ID tag?

    a. To indicate the dog's breed

    b. To provide information about the dog's vaccinations

    c. To display the owner's contact information

    d. To indicate the dog's age

Answer: c) To display the owner's contact information

35. Which command is commonly used to teach a dog to come back to the owner?

    a) "Stay"

    b) "Down"

    c) "Come"

    d) "Sit"

Answer: c) "Come"

a)

b)

c)

36. Which dog sport involves dogs tracking scents and locating hidden objects?

    Canicross

    Rally Obedience

    Flyball

    d) Nose work

    Answer: d) Nose work

37. What is the purpose of a dog license?

    a) To identify the dog's breed

    b) To prove the dog's training abilities

    c) To certify the dog's pedigree

    d) To comply with local regulations and ensure the dog is vaccinated

    Answer: d) To comply with local regulations and ensure the dog is vaccinated

38. What is the ideal time to start training a puppy?

    a) 1-year-old

    b) 6 months old

    c) 8 weeks old

b)

c)

d) 2 years old

Answer: c) 8 weeks old

39. Which of the following is an important aspect of responsible dog ownership regarding their health?

   Regular exercise and mental stimulation

   Providing a balanced diet and freshwater

   Regular vet check-ups and vaccinations

d) All of the above

Answer: d) All of the above

40. What is the purpose of a spay/neuter surgery for a dog?

   a) To prevent unwanted behaviors

   b) To enhance their athletic abilities

   c) To extend their lifespan

   d) To control the dog's population and prevent certain health issues

Answer: d) To control the dog's population and prevent certain health issues

41. Which dog sport involves dogs jumping into a pool and retrieving an object?

a)

b)

c)

   a) Weight Pulling

   b) Dock diving

   c) Lure coursing

   d) Disc dog

Answer: b) Dock diving

42.   What is the correct way to reward a dog during Training?

a) Yelling loudly

b) Providing a treat or praise

c) Using physical force

d) Ignoring the dog's behavior

Answer: b) Providing a treat or praise

43. Which of the following is an important responsibility of dog owners regarding their safety?

a) Providing a well-fenced yard or secure living area

b) Allowing them to roam freely in public spaces

c) Leaving them unattended for long periods of time

d) Encouraging them to interact with unfamiliar dogs without supervision

Answer: a) Providing a well-fenced yard or secure living area

44. Which dog sport involves training dogs to perform various tricks and behaviors?

a) Rally Obedience

b) Schutzhund

c) Flyball

d) Freestyle obedience

Answer: d) Freestyle obedience

45. What is the purpose of a dog's collar?

    a) To provide a comfortable sleeping area

    b) To display the owner's fashion sense

    c) To attach a leash for control and identification purposes

    d) To prevent the dog from barking

    Answer: c) To attach a leash for control and identification purposes

46. Which of the following is an important aspect of responsible dog ownership regarding their social needs?

    a) Providing opportunities for interaction with other dogs and people

    b) Isolating the dog from social situations to prevent aggressive behavior

    c) Allowing the dog to roam freely in public spaces

    d) Limiting their exposure to different environments

    Answer: a) Providing opportunities for interaction with other dogs and people

47. Which dog sport involves dogs chasing a mechanically operated lure?

    a) Dock diving

b) Nose work

c) Lure coursing

d) Canicross

Answer: c) Lure coursing

48. What is the purpose of regular exercise for a dog?

a) To tire them out and prevent unwanted behaviors

b) To increase their weight and muscle mass

c) To enhance their hunting skills

d) To limit their energy and prevent playfulness

Answer: a) To tire them out and prevent unwanted behaviors

49. Which of the following is an important aspect of responsible dog ownership regarding their mental stimulation?

a) Providing interactive toys and puzzles

b) Allowing them to roam freely in the neighborhood

c) Keeping them isolated without any social interaction

d) Restricting their access to different environments
   Answer: a) Providing interactive toys and puzzles

50. What is the recommended frequency for grooming a dog's coat?

    a) Once a year

    b) Once a month

    c) Once a week

    d) It depends on the breed and coat type

    Answer: d) It depends on the breed and coat type

E-mail: gotadog1gmail.com for grading and certificate

Made in the USA
Monee, IL
10 November 2023

46148943R00299